One Trick pony

Daniella
Brodsky

DELACORTE PRESS

Published by Delacorte Press
an imprint of Random House Children's Books
a division of Random House, Inc.
New York

This is a work of fiction. Names, characters, places, and incidents
either are the product of the author's imagination or are used
fictitiously. Any resemblance to actual persons, living or dead,
events, or locales is entirely coincidental.

Delacorte Press and colophon are registered trademarks
of Random House, Inc.

Visit us on the Web! www.randomhouse.com/teens
Educators and librarians, for a variety of teaching tools,
visit us at www.randomhouse.com/teachers

Library of Congress Cataloging-in-Publication Data is available
upon request.

ISBN: 978-0-385-73452-3 (trade)
ISBN: 978-0-385-90452-0 (glb)

The text of this book is set in 11-point Galliard.
Printed in the United States of America
10 9 8 7 6 5 4 3 2 1
First Edition

Random House Children's Books supports the First Amendment
and celebrates the right to read.

To Niki and Steven—
may all your dreams come true.

1

"Crap," Jesse Majors barked as he pushed open the front door of the apartment building with the tire of his bike. It was pouring again. And he had a hangover. From the way that girl Cassie or Carrie or Cammie or whoever was kissing him all over the face a second ago, he just knew she wasn't going to handle this one-night stand—which he hadn't made any attempt to disguise as anything but—very well at all.

He pulled his Saint Martin cap from his back jeans pocket and covered his freshly buzzed hair with it, the bill shading his face. The hat—like his Italian key fob; too-mature steel-rimmed sunglasses from Paris; and expensive Hawaiian shirt—was a souvenir from his parents. Armored up in all this stuff, Jesse felt like a walking, talking souvenir himself, something you bring home from a trip and forget about.

His cell phone rang right as he started pedaling home. It was his movie exec dad. "We're going to stay another week out here. This producer is really trying to ruin Kevin Sting's book. Could you imagine doing a *musical* of a horror picture?" No, as a matter of fact, Jesse couldn't. He couldn't imagine leaving his own seventeen-year-old son for months at a time, either, but that was something Jesse kept close to the vest.

"Don't worry about it, Dad," he managed to say, mustering up his most carefree voice. "I know you've got to do a good job. We'll do the hiking thing next month." They'd planned on heading up to the Catskills, where his mom had picked out an old Greek Revival place the previous year, but Jesse hadn't actually assumed they'd be going. They'd only been up there once since they bought it. Surely there was some rotting crap in the fridge by now.

"All right, Jess. Thanks for understanding. Why don't you go out and get yourself one of those new Nintendo Wii game systems? You've got the credit card. Everyone's talking about them over here. We've got two on the set. The Road Rage game is pretty awesome."

"Yeah, sure, Dad. Thanks. Talk later." Jesse tucked his phone back into the Velcro pocket on his left jacket sleeve and slipped his ear buds into his ears. Lately, he'd been listening to this garage band, the Flash, he'd heard at the One Trick Pony the previous month. The Flash had sort of a British punk sound and they'd played on the last night the place was open. Right when Jesse finished cleaning out the espresso machine and counting out his drawer, Jimmy had pulled a chair up in front of the coffee bar, settled his hands on the roundest part of his belly, and said, "This is it, Jesse.

We're closing up for good. I'm bankrupt. Kaput. Dead. Over. If I thought you needed the money, I'd feel pretty bad about it. But I'm sure you can find a new place to pick up girls," he added with a wink.

"What are you gonna do now?" Jesse had asked. Jimmy was just about the worst businessman in the world—more into music and hanging out than keeping consistent business hours, or serving good coffee—and it wasn't shocking that the One Trick had gone under. But at least Jimmy had been around a lot, and he *knew* Jesse. He hated to admit it, but Jesse missed the whole scene.

Ah, but that was all history now. Jimmy had moved down to Miami and planned to waiter at a tapas joint. "People, possessions, money . . . it all comes and goes in life," Jimmy said before he left. That was exactly the way Jesse himself saw things. He found that if you didn't worry, life had a way of working out—ups and downs, ins and outs. There wasn't much point to any of it, so far as he could tell.

"Yeah, yeah, kiss her where it huurrrrrrrrts!" The music thumped in his ear as he coasted along Smith Street toward his family's luxury apartment, ready for a final school-free Friday of nothing and a whole lot more nothing. Maybe he'd order some wings later. Or take his car out to Brighton Beach for some Roll-n-Roaster. Maybe Randall would join him, if he wasn't too busy waiting around for Abigail to fall in love with him. Randall sure knew how to make things difficult.

All of a sudden, Jesse's gaze was attracted skyward. As his eyes widened, he felt the scar through his right eyebrow tug a little. The dark clouds that had layered Brooklyn for the past month—making the air hazy, so thick you could grab a handful of it—now broke, and right above the chained-up façade of the One Trick, there was a sliver of crystal-clear blue. A huge gray bird of a variety you didn't normally see on Smith Street swooped down and Jesse slammed on his brakes in surprise. His eyes followed the bird soaring right down to the door of the One Trick. Jesse was shocked to see a black-haired woman crouched down, fumbling with the lock.

Jesse weaved seamlessly between a few cars across the street to the woman as the bird flew off frantically. He leaned his bike against the brick wall and asked, "Can I help you with that?"

She didn't seem surprised or frightened by the voice coming from behind her. Instead, she smoothly answered, *"Oui,* that would be wonderful."

A Frenchwoman, Jesse thought. He'd had plenty of dreams about them. But when she stood and turned to face him, Jesse had the weirdest feeling; he thought she could have stepped off the set of a 1940s movie. She had shiny, unfussy hair, pulled back into a lacy band, so that her milky white neck was revealed. It was the kind of neck Jesse had the urge to reach out and touch, ditto her tiny ears. She had enormous, almond-shaped eyes—as dark as her hair—and they seemed miles deep as Jesse's gaze was caught in them. Her thick lashes blinked and snapped him out of it with a start. The woman wore a classic trench coat, tied tight at the waist and flowing to her high-heeled shoes. She was beautiful, with her heady perfume and curved smile, and though she was older—he guessed twenty-something—he was very attracted to her.

He held his palm out for her to drop the key into it and

fit it into the lock. "It's a little finicky. You have to finesse it gently to the left," he said, clicking it open with ease.

"Have you bought the place?" he asked.

"*Oui*, I've been setting up all week. I am Caroline Deneuve, and you are . . . ?"

"Jesse. I used to work here as a barista when Jimmy the Dude owned it."

"The 'Dude'?" she asked, a smile forming on her lips as Jesse pulled the gate up.

"Yeah. Everyone called him that."

"Why?" Caroline asked, gathering her things. Jesse reached for the couple of tote bags and the big cardboard box to carry them inside for her.

"Because he told them to, I guess." They both laughed easily, as if they'd known each other forever. People always told Jesse he had a nice laugh . . . that and "intense eyes."

"Would you like your job back?" Caroline asked.

"As a matter of fact, I would," he responded, smiling at the old place. He'd missed it. Originally, he'd loved it for the chicks—he'd found that baristas seemed to have the same allure as bartenders. But the hum and flow of a coffeehouse had grown on him—the click-clack of the espresso machine, the porta-filter against the rim of the knock box (where used coffee grounds were stored), the chitchat with the regular patrons.

"Great," Caroline said. "You can start by bringing this carton down to the basement." She pushed it over the coffee bar in his direction, sending dust particles dancing through the dim air between them so that they were subtly illuminated in the slivers of light that came through the window.

Jesse lifted it off the bar. It was heavier than he'd

5

expected. He shoved the basement door open with his left shoulder and descended the creaky wood staircase, flicking on the light about halfway down. Where there used to be nothing, there were boxes and wooden crates. Jimmy had never stored much down here, but it looked as if Caroline had half of France tidily labeled and stacked against the brick walls. At the last stair, Jesse felt the box give way on the bottom and heard a flap as something from inside fluttered to the floor.

He walked the box over to a round wooden table and went back to pick up a photograph. It was a black-and-white with a rough black border. There was Caroline, and some French guy with a bulbous nose and heavy brows, passionate eyes and long arms. They were sitting at a table and regarding each other so deeply, Jesse felt as if he were intruding just looking at the picture.

"Jesse?" Caroline called, pulling him out of his thoughts. He slipped the picture back into the box, but in his mind he was still gazing at that image. There was something about it that intrigued him. *Why haven't I ever looked at anyone like that?* He hoped this was a bad side effect of his hangover and climbed the stairs, trying to shake it off.

Caroline was already at work making things smell good. Real good. "Here, you wash these," she said, plucking a coffee cup from a compartmented cardboard box. She handed him a blue-and-white-checked towel that smelled of lavender. "You can use this to dry."

She walked over to a huge, ornate copper cylinder with copper daisies soldered all around it and turned a dial to the right.

"What is that?" Jesse asked.

"This? Ah . . . this is the center of my family's history.

It is a coffee roaster and it is over two hundred years old." Caroline opened a small door and pulled out a plate that looked as if it was made from tile. She searched through a couple of boxes until she came upon a huge woven sack, and then she scooped out a mound of coffee beans.

"Are those still good? They look kind of green," Jesse said. All the beans he'd ever seen were brown.

Caroline giggled and said, "Ah, darling, this is the *real* way to make coffee. These are fresh beans that haven't been roasted weeks or months ago like the ones you're probably used to. And now we will roast them and then you'll recognize them . . . and you will grow to love their magical smell."

Caroline is way into her coffee, Jesse thought sarcastically, but even while he mocked her seriousness, he couldn't deny he was enchanted by it.

"The beans actually grow inside a berry—two nestled inside together, like lovers," she said, her tone distant, evoking in Jesse's head that beautiful, somehow heart-breaking photograph.

Jesse continued dipping the cups into the soapy liquid, pulling them out, drying them with the towel, and arranging them on the hooks Caroline had designated for their storage. He thought about calling that Carrie or Cassie girl but shook the idea off like the soapsuds on his hands. He didn't want to be attached.

"Hey, Caroline, what's this candle mean?" Jesse asked, looking at the design that adorned the side of each black-rimmed cup—a candle on an old-fashioned handled base, the kind people used to carry around dark hallways before electricity.

"That is my family symbol. It means light, life, and

spirituality," she said. "If you see candles in your dreams, it can mean a bright future, good luck, and hope. Candles are all about the growth of your spirit. From way back in ancient times, people have believed that for each of us there is a candle, a symbol of our own inner light, but that no one can kindle his or her own candle. Each of us needs someone else to kindle it for us."

Jesse was taken by that idea—so many girls he'd been with . . . how come none of them had kindled his candle? How come he hadn't even realized he had one? Probably because nobody had ever taken the time to show him. If his family had a symbol, it would probably be a dollar sign. He thought again of that picture and wondered if this symbol had anything to do with that passionate stare. "Do you really believe that?" he asked. "I mean, do you really think there is so much meaning in life, that we aren't all just coasting along?"

"'Coasting along'?" She repeated his phrase unfamiliarly.

Jesse tried to clarify. "Yeah, my theory on life is that you just go with the flow."

Caroline smiled immensely. "You have more control than you think," she said, leaning in close, looking at his Saint Martin hat as if maybe she knew something about it. "But it takes time to learn how to harness it, to find your destiny and go after it." She was roasting a second batch of the beans now and the smoky smell curled around them. "You listen for the first crack, which is loud and obvious," she said, cupping a hand over her ear just seconds before Jesse could hear the popcorn-like sound for himself. "It's the second, more subtle one that actually fractures the exterior. You have to be more attentive and focused to hear. If you miss that one, you could ruin the whole batch. Like people, each bean is different, has its own threshold and personality that makes it react uniquely."

Jesse hadn't noticed he'd been holding his breath while he watched her.

"Here," Caroline said with that enigmatic smile, and passed him a cup with the candle insignia, a fragrant, dark drink sending up a coil of smoke from inside. "Drink this."

Jesse didn't know if he'd been put under a spell or what, but sipping that coffee seemed so intimate, like a long, lingering kiss, that he felt his cheeks burn as she watched.

2

"I just keep thinking of that day at the hospital when my mom was talking about fresh blackberries. 'Fresh blackberries would be so wonderful now, don't you think?' She twisted herself around in her bed as if it were any old day, not two or three days before she was going to die, and asked me that. Mom never wanted me to worry, never wanted to do anything but care for me."

Abigail Jones didn't want to cry in front of another human being even if it was her close friend Randall. She sipped from her water bottle and allowed the longer layers of her pixie cut to cover her eyes. It was probably obvious now that she was trying to cover up her crying. She could see that some of her dirty blond hair was darkening from the tears.

Now that her mother was gone, it was up to her father

to take care of her—the man who'd once lost her at the Bronx Zoo in front of the lions' den.

Randall moved closer to her where she sat on the wood floor of his bedroom, her back resting against his bed. He put his arms around her, thankfully not asking if she was okay or saying anything about the crying, or the covering it up. Randall just pulled Abigail in tight and rubbed his hands up and down her arm. Finally he said, just as she was thinking it, just as he pushed the dampened layers of hair out of her eyes, "Your dad's a little clueless, isn't he?"

They giggled; she started it, and this eased the mood immensely. "Yeah, nothing at all like yours," she joked.

"Maybe they could get together and start the Clueless Dads Club," he suggested with a shrug.

"Yeah, but they'd never be able to get their act together to actually have a meeting," Abigail said, stretching her legs now, looking up at the ceiling. She'd been here many, many times before her mother died, but now she noticed everything—cracks in the ceiling, peeling posters—as if taking note of her new world, of this empty way of living she'd been forced into.

Still, there was something about being here with Randall that felt comfortable. Lately that was all Abigail could hope for, small moments of comfort, and this one ranked high.

"Wanna go see that new Spanish movie over at the Angelika later?" he asked, standing and shifting his weight from one foot to the other, as Abigail pulled herself up.

It wasn't a strange question. They saw every movie at the Angelika. It was their thing. They smuggled in cherry Twizzlers and Sno-Caps "to fight the man," and sometimes stayed for two movies, even though they'd only paid for one. Then they went to the One Trick Pony, when it was open, to talk it all over.

They hadn't seen a flick since Abigail's mom died, and it sounded like a nice return to routine, but Abigail was pulled away from the idea by a light jingle on her cell phone. "Another text message," she said, shrugging. Abigail acted annoyed, as if the text messages that her boyfriend, Nick, sent her all the time with fortune cookie sayings, such as "You shall live long and have many children," were excessive displays of attention. But secretly they made her feel special. She couldn't help feeling that no matter where she was, someone was thinking of her. Now she pressed a couple of buttons so she could see what he'd written: "There is a good-looking blond man in your future." This was a reminder that they had plans to meet, and a quick look at her watch told her she was already running late.

"Sorry, Ran. I have to head to NYU and meet Nick." Abigail couldn't believe they'd been talking up in Randall's room for three hours already. Now she was going to have to rush over to Washington Square.

"Ah, Nick . . . Mr. Good Times." Randall always spoke condescendingly of Abigail's college boyfriend. He argued that Nick was the type of guy who came to New York to have an "experience." Randall once said Nick didn't have an authentic bone in his body, that he'd lost the very last one eating at the TGIF in Times Square. Abigail had laughed, but what Randall didn't always know was that Nick could show her how to take life less seriously, how to live for the moment, how to grab on to those flashes of comfort or happiness, like that one a second ago . . .

something that had become increasingly difficult for Abigail since her mom died. She always felt as though she was holding back, conserving herself. But for what? Things would never go back to the way they were. She knew this, but at the same time, she didn't.

Abigail smiled knowingly at Randall. He kissed her on the cheek and wrapped her in a warm, strong hug—one of his specialties.

"I hate to sound like someone we both know and I for one hate, but have a good time tonight. You deserve it. And remember what we talked about . . . just go with your emotions, don't fight them. If you don't want to be nice to someone—including Ginny, and especially Nick—then don't be," he said. Abigail understood how Randall felt about Nick; the two couldn't be more different . . . and in many ways she knew Randall was right about him. As for her dad's girlfriend, Ginny, the less Abigail thought about her, the better.

Outside, the sky had cleared dramatically. Maybe this was a sign that things would clear up for Abigail, too. But no . . . she knew it was more complicated than that.

As she walked down Smith Street in the sunlight, Abigail practiced capturing in words the images she saw. It was a technique she used to improve her poetry. The Chinese furniture shop had a branch of dogwood in the window. *Delicate.* The bakery displayed three tiers of pastel cupcakes. *Easter hues.* The necklace in the window of the clothing boutique Frida was a shiny red laminate. *Pop art.* The One Trick Pony had a chalkboard outside, on which someone had written, "If you want to improve your understanding, drink coffee; it is the intelligent beverage.—Sydney Smith."

Now Abigail's mind was yanked from her game. Who

had reopened the One Trick? Who had written this quote that seemed to speak directly to her thoughts? She pushed the door open and there was Jesse, as he'd always been.

"Abigail, how are you?" He jumped over the counter and enfolded his wheat-haired friend in a big hug.

"I'm okay," she said, looking up—Jesse was substantially taller than she was. Abigail didn't speak with anyone the way she spoke with Randall. He'd asked that same question earlier, and three hours later they'd come up for air.

"Glad to hear it," Jesse said.

Abigail adjusted her jeans—pulling them up under her "Drink Milk" T-shirt. It seemed all of her clothes were becoming loose lately.

Just then a woman with glossy dark hair appeared at the basement door, holding a woven basket lined with a blue-and-white-checked towel. *Lovely.*

"Ah, and who are you, my dear?"

"Caroline, this is my friend Abigail," Jesse said.

"Hello, Abigail," Caroline sang in the warmest voice. She plunked the basket onto a nearby table and took Abigail's hand in both of her soft ones. "A beautiful name, for a restless spirit, trying to break free . . . I have just the coffee for you," she said, and winked.

Abigail glanced at Jesse curiously as Caroline headed toward an old-fashioned espresso machine. He shrugged and smiled, but she noticed that his grin was not altogether mocking. Abigail was entranced with the woman's musical way of speaking, her vintage way of dressing, her pretty gold-filigree earrings. Abigail watched Caroline's fingers flutter around the shiny machine, pinch a bit of purple seed and spoon some sugar, her chunky purple ring catching the light.

14

"Did you know that when coffee was first introduced in Italy, some fanatical Christians urged Pope Clement the Seventh to forbid the faithful to drink the 'devil's beverage'—that's what they called it! Because it was so powerfully delicious." Caroline was animated and elegant as she danced around the machine, making delightful noises, adding still another pinch of this and a curl of that.

Abigail took a sip of the pretty drink, with its hilltop of foam, and was reminded of her mother—an image of her when she'd been well, which Abigail had not thought of since her mother died of cancer nine months ago. Penelope Jones had been a dancer, so graceful as she turned pirouette after pirouette, her sheer wraparound skirt twirling, "like flower petals," Abigail used to say as a child. She felt a tear well up at the strength and clarity of the memory. She tried her hardest to will it back where it came from; she did not like to expose herself to this kind of torment, thinking of things she could never have again.

"That is . . . different," she said of the beverage, unnerved at not being able to shake off the memory.

Jesse looked sympathetic, as if maybe he'd seen the tear surface and guessed at the reason. He'd been at the funeral and had dropped by a bunch of times when she was riding it out at home. He brought candy and junk food she politely picked at for his benefit. Abigail had always been a pleaser, a "do what people think you should" kind of girl. But now that she felt so lost, that part of her had seemed to swell even more—she sought out some direction, looked for ways to blend deeper into the scenery.

After weeks of being watched like an exotic animal in a zoo—*Step up, folks, and see the girl who lost her mother!*—Abigail stuffed her emotions away, especially in public. She didn't like to be met with pity. It was the worst kind of attention you could get, as far as she was concerned. Pity just served to make her shyer. Was she allowed to laugh? To smile? Under the critical eye of others' expectations, Abigail's insecurity was intensified by the thousands.

"I knew you'd appreciate it." Caroline leaned over the counter and rested her chin on the knuckles of her left hand. The nails were perfect half moons, painted red as the apples Abigail's mother had always piled into the Hawaiian bamboo bowl on their kitchen table.

"Caroline, what brings you to Cobble Hill?" Abigail asked, feeling her own bitten-down nails with her fingertips. She tried to move the conversation toward more comfortable territory.

Jesse was drying a mug. He looked up as she asked the question.

Caroline didn't answer right away. Instead she inhaled and exhaled deeply, spun around toward the machine and then back, her flowery dress swishing right and left hypnotically. "I can't stay in one place forever, now can I?" She smiled immensely and then winked.

Abigail inhaled the sweet aroma of the coffee and sighed softly. She still couldn't pin a word on the taste of it. Her eyes darted around the room, as if they'd found some new energy source. The whole place had changed. The room was filled with pretty little café tables, and old photos leaned against the wall in spots, as if Caroline was testing out where to hang them.

Abigail twirled the funny white stick that had been propped in her coffee between two fingers. She wanted to ask what it was—it had a sweet scent—but if it was something she should already know about, like vanilla or a spice

16

or something she'd only ever seen in a jar before, she'd feel dumb.

Caroline caught her looking and answered the unasked question. "It's coconut," she said, "the way they like it in the Caribbean."

Coconut in her coffee. What an idea! Her mother would have loved that. She was always doing something special with meals or hot chocolate—adding pretty syrup drizzles or edible flowers. Abigail reveled in memories of her mother and the delicious aroma of coffee. She wished she could stay forever in this warm, inviting place, instead of living in her empty home. But . . . oh *crap!* She had to go. She'd already been late when she stumbled upon the chalkboard outside. How could she have forgotten about Nick?

Abigail backed off the stool she'd been sitting on. "Jesse, I'll catch you later. Caroline, it's been a pleasure. What do I owe you?"

"Oh, nothing, *chérie*. For you . . . nothing at all."

Abigail reddened at the kindness, garbled her thank-you, and turned to go.

3

Randall Gold never found guitar scales boring. He did them every day before practicing songs. They were process, something he knew inside and out, with his eyes closed and his ears covered. Jesse had once asked him how he could do the very same thing over and over. Didn't it drive him nuts? No, it didn't.

As his fingers moved along the frets of the guitar's neck, there came that sweet feeling of familiarity. Randall didn't think about the Live Records producer he'd met two months ago and had since avoided calling. He didn't think about his dad's life—working as a business consultant in his pajamas all day and then sitting on the couch eating expired food all night—or how his mother had told Randall last year she'd fallen out of love with his father and would be moving back to her mom's house in Texas. He especially didn't think about the way she'd told Randall that she had to go off and start a new life for herself. "You only get one, honey," she'd said, like that made the whole thing okay.

Randall always turned the amp way up when he did the scales. He wouldn't say he was proud of his ability, because that would be lame, but he did like the idea that he could do this well. His callused fingertips slid over the strings by pure instinct.

After about an hour, Randall finished the exercise and hesitantly pulled out the notebook he'd been writing songs in lately. There was a lot of scribbling on the front—band logos and lightning bolts, and Abigail's signature in one corner below the words "You are my idol." She'd been joking, of course, but he looked at that every day, maybe growing a little superstitious about what might happen if he didn't—like, would it ruin the chances of Abigail's ever realizing how he felt about her? It was ridiculous, but what else did Randall have to go on while she was with Nick the Dick?

Abigail had once pointed out that Randall had a habit of running his hand through his hair when he was deep in thought, and he caught himself doing that now. His hair was a dark, dark brown, just like his mother's. It was really the only feature he'd inherited from her. She was Italian and his father was Jewish. Everyone said Randall had only gotten the Jewish genes. His know-it-all buddy Kate joked that he could have filled in for Jerry Seinfeld, when he retired. Randall didn't know if that was good or bad, although he didn't mind either way. He liked being Jewish, insofar as his family was, eating potato latkes and matzo balls every once in a while, weekly corned beef sandwiches and half-sour pickles from Katz's, and going to a jazzy bar mitzvah every few years.

Randall wasn't nerdy, Kate said, but intellectual-looking. She said he was very handsome "in that kind of way." And although he realized this wasn't the same as the "best-looking" title Jesse won in the unofficial student body polls that were constantly being passed around, Randall took it as a major compliment, since Kate didn't say things she didn't mean—which usually was a bad thing, but not in this case.

He looked down at the bottoms of his jeans—which were severely frayed, just the way he liked, and he started to pick at them. This led him to tying a couple of threads that had come loose into a knot, and finally he realized he was procrastinating. It wasn't that Randall was lazy, because he wasn't. It was just that the sweet perfection of ideas swimming around in his head never made it onto the paper; he never achieved on a concrete level what he knew in the abstract. If he procrastinated long enough he wouldn't write anything today. Jesse was coming around to pick him up in a little while. Jesse's parents had bought him a huge SUV and now he was driving everyone around, since none of them were seventeen yet except for Jesse. He was nearly a full year older than Abigail, Randall, and Kate.

This wasn't going to be Randall's night for achievement. He closed the spiral notebook and changed into a long-sleeved T-shirt—orange with navy sleeves—since it was a bit chilly at night now. He turned on his computer. There were no messages from Abigail, not that he was expecting any. Randall read through the news, checked his stocks, installed a new program his dad had e-mailed to him, and went down to hang with his father for a few minutes before he left.

Randall found him on the floral sofa—a pathetically

blatant remnant of his mother—where his butt print had been worn in over the past three years. His dad was watching a musical documentary on Steely Dan.

"What's going on?" Randall asked.

"Not too much."

"Got any plans tonight?" Randall stole a look at the giant flat-screen before glancing back at his dad. Six o'clock and he was already in his ugly old Columbia University sweats.

"Oh yeah, I got big Friday-night plans for that microwave popcorn in the cabinet." His dad smiled, aware of his weaknesses. After Randall's mom had left him, his confidence had been shattered. He hadn't done one thing to piece his life back together; it was as if he was afraid to try and fail. Randall didn't have to work too hard to figure out how he had developed those same fears. Like father, like son.

"Whatever happened with that woman you met in the park?"

"I'll call her . . . maybe next week."

"Dad, you met her six months ago!" Randall said.

"I like to take things slow." His dad half smiled.

"There's slow and then there's dead, Dad."

"What did I do to get stuck with such a wiseass son, huh?" His dad grabbed Randall in a headlock and started knuckling him.

"Dad, you're gonna ruin my hair," Randall cracked.

Finally he heard Jesse's honk and told his father he had to go. "See you later, Dad," Randall said, pulling himself from the sofa and tossing one of the pillows at his father's head. He felt terrible about leaving. "Hey . . . you wanna join us at Roll-n-Roaster?"

"Nah. Bring me back something, though. You know what I like . . . a classic roast beef, some curly fries, and, um, some of that horseradish sauce."

"Cool. Catch you on the flip."

Aside from the fact that he was brokenhearted and incapable of moving on, Randall thought his dad was great. But the divorce had been rough on both of them. When his mother left, she'd actually gone right up to Randall and explained to him about how people's feelings change, but it doesn't mean they don't love their family. The speech came off as something out of a self-help book, and Randall had wondered if she'd said the same thing to his father. It would explain why his father hadn't cleaned the house or gone out with friends since she'd left.

"Hey, Ran," Jesse said from behind the steering wheel of his SUV. They had met way back in Little League—the two kids who never wanted to be played. They shared headphones under the bleachers.

"You do realize you're killing our planet with your super-size ride here, right?" Randall had just read a compelling *New York Times* article on the subject and wished he could do something about it. But what? He was just one person, and even getting out of bed in the morning sometimes seemed a little too daunting.

"It's getting you to Roll-n-Roaster, isn't it? Really, why do you have to be such a tree hugger? What has this planet ever done for you? Give and take, my friend—give me this car and I'll take you to get some grub." Jesse laughed lightly. He twisted his Saint Martin cap on the diagonal to imply he was tough.

Randall understood that Jesse was trying to press his buttons and that he wasn't serious, but something about that last question got to him. "You're right. What has it done for me? I've got all the tools—ability; a connected, genius—if miserable—dad; money—but somehow I can't muster up the energy to get my music off the ground."

"I've got an idea. Why don't you give yourself some kind of deadline, like tell yourself you'll finish putting a demo together by next month, and whatever it is by then, it is." Jesse turned to Randall while he spoke, the car never once swaying. He was the only person Randall knew who could be insightful while wearing a crooked baseball cap. If only Randall could tap into that kind of confidence.

"It's just . . . I don't know, let's put it this way . . . what if they don't *get* me? Or what if they get me, but want to repackage me into some manufactured pop star without a shred of integrity?" There were so many "what ifs," they could drive Randall nuts . . . or drive him to go back to bed and pull the covers over his head.

"You gotta take a chance, man. Otherwise there'll always be an excuse to hide behind."

Randall changed the subject. "So what did you do today?"

Jesse drove like he spoke—relaxed, confident, but not aggressive or in your face. He made driving and everything else seem like common sense.

"The One Trick opened up again, so I'm back there." He turned onto the Brooklyn-Queens Expressway, and across the river they could see the Manhattan skyline.

"Jimmy the Dude called in a favor?" Randall asked, his face at the window like a puppy's. If only he could be as up-front and comfortable with the world out there as he was with his friends.

"Nah, some new chick from France named Caroline."
Jesse raised his eyebrows to bait his friend.

"Let me guess, you spent the afternoon in the basement 'getting to know each other'?" Jesse wouldn't know love if it came up and mugged him on the sidewalk. Randall had to hand it to him, Jesse sure did make life easier with that attitude. If only he could be that way himself. But no, Randall had to be plagued with the worst kind of love—the unreciprocated kind he felt for Abigail, his best friend.

He could remember the precise moment it had happened. They were doing geometry homework last year. It was the very beginning of the semester, and Abigail didn't understand a thing about it. She kept asking, "But *why* does $A^2 + B^2 = C^2$?" Her hair was a little longer then and it kept slipping down in front of her shoulders. They were sitting at her kitchen table.

Randall had showed her over and over again—the whole thing was quite elementary—but she just couldn't get it. And for some reason this made him smile uncontrollably, the kind of smile that stretches your mouth as far as it goes. Her mother had some kind of opera music playing, and though Randall didn't exactly like it, the drama and importance of it had heightened his senses. When they both looked up from the book at the exact same moment, his breath had been drained from his lungs altogether. Randall had choked and eventually Mrs. Jones had come running, patting him on the back like a child. It was mortifying.

"Nope. Honestly. It's not like that."

"Okay, ha ha, April Fools', I get it."

"First of all, it's September. Remember, school starts in

a couple of days? Second of all, what's going on with Abigail? She said she saw you earlier."

"Oh yeah? What did she say?" Randall asked, his attention torn from the water and the cityscape beyond.

"She said she wanted to kiss your big, pouty lips and then . . ."

Randall screwed up his mouth and let out a huge sigh. When Jesse joked around like that, he minimized the difficulties and delicacies of the situation. "I actually think we're making some progress," Randall said, half-believing himself. In the past week it had seemed as though Abigail was opening up to him more and more. Surely that had to mean something, had to signal some type of innate connection.

"Well, I guess that's good, right?"

"Yeah, great," Randall said.

Jesse rolled his eyes. "Hey, look at it this way, if you continue at this pace, then by retirement age, I'm sure you'll get to first base. And then you can get the senior discount on bus fare wherever you take her."

"You're hysterical, Jesse." He wasn't going to think about how similar that comment was to the one he'd made to his dad earlier.

They listened to the Flash real loud until they pulled into a parking space and piled out of the car. "Maybe that thing is a little big," Jesse said, looking back at the SUV, which covered one and a half spots. Then they made their way inside the fast-food restaurant.

"Mmmmmmmm," Randall said when finally he bit into his first roast beef sandwich. "This is some amazingly good crap." The woman had gotten his order wrong, but he

25

hadn't said anything. It was okay that he didn't have cheese. This way, maybe it would take a little longer until he suffered his first heart attack. Randall hated to make waves. He avoided them at all costs.

"You got that right," Jesse said. Just then his cell phone rang—the theme from *Rocky*. His face turned serious, something Jesse's face didn't often do.

"Who's that?"

"It's the chick I hooked up with last night."

"And you're considering answering it?" Randall couldn't believe his ears. He turned his face up to the sky. "Excuse me, God? What have you done with my friend Jesse? And who is this guy? He's turning into . . . me? And then who will I become?" He had the strangest feeling Jesse really hadn't been pulling his leg in the car.

"Ssshhhh." Jesse placed his finger over his lips and picked up the phone. "Hello?" he said.

Randall could hear the girl's voice, uncertain, on the other end. "Jesse? It's Cammie, from last night?"

Randall cupped his hand over his mouth. He waited for Jesse to do his usual and give her the brush-off. He was king of the brush-off. "Okay, pretty baby, stay cool," he could say, or "I'll be around," and nonchalantly break hearts without a second thought. Jesse made it look so easy. But sometimes Randall wondered if Jesse was afraid of actually having some real feelings. Would it be possible, though, to keep up the act as long as his friend had? Maybe nothing was easy, no matter how it might look from the other side.

"Hey, pretty girl," Jesse said. "How's your Friday?"

"It's okay . . . but I miss you," she said.

Even to Randall this sounded a bit desperate. But Jesse,

the biggest commitment-phobe of all time, stayed right on the phone. "Okay. You want to do something tomorrow night?"

"Sure. Why don't you pick me up at eight?"

"See you then," he said, and hung up the phone.

"I think I'm gonna be sick." Randall balled up his empty sandwich wrapper. "This is too confusing. I'm emotionally drained. I don't even know you anymore. The one thing I could count on . . . gone." He faked a couple of sniffles for effect. "Could you be . . . in love?"

"Relax. I'm simply giving her another shot before I blow her off. I just felt like I should."

Randall knew that no matter what Jesse was doing with this girl, it was more than he was doing with Abigail, so he let it go.

Back at home, his dad was passed out on the couch with his arms and legs splayed like a rag doll. The man had the potential to be so much more than this. He *was* more than this. He'd invented the second most popular Web browser in the country—dig.com—but since the company had gone public, he'd basically stopped making goals for himself. He was stagnant, working from home almost every day, sometimes skipping his shower.

Randall took one last look at him lying there—his hair still thick as a lawn, but partially gray now and more than a little too overgrown; he had put on a little weight as well, mostly around the middle. Finally, Randall looked away, and then retreated to the kitchen to stuff his dad's bag of Roll-n-Roaster into the fridge. His father probably wouldn't heat it up. He could eat food cold without a second thought. Randall's mom used to say it drove her nuts. But you could tell from the way she said it that the funny habit only further endeared him to her. It still boggled Randall's mind that his mom could up and leave. How could you get so far, only to turn around and go all the way back?

Randall grabbed a bottled water from the fridge and jogged up the stairs. He wished his father would take down that photo of the three of them—a happy family out on the lawn in Cobble Hill, green grapes and Frisbee and library books. What a joke. But Randall wouldn't tell his dad because he knew that picture represented a bit of hope for him. It reminded his father that he'd once been happy and possibly he could be again. He just didn't know how to get there, was all.

In his room, Randall plugged his Ibanez into the jack on his amplifier. His walls were all soundproofed with wavy foam, so he could turn it up all the way. About six months ago, before his dad had retreated to the living room for good, he'd introduced Randall to Jonathan Sizemore, a producer from Live Records—the guy responsible for his favorite band, Empire, who were a cross between Green Day and Foo Fighters. "Here's my card," Mr. Sizemore had told Randall. "Give me a call in September. I'll have some time then and I'd love to take a listen to your demo."

Well, the story kind of fizzled out after that. Randall had equipment, and he could easily afford the studio time over at Day-Glo Studios. He spent time on songs—had dozens of them recorded—but nothing felt good enough. Randall thought he couldn't get the words to fit, that they didn't really say what he wanted them to, or the next time it was the guitar solo that wasn't working.

The business card would disintegrate pretty soon if Randall kept on this way. And then he wouldn't need an excuse for not doing anything . . . he'd have lost his chance for good. Randall looked at the softened card long and hard before putting it back in his wallet and doing nothing about it. Sure, he'd advised Abigail earlier that she should follow her gut, take charge of her situation, but here he was . . . a complete hypocrite, with the exact same problems holding him back.

Randall looked at the poem Abigail had given him the previous week. He'd been surprised that she allowed him to read it, and he wanted to show her how much that meant to him by putting it to music. But even that never seemed to crystallize from an idea into something concrete enough.

> *Go on, he says.*
> *Sauté, jeté, pas de bourrée.*
> *Kick and tuck and slide.*
> *She died.*
> *But life and the words. Sway leaf and hail cab*
>   *and sweep the floor.*
> *More, more. We must always want more.*
> *Are you sure?*

There was something special here and Randall knew it, something deeply beautiful to sing, but he feared he wouldn't do it justice, so he slipped it back into his notebook for another time.

It was late anyway. After Roll-n-Roaster, Randall and

Jesse had sat by the Promenade in Brooklyn Heights and shared a joint. And now, Randall felt like a douche for moaning about Abigail.

"You make everything so difficult," Jesse had told him.

Was he right? Was there an easier way that Randall just wasn't aware of? If there was, it eluded him. He ticked off the details of the situation: Abigail had just lost her mom, leaving her more unsure of herself than ever; she already had a boyfriend (who wasn't worth the dirt on Abigail's shoe); and lastly, if Randall ever did get the balls to actually tell Abigail how he felt, there was a very good possibility he could destroy their friendship.

If she didn't like him back, things would be awkward and she'd stop opening up to him, which was this amazing road-to-recovery thing she'd started to do lately only with him. On the other hand, if Abigail did return his feelings initially, but they wound up eventually breaking up, they wouldn't even be casual friends anymore. The whole group—Jesse and Kate, too—could become victims of the aftermath.

With all that risk, how *could* Randall make a move? He shook the weight of all that out of his head, plopped onto his bed, and turned on the television. Downstairs, he heard his dad plod into the bathroom.

"Randall," he heard his father call, and for some reason the name hit him oddly, as if it were a thing he didn't want to be associated with. *Fear*, Abigail would say in that charming way she had of naming things as they passed by.

"Yes, Dad?" he croaked through the narrowed space in his throat.

"Why don't you sit with your old man and watch some television?"

"Be down in a minute," Randall called, glancing briefly at the time, the guitar, thinking tomorrow would be another day.

4

When she reached Ellen Saneman's office on the last Friday before school was about to begin, Kate Foster glided right in through the open door with the stenciled black name over the word "President." Kate knew firsthand that in small companies the owners used titles like that to create the air of professionalism that simply did not exist. Just yesterday she'd sent out a company-wide e-mail informing everyone that she herself should now be referred to as account associate. Kate had researched a bunch of other public relations firms online and found that title worked best.

Ellen Saneman was once again wearing an untucked blouse that truly should have been tucked, not to mention paired with a skinny belt and a brooch at the very least. How could a "president" present herself this way? Without a single accessory?

"Well, come on in, Account Associate Kate," Ellen said sarcastically.

Was that tone really necessary? After all, Ellen had just called her in, saying, "Please come to my office to talk."

"What can I do for you, boss?" Kate asked. She'd been at this internship two weeks now and could count on her hands, toes, and then other people's appendages the ways in which this public relations firm could be drastically improved. She'd drafted memos to Ellen suggesting each. They'd probably make her vice president before she even graduated from high school. But then, of course, they'd better start paying her, because she wasn't going to fix up an entire company for four lousy credits.

"Honestly, Kate . . . nothing more."

"I'm sorry, what do you mean?" Kate was determined. She was not going to be fired again. If she didn't stop getting fired, she was going to wind up in summer school next year taking another course for those four credits.

"I have to let you go."

"But why?" She'd had it! Everyone in this world was a moron. How were you supposed to get anywhere under those conditions?

Ellen Saneman laughed wildly. "You really don't know, do you? I keep forgetting how young you are." She shook her head, curled a finger at her chin, and angled her head to one side.

"I was helping you out, showing you how to make things work better, and, honestly, I thought I'd be rewarded."

"Let me tell you something, Miss Kate. You cannot go around telling your superiors that they are doing everything wrong and that you can do everything so much better, that it's so easy a kid could do it. You're going to make a lot of enemies that way."

"Are you saying those aren't solid ideas that would benefit your company?" No matter how young she was, when Kate saw inefficiency, she was going to point it out. Period. This was the way things were done in her family. Lord, she couldn't wait to see how her mom would make an example of this most recent internship failure. "How difficult could this be? It's a *nonpaying* job!" Her mother had said last time.

"Kate, that is irrelevant. You are smart as a whip and painfully confident, intimidating even. But you need to learn tolerance, respect, and patience, or you are going to have a long, lonely road ahead of you. If you take one thing from this experience, please, let it be that. I know you don't want to hear this, but eventually you'll see I'm right."

The air outside was still, as if nature were taking a break. The sun shone on Kate's bad luck as if it couldn't give a crap. If God hadn't wanted her to be aggressive, then he shouldn't have made her beautiful, tall and thin and with ample cleavage and blue eyes, and so freaking smart. It was ridiculous, the way people danced around everything instead of just going for it. And now it seemed as if everyone was trying to tell Kate that she should start behaving this way. Life was short, and Kate was determined to squeeze every single ounce of happiness from it.

"Taxi!" She wasn't about to get on the grungy subway after a day like this. Screw that.

Two taxis nearly collided, competing over the few feet

of sidewalk in front of her. See? She looked too good to be so miserable. And she was wearing an amazing vintage Pucci shirtdress with a glittery gold chain belt, and round-toed, stacked-heel pumps that looked absolutely perfect. What a waste of a great outfit.

"Take the Brooklyn Bridge to the Cadman Plaza exit," she said. Once settled in the backseat, she fished around in her purse for her cell phone. She hadn't called Ken, the most recent guy she was flinging with, in four days, despite the two messages he'd left. But the Foster women did not do failure well, and at the moment Kate needed to feel that something was right in her life, that she could succeed somewhere, so she thought she'd give this guy a try.

Kate scrolled down through a sea of other names: James, Christopher, Luke, Ronald, Jefferson, Linus, Steven—she'd tossed them all aside after an equally short time because of their lack of gumption, or fear of a real relationship, or whatever. She pressed "send" when she came to Ken's entry.

"Ken Digson," he answered.

"It's me," she cooed, trying to be enthusiastic. They'd met on the 6 train and talked all the way up to Sixty-eighth Street. Kate suggested they grab a cocktail at a local pub that never checked ID, and after that they couldn't keep their hands off each other. But Ken hadn't seemed very cultured. He'd never even heard of the New York City Ballet, which Abigail's mother had been a part of.

"Oh yeah, hey, Kate. I was just thinking of you. Do you wanna grab some dinner later?"

But something too eager in his voice turned her off. She'd wanted this to work, to give the guy a chance, but her heart wasn't in it. "I can't, I'm afraid," she said.

"How about tomorrow?" he tried, sounding almost desperate.

She answered directly, before things got sticky. It was so disappointing for this to happen to her again. Was there no one in the world right for her? How much failure could a person stand? Kate searched for her most heartfelt voice. "Ken, I just called to say that I don't think we have very much in common. I think it's best if we part ways." She longed to hang up the phone and just be done with this latest failure so she could move on, but she waited for him to respond.

"I'm sorry you feel that way, Kate. But . . . can I ask you one thing?"

Oh God, she thought, *here we go.* He's going to try to change my mind. She should have left well enough alone. "Sure," she said.

"How do you even know what we have in common? We only hung out for about four hours."

"I just know myself," Kate said.

"All right," he said. "Good luck with that."

Good luck with that? What was *that* supposed to mean? Was there something wrong with a girl who was confident about herself, who just happened to have an instinct about things?

Kate hung up the phone, wanting it to make a serious slam but achieving only a dainty click.

The driver caught sight of her in the mirror with a look of shock around his eyes.

"You wouldn't find yourself saying those things about me, beautiful miss. If you ever want to give it a whirl, here's my card."

Kate took it between two fingers with a fake smile. She knew you didn't screw with your taxi driver before you even got to the bridge. But honestly, this man had more guts than any of the other guys had showed after a couple of dates. The beginnings, Kate was great at those—the initial attraction and flirtation—she barely had to bat her lashes and guys were lining up to take her out. But give it a week and . . . pow! . . . off they went.

There was only one person she wanted to talk to now. Abigail . . . now there was someone she could rely on.

"Hey," Abigail answered. Kate missed the funny things Abigail used to say when she'd answer the phone. "Ed's Repair Shop," she might say, or, "Exotic Birds and Fish on Third."

"Hi. How are you?" Kate said, her eyes on the river, glittering in the sunlight.

"Uh-oh, what's wrong?" Abigail asked.

"Oh, nothing," Kate said.

"Come on, you can tell Madame Abigail."

"I got fired."

"*Again?*" Abigail asked in her best impression of Kate's mother.

"Come on!" Kate couldn't help laughing.

"Well, look at it this way . . . at least you might have a chance at getting your name into the *Guinness Book of World Records*. I think it was Darryl Schminglington who took the title of Most Firings in a Single Month back in 1987 with a whopping three. One more and you've got him."

"Ha ha ha." Kate tried to be sarcastic, though she couldn't help lightening up a bit at Abigail's take on things.

"Seriously, though, I need an internship or I won't be able to go to London in the spring."

"That's the good thing about you, Kate. You always figure things out. You always find a way to make it work in the end. I have faith in you, wouldn't have you as my friend if I didn't."

Abigail and Kate had become friends in the second grade. The private school they attended was a kindergarten-through-twelfth-grade institution, and when Kate saw young girls swinging hands on the way to school, she always thought of herself and Abigail. They'd been inseparable. Everyone had wanted to be Kate's friend except Abigail, who'd once walked up to Kate during quiet math time and asked her why she didn't let someone else answer a question once in a while. And that was when Kate knew they'd be friends forever. Abigail had always been introverted, and that was what made her attempts at assertion so fantastic—if you knew her, you understood how much it cost her to accomplish them. Those fleeting moments were entirely gone since Abigail's mother had died; Kate sorely missed them.

"Well, shucks. You know what I could use now, though?"

"Some Korean noodle soup?"

"You read my mind."

"I wish I could, Kate, but I'm on my way to meet Nick."

"Fine, I'll talk to you tomorrow," Kate said, snapping the phone shut in disappointment. She loved that soup, but wouldn't dare eat at the noodle shop by herself. How tacky.

Kate arrived at her block. She never had taxis drop her

off directly in front of her house in case they were lunatics who'd come back later to kill her. She folded a twenty in half the long way and gave it to the driver. "Keep the change," she said. "And thanks for the compliment. It was thoughtful."

He replied, "It was true." He didn't seem like a lunatic, but Kate knew better than to take chances.

She smiled and was careful not to slam the door behind her. She hoped, but didn't depend on, the possibility that her goodwill might circle back her way. On the record, Kate strongly believed you made your own luck, but after the day's events she wasn't convinced that her theory held water.

She steeled herself to face her mother. *Just get it done with,* she told herself again and again as she stepped over the cracks in the sidewalk on the way to her own stoop halfway up the block. The house was a double-wide brownstone—they'd taken over the neighbor's unit the second her parents bought the movie and subsidiary rights to the mystical children's book series The Young Wizard, which became a four-part movie, a card game, a video game, a board game, an interactive computer game, a collection of figurines, a line of plush toys, and a McDonald's Happy Meal prize. The place hadn't been for sale, but that hadn't stopped her parents.

Kate lifted the latch on the wrought-iron fence, walked past the pretty Colonial streetlamp her mother had had installed on their minuscule patch of grass a few months ago, and climbed the six brown cement stairs to the red front door. Inside, their housekeeper, Selma—always discreet and barely detectable—had neatly placed the mail in order of size inside the painted African box they kept on the table in the foyer. Kate hung her bag on the hook above and tried not to look around at all the perfect things staring back at her on her way upstairs—the Mexican masks, the real Degas painting, the series of Turkish rugs underfoot. They would just be mocking her when she admitted to yet another failure—one that was absolutely not her fault. It wasn't fair, that was for sure. But she knew what her mother would say to that. "Life's not fair, Katey-poo." She hated when her mother called her that. "Any fool knows that. It's how you work around it that really counts."

Kate climbed the stairs, looking at all the black-and-white photos of her award-winning moments—first-grade science fair, mathletes champion, first-place spelling bee prize, swim team champ, Camp Minnekonda color war most valuable player, and so on, until she reached the top stair and turned down the hallway to her part of the house.

Atop her stiffly made bed, the Italian white linens with their black hotel borders, Selma had piled a few of the items Kate had asked her to pick up at the store—the face wash she loved, a bottle of rosewater, shea butter, and the shampoo and conditioner she used. *Miss Kate, here are your things, dear. Let me know if you need anything else.* She'd written that on a pretty square of parchment Kate's mother kept around the house in stitched leather boxes so no one could excuse themselves from leaving a note about something. Her penmanship was perfect. Selma herself was perfect. In all these years, she'd never gotten one thing wrong. It wasn't that it was a burden; it wasn't that Kate couldn't follow in all these impeccable footsteps. It was that all the other blundering idiots were always getting in her way, and she was getting very, very tired of it all.

40

"Blah blah blah," Kate said to the flawless, empty house as she shed her pretty dress and pulled on a pair of dark denim jeans and a comfortable mint green cotton polo shirt. Then she retreated to her bed and thought about what Abigail had said: "You always find a way to make it work in the end." Kate knew that was true, but for some reason faith wasn't enough to keep her from pulling the covers over her head and hiding.

5

Why am I doing this again? Jesse asked himself as he drove over to pick up Cammie on Saturday night. He could barely remember what she looked like. He was king of the one-date romance, master of the one-night stand. Jesse didn't do follow-ups. He didn't do commitments. In his experience, most relationships in this life disappointed you if you let them, though you wouldn't hear him sharing that perspective.

"I'm here," he said into his cell phone when he was outside Cammie's door. She was taller than he remembered, leggier. Hot. She had that severely layered hair that fell to her shoulders, kind of like Kate's. But when Cammie opened her mouth it was a different story. "I wasn't sure you were gonna make it," she said as she buckled herself into the gigantic passenger seat.

Jesse was barely five minutes late. See this? She was

already expecting all kinds of things from him, and they hadn't even technically gone on a date yet. They'd met at a party and then gone back to her apartment. He was already thinking he should have left it at that.

Still, Jesse tried to ignore the awkward start to the evening and leaned in to kiss her. First he moved in real close but didn't actually make contact. Girls loved that stuff . . . the anticipation. He closed his eyes and then opened them again and then he gave a soft tug on her bottom lip and then her top and then . . . pow! Jesse went in for the kiss. Cammie smelled too sugary, like strawberry-flavored Chap Stick, which smelled nothing like a real strawberry. Suddenly Jesse was struck with a comparison between that scent and the trail of real lavender that seemed to follow Caroline wherever she went. He faked a scratch to his nose to see if he could still smell a slight whiff of it on his own hand.

"You're forgiven," Cammie said as he shifted into drive and made his way toward a new restaurant, Copper, somewhere on Atlantic Avenue.

When they reached Copper, Jesse was glad to see a parking valet, because he didn't feel like being stuck in the car with Cammie much longer. He didn't know about second dates. He wasn't sure what was expected, and nothing was really coming to him. What was he looking for exactly? Well, he wouldn't have minded if, when he'd leaned in for that kiss, it wasn't all choreographed, if instead he'd felt something . . . something like in that photo of Caroline's. Sure, it was his own routine he'd followed—the old wait, open, tug—but now it seemed hollow and phony and for some reason it bothered him.

"Mademoiselle, Monsieur." The hostess cooed a

greeting to them, but really just to him. She wore a slinky black dress, barely covering her ass and her chest, and she made the most of it as she showed them to their table. She waved her hips back and forth in a message to Jesse. He'd gotten that message before, so he recognized it now, loud and clear. But he couldn't do anything about it. Not now that he was on a second damned date!

The place lived up to its name—a copper-coated tin ceiling, hammered-copper tables, low-slung copper chandeliers with flickering lightbulbs.

Once they reached the table, Jesse pulled Cammie's cushy blue velvet chair out while the hostess placed the menus on their coordinated blue plates. From that vantage point he mirrored the hostess's interest with a knowing glance, and she gathered her puffed lips in and then bit down on the bottom one. When Cammie had sat down, shimmied in close to the table, and looked up, the hostess said, *"Bon appétit,"* and turned to go. Jesse sat his lower half under the table before he could be arrested for indecency.

"You think that hostess is hot, don't you?" Cammie said, her chin back so far, it was indistinguishable from the rest of her face. Her eyebrows looked pretty scary raised up that high.

"Which hostess?" Jesse asked, shifting his long legs under the small table.

"The one you were making eyes at when you thought I wasn't looking."

Cammie is pretty smart, Jesse thought. Maybe he should give her another chance before he closed the book on her, which he'd nearly done before they'd even arrived.

Rather than talk, Jesse thought action would speak to that point best, so he felt for her knee under the table, and then he allowed his hand to travel north a bit. As he suspected, Cammie responded positively. She softened her features, leaned in a little, and removed her shoe to tickle Jesse's ankle with her foot.

"I'm starving," she said, likely not talking about the food.

Jesse cleared his throat and thought maybe second dates weren't that bad after all.

"What are you in the mood for?" he asked.

She ignored the question completely. "Has anyone ever told you how intense your eyes are?" she said seductively.

"No, they're just ordinary," he said, twisting the tiny bud vase in the middle of the table so the single tulip inside waved slightly. He let her think she'd discovered him in a way nobody else had before.

"Not ordinary at all," she said, lingering on the last word.

He licked his lips.

She readjusted herself in her seat and breathed deeply before they opened their menus. Shortly after that, the waitress came by to take their drink order. Jesse looked up and saw another gorgeous woman with long wavy hair the color of honey, a couple of delicate freckles over her nose and cheeks. When she spoke she had a British accent. Oh Jesus! Did every woman here have to be this unbelievable? How was he supposed to follow through with this? It seemed like all signs were blinking ABORT! ABORT!

But the waitress seemed not to have any interest in

Jesse. "I'm Georgianne, and I'll be your waitress this evening. Can I interest you in a cocktail?" She turned to Cammie first.

"What would you recommend?" Cammie asked.

"Oh, we make an amazing mojito," the waitress said. She had an easy way that made Jesse want to chum up to her.

"That sounds great," Cammie responded.

"Make it two," Jesse said when finally the girl looked his way.

"Are you old enough?" the waitress asked.

Jesse was stunned. He was never carded. Never! Not since he was fourteen years old. This was crazy. He had a fake ID, though. No problem. He reached into his wallet, pulled out the California license he'd bought with Abigail, Randall, and Kate in a Greenwich Village head shop last year, and passed it to the waitress. They were great fakes— worked everywhere.

"Oh, you're from Escondido," she said. "Where-abouts?"

Was this girl kidding? He had no freaking idea about Escondido or wherever. He wasn't even sure if that was a real place or not. "By the water." Jesse figured that was a safe answer for anywhere in California.

The waitress smiled, shook her head, and handed the card back. "I'll bring your Coke right over," she said.

Jesse screwed up his face. Whose life was he living, exactly? These things just did not happen to him. He felt the heat rise in his face as he watched their waitress walk over to the bar.

"How old *are* you?" Cammie asked. She had said

earlier that she was twenty-one and in her senior year at Parsons because she wanted to become some kind of commercial artist.

"I'm nineteen," he lied, annoyed as hell.

"Oh, a younger man, huh?" she joked.

Jesse accepted his carbonated beverage silently and looked closely at Cammie. She didn't have a touch of that "just out of reach" quality he'd noticed about Caroline. Cammie seemed as though she put it all out there, like she was completely exposed and there was nothing really to wonder about. He'd known Cammies before. Plenty of them. What he needed was someone he couldn't figure out at a glance.

"Do you drink coffee?" Jesse asked out of the blue.

"Oh, I like that instant flavored stuff. You know . . . the kind you just add water to. I'm always rushing around."

"Yeah, I know that stuff," he said, trying not to get caught sniffing his own palm for the fifth time. He wondered what kind of reaction Caroline would have to instant coffee.

When a wire basket of fancy breads with lots of poppy and sesame seeds came out, Cammie grew talkative. "Have you heard about that new club Marrakesh that opened in the Meatpacking District?"

"No, I haven't," Jesse said. He hated the velvet rope scene—pretentious spots where people were trying too hard to prove how cool they were. Jesse only ever went when Kate threw a must-attend event like a birthday party for one of them. He'd rather something off the beaten path, something that had its own identity; this was just exactly what had originally attracted him to the One Trick

Pony. It was offbeat now, too, but in an entirely different way. It was funny how a single person could have such an effect on a place. In less than a day, Caroline had made such an impression on him. And considering how delicious her coffee was, he knew that everyone in the neighborhood would be knocking down the One Trick's door, just to get a taste of it—and gaze at the enigmatic woman who made life sweeter.

At closing time the previous night, Caroline had pulled the elastic from her hair and it had tumbled over her shoulders in pretty kinks. She flopped into one of the chairs and sighed. Jesse had expected her to say she was tired or that it had been a long day, but instead she tossed off her shoes and exclaimed, "Put on some music, Jesse! It's time to dance." He wasn't much of a dancer. Sure, he could if he wanted to, but he hadn't ever really wanted to. He had stood hesitantly a few feet away from where Caroline sat, unsure about the idea yet feeling the thrill rise.

"Come on! What are you waiting for?" She stood up and went to the antique radio she kept on a shelf along the wall. The music that came through had sounded as though it was from a World War I movie.

"Where did you find this station?" he'd asked.

"You like it?" Caroline answered his question with another, which, he was noticing, she often did.

Jesse had shook his head, his eyes narrowing. There was a deep romance to the sad saxophone and the light piano that stirred up the questions and feelings that had been brewing within him. Caroline pulled Jesse in by taking both of his hands and then placing them on her shoulders. She was about three inches shorter than he was, and he looked down at her with their chests nearly touching, her warmth spreading through him. He took the liberty of breathing her in fully. He found himself admiring her cheeks, which were thick with a rosy hue, probably from the hot coffee steam that had been in her face. It made her look so . . . alive.

Caroline had closed her eyes a couple of minutes into the music, gliding Jesse around with wide steps and turning them every few beats. She had a smile on her face, like she was escaping to some place the music reminded her of. "La la la," she sang, following along.

"This is pretty cool music," Jesse had said. "Different."

"I'm glad you like it."

They had danced for a while like that and then talked afterward as they washed, swept, stored, and wrapped. It was ten-thirty when they parted ways.

"Can I come upstairs for a bit?" Jessie had asked.

"Oh, I've got to run some errands," Caroline had replied, leaving Jesse to wonder what kind of errands could be run so late at night. He comforted himself with the fact that this was New York and most things were available twenty-four hours a day.

"So have you?" Cammie asked. She'd been talking all the while, but Jesse had been lost in his memories and he didn't know what she meant.

"I'm sorry, what's that?"

"I said have you ever gone to Bungalow Eight?"

"Yup." It was Kate's last birthday, just a couple of weeks before Abigail's mom went into the hospital. He thought of the way Kate had danced on top of their table (and other people's tables), the look in her eye, as if maybe she wanted to hook up with Jesse again. But he hadn't followed up. He didn't want to mix romance and friendship again. She was gorgeous and they'd had a hot time, if memory served him correctly, but Jesse didn't think they could escape a mess if they tried that again.

Cammie laundry-listed through a bunch of other spots, boring Jesse to tears with accounts of celebrity sightings, until their entrées came out. Rather than plot the route that would take him directly to Cammie's bedroom, he spent the time doubting whether Cammie had a candle inside her. There was something off about him, and he hoped it would fix itself quickly.

The evening did not improve. After they each ate a bowl of pasta, Cammie excused herself to the ladies' room, and the hostess returned to Jesse to pass him her number and make sure her thigh brushed against his arm. But Jesse was still off his game—he'd been thinking about this thing Caroline had done at closing time, how she'd put the remaining muffins out on one of the sidewalk tables with a little sign that said "FREE"—and so the touch startled him and he jumped, knocking the table loudly. The hostess giggled, but Jesse didn't see the humor.

Cammie returned earlier than expected and caught that last bit, getting the wrong idea altogether. "You're disgusting," she said, though this one time he'd been trying to do the right thing. "You have no idea how to treat people, and I guarantee you will never have a meaningful relationship in your life because of it."

People had said that kind of thing to him before, but now it spread hollowness through his chest. As her figure shrank toward the door, Jesse realized he should follow her, explain it hadn't been his fault. He threw some cash onto the table and made his way outside. But when he got to the street, she was gone. There was a soiled, torn newspaper page at his feet and the headline read "It's Over!" This seemed to be speaking to him. It did appear his run had ended, and now . . . he didn't know what to expect. He realized he'd left his valet ticket on the table and pushed the door open to retrieve it.

The waitress was already clearing their glasses and napkins. Damn, she really was breathtaking. Maybe Jesse could salvage the night, prove to himself he hadn't lost it. He smiled at her as he reached for the ticket, about to ask, "Would you like to grab a drink later?" But he didn't.

She smiled encouragingly—a lively, bright, beautiful thing—though she'd given him a hard time before.

Jesse stood there for a second, holding on to his ticket. Why hadn't he asked her out? What had made him pass up this opportunity? He was completely stunned at his inaction. Would he really go home alone?

Jesse watched the waitress for a second as she took an order at a table not far from where he stood—a couple in their thirties, he guessed, dressed up like it was Christmas Eve or something. But his attention turned to the couple, the way they held hands, the way their eyes shot directly to each other at something Georgianne said, like they shared a secret joke.

Outside, he gave the valet a five-dollar bill and closed himself inside his car. He started to drive slowly toward his house. The streetlights streaked his car in the darkness. Jesse fiddled around with the radio, looking for that old-time station. Finally he found it on the AM register. The slow sway of a high-pitched guitar—a ukulele, maybe—and a tinkling piano came over his car stereo clearly. He pictured himself in an old music hall, an orchestra playing on an elevated stage. He was wearing a tuxedo with a sharp bow tie and on his arm was Caroline in a glittering evening gown, dancing just as they had the day before. This comforted him immensely.

Jesse passed the Laundromat, the Chinese grocer, the Korean vegetable stand with a remarkable hill of cabbages out front. The song was long and it had great movement. Against it, the familiar, worn avenue with its intricate web of cracks and millions of black gum spots was rejuvenated. A couple of women chatting looked extraordinarily elegant in black dresses and heels; the trees swayed importantly; the moon looked down at him with something to say, if only he could figure it out.

It was outside the International Food Market that Jesse saw Caroline. At first he couldn't be sure it was her. She looked so plain and ordinary outside the One Trick. Caroline's hair was pulled back into a bun this time, and he could see the profile of her face as he came nearer. She looked sad, lonely, like a stranger in a strange land, and his heart contracted at the thought of that.

Jesse pulled the car over at the bus stop—the only place where another car wasn't parked—and jumped out. "Caroline!" he called a little too frantically.

When she turned and recognized him, one side of Caroline's mouth twisted up into a familiar smile.

To be responsible for a smile like that! Jesse was overcome.

" 'Allo, Jesse."

He grabbed the bags from her. "Hi."

"Thanks," she said. People passed by, walking around her without recognizing anything special, and this seemed odd to Jesse—that she could be just like anyone else on the street, heads shaking at Caroline like she was a nuisance holding up the flow of foot traffic.

"Let me drive you home," Jesse offered.

"Okay. Yes," Caroline said. "That would be nice."

"Where do you live?" he asked.

"Upstairs from the café." She watched him pack the bags into the back of the giant SUV. They hardly took up any of the enormous space at all. "I should have bought more," Caroline joked.

Jesse looked at her with his eyes gleaming. "You could've bought the whole store," he said. "My parents believe bigger is better. You should see our dog."

He made her laugh. At the end of it, she sighed a little and pulled her loose raincoat tighter over her shoulders.

"Are you cold?" he asked as he closed the rear door. Instinctively, he placed his hand in that place under her neck where he'd looked so many times when he assumed she wouldn't notice.

"A little." Caroline didn't say anything about the hand. He wished they had longer to walk. But alas, they reached the front passenger door and he had to remove his palm to open the door and help her up. Now his hand was on her hand as she jumped up into the passenger seat, and he couldn't keep himself from holding it there a second too long. Did that look say she didn't mind?

Jesse walked around the SUV, taking his time, not wanting this experience to end too quickly. He slid into the seat and turned the key in the ignition, and that radio station came on. This time the song was very brassy— trumpets and trombones moaning sadly. Immediately, he was embarrassed. What would she think of him, listening to this?

He avoided looking at her directly, but he could see out of the corner of his eye that she had turned to him. After a moment she asked, "Do you really have a dog?"

"Nah. Always wanted one, but I'm deathly allergic."

"You are kidding me!"

"No, I am. When I was a kid I had to be hospitalized once after a playdate."

She laughed and Jesse turned in mock horror. "I almost died and you find this hysterical?" he said.

"I am sorry." Caroline rested her hand on his arm. "It's just that you don't look like the kind of guy who'd be allergic to dogs, or one who'd have a 'playdate.'"

"I'm gonna let you off the hook," he said, "and take that as a compliment."

Remembering that Caroline was cold, Jesse turned the heat on.

She rubbed her hands in front of the vent. "Thank you."

Inside the car, Jesse thought, they could be anywhere— far, far away from the row of signs and awnings, the army of meters and alternate-side-of-the-street parking signs.

They pulled up to the One Trick and Jesse double-parked alongside a beat-up Volkswagen Beetle.

He turned the car off and slid the keys into his jeans pocket, hopeful he might get invited up. He walked around to let Caroline out, but she was already stepping down. He stretched his hand out, and she grabbed for it. His heart jumped in his chest. Jesse wanted to keep his hand on hers, but she was quick to let go and feel for her own keys inside her coat pocket. He walked around to the back and gathered her bags.

"So what are you going to make for me?" he asked.

"I'd love to make dinner for you one day, Jesse. But tonight I have some things I have to do."

All the blood drained out of his face and he thought he might fall over. *So this is what rejection feels like,* he thought as he got back into the car.

6

That same evening, at her home on Douglass Street—a brownstone whose original integrity had been maintained thanks to her mother's care—Abigail spruced herself up as best she could in a couple of minutes. It wasn't possible to hold her attention to the task any longer than that. She thought of changing into a chocolate brown peasant blouse and switching from her sneakers to woven wedge shoes, but she couldn't bring herself to care enough. She tossed the blouse, still on its hanger, onto her bed.

This had been pretty common since her mom died. She didn't know what she'd do to get through the coming school year, but hopefully, she would feel more alive when next September rolled around. She was putting off her SATs until next year in the hopes of just that.

Abigail stood before the antique gold mirror with its mysterious orchid at the top, which hung over her low bureau. She applied deep maroon liner above her lashes with a brush and slicked on some pink lip gloss. She bent over and worked some gel into her short pixie cut—the easiest hairstyle she'd ever had. It would have to do. She didn't have the patience for primping just then. That memory of her mother from yesterday had really weirded her out, and though she had tried to shake it off, now she wanted to explore how she'd felt when she drank that interesting cup of coffee. She thought again of the taste that had lingered on her tongue during her walk to the subway and the train ride to Manhattan.

"Aaaaghhh!" Abigail stood upright and was shocked by the appearance of Ginny, her father's grasshopper of a girlfriend, right there in her room. Didn't she know how to knock? If she had knocked, Abigail would have politely said, "I'm busy." Her heart pounded. Wasn't this just like Ginny? Showing up where she wasn't wanted, appearing out of nowhere to ruin everything? Here she was . . . trapped.

Abigail held on to the corner of her tall flea-market dresser, the one with the seashell-shaped handles she and her mother had bought in Manhattan. *Mystical.* What a contrast the whimsical elegance of the dresser made with Ginny's mass-market look—in her tight pinstripe chainstore suit, fading into the crowd, but trying to force her way through as if there were something different about her. *Ordinary.* Abigail knew just what it was Ginny wanted—her father's money—and it made her sick just to think about it.

Get out! If only she could yell it, and hurl a few heavy knickknacks. "Can I help you, Ginny?"

"Oh gracious me! I was thinking I could help *you* . . .

you know, do something girly like help you get dressed to go out. Doesn't that sound like fun?"

Oh God, oh God. Anything but that. "Well, I'm dressed already, and I've really got to go." Abigail tried to keep her tone light and civil. She held on to the iron drawer handle tightly, feeling the striated lines of the shell shape, desperately trying to find the strength to get through this.

Sometimes, when her mother was well, she would lie on Abigail's bed while Abigail tried on different outfits she was considering for a party, and they would discuss the merits of one T-shirt versus another. They would get off on all kinds of tangents, talking about books and songs because they liked so many of the same things. Other times they'd get the craving for ice cream sundaes with caramel and her mother would run to the kitchen like a little kid, her feet heavy down the stairs, and make one for each of them—really big ones in cereal bowls, with clouds of whipped cream over the top. Her mother would look up sometimes, turn her head to the side, and just shake it back and forth.

"What?" Abigail would demand, smiling hugely.

Her mother's hair was so shiny it glowed. "I just can't believe how alike we are."

Hearing this made Abigail feel wonderful. Afterward, she would want to do whatever her mother suggested— wear the shirt she liked best or order the same dinner at a restaurant. Now here was Ginny in Abigail's space, on the hallowed ground of these memories, spitting and stamping on them.

"Aw, come on. I thought we could put something really chic together for you." Ginny clapped her hands together, as if this were very exciting. Her long red nails clicked.

How could her father go for someone like this, and less than five months since the funeral? Her mother was so . . . unique . . . and strong, beautiful and glowing. Abigail couldn't help glancing at her mom's photo on the nightstand. This was too much. She felt a tear and turned her head away. She'd have to go before Ginny noticed. But Ginny kept talking!

". . . Something more . . . feminine . . . something that makes you . . . you know . . . look good." Ginny walked to the closet and opened the door. "Oh well, what have we got here? T-shirts . . ." She sighed, poked through the piles on the top shelf, and continued, cataloging all the garments. "Jeans, jean shorts . . ."

Without a better plan, Abigail pulled her purse off the dresser, grabbed her cell phone and keys, and walked away as Ginny gabbed on without noticing.

"I'm leaving," she yelled to her dad once she reached the front door, hoping she could skip the "family" meeting her father had asked her to schedule for precisely this moment. Abigail wanted to be out the door, in peace, with her mother twirling and twirling so beautifully in her mind, the arc of her arm overhead strong yet still delicate somehow. But she had no such luck.

"Can you come in here for a second, Abby?" her father asked from behind the staircase, in the family room.

Would there be any peace at all? Abigail let her bag fall to the floor in frustration. At that precise moment, Ginny, having realized she had disappeared, descended the stairs with her hands planted on her hips. She didn't say anything but blinked wildly, as if Abigail should apologize. Well, maybe Abigail would have done that some other time, but she felt a new tide rise inside her. She longed to be free-floating, like her mother's flower petal skirt, weightless, flying. Now she could see the beginning of the path: there were certain choices you could make that brought you closer to such a thing. For one, you could not allow your father's girlfriend to stomp her way over your sense of self.

Ginny stood at the bottommost stair for a second and glared at Abigail. Then she turned left into the family room, where Abigail's dad was waiting. "I was helping Abby pick out something more festive to wear to her party, and I turned around and well, she had snuck out of the room."

Mr. Jones didn't yell at his daughter. He looked at her as if he might have been a stranger sitting near her in a restaurant. They'd always been close, but they'd existed in a pattern—Abby and Mom and Dad—and now, without her mother, neither of them really knew how to cut a new pattern. They just sort of winged it, and it wasn't working well. "Abby, can you please come here? You know we've got this meeting now."

"Sure, Daddy," she said, agreeable as always.

Abigail breathed deeply and sauntered into the family room. As if mocking the idea of family altogether, there was her father with his arm around Ginny, his account assistant who had turned into his girlfriend in a matter of weeks. Abigail didn't want to consider how they'd spent their "brainstorming sessions" for the Sun Safe suntan lotion account. She didn't want to think about them, period. It seemed unbelievable that her dad had once played piano so passionately alongside her mother's stage, that he'd once been part of that exclusive club of dancers Abigail had studied with such awe—

60

their steady, knowledgeable gazes; their rolled shirtsleeves; the secrets they looked to have held.

Now she looked upon her dad with disdain, his hair too styled, his clothing too new, sections of the *Times* all around the couple, as if her mother had been vaporized from existence and replaced with something mediocre she would have hated. Surely Ginny couldn't be more than twenty-six.

Abigail stood before the two of them, knowing that the world as she knew it had disappeared and this was all she was left with, take it or leave it. "What did you want to talk about?" she said, dropping onto the couch opposite. If only she could yell, "Get this ho bag out of my mother's house!" But she wouldn't, couldn't. Abigail was the polite, docile one. When everything was going well, this trait hadn't bothered her so much, but lately she was infuriated by it.

"Well, honey, you look nice," her dad said to her while running his hand over the sofa arm. He'd taken his ring off, and the windup watch her mother had given him on their second date. He looked like a vanilla version of himself— his dark hair had been cut shorter, neater; his shirt was plaid; and there wasn't a single crease in his pants.

"Thanks," Abigail said, trying not to look at Ginny.

Her father cleared his throat and kept the eye contact to a minimum. "What Ginny called this family meeting for, was to, ummm . . ."

Ginny had called the meeting? Didn't you technically have to be *in* the family to call a family meeting?

". . . to talk to you, ummm, about how Ginny and I were thinking about how good it would be for all of us to get a fresh start, somewhere new where we can put every-thing behind us and start, well, completely—"

"Fresh?" Abigail finished this ridiculous sentence for her father. She shouldn't have been so surprised. This was the way he'd handled the entire ordeal—out with the old, in with the new. Sure, he'd asked her a few times if she needed to talk about things, but he'd looked so entirely relieved when she had lied and said, "No, I'm fine."

Abigail's eyes moved to the Ballets Russes poster that hung behind him, the curves of the dancers' legs, the paint splodges she'd told her mother looked like a cow's spots, the mysterious one shoe, the billowing scarf suspended as if by magic—her life was missing all that beauty now. It seemed it had died with her mother, and now her father was going to see to it that even the unreachable relics, the scattered leaves of her they could still tread through, would be raked away, too.

Normally Abigail tried not to look Ginny directly in the face, but when Ginny spoke now, Abigail was forced to look in her deeply set dark eyes. "We thought you would love Aspen because there's a very established arts community there, you know." Then Ginny glanced at Abigail's dad and nodded, as if she'd said this just the way they'd rehearsed it.

"That's where Ginny's from," he said.

Abigail was definitely going to be ill. The words pounded in her eardrums, and amazingly, magically, some spike of determination welled up inside her and allowed her to do exactly what she had wanted to do . . . walk out without saying a word.

"Abigail? Abigail!" her dad called after her, amazed that his compliant daughter had done something so bold—but she *had*. And it felt wonderful. Abigail was already making her way to Smith Street to catch the F train to NYU.

Abigail had never been so glad to be outside. The air was exhilarating. She felt more alive than she could remember. There was a smile on her face . . . she'd nearly forgotten what that felt like. Something was happening now. She was free to roam around the perimeter of her memory, to feel in her mind the smooth wood floor of the dance studio against her palm, to remember how beautiful her mother was, with her studied, far-off look, her calves beating together like an instrument in the air; how Abigail had longed so much to possess that same grace. She thought of her mother in toe shoes, lengths of tape wrapped around them, as she levered her leg high above the back of her head, her entire body one endless curve.

Abigail caught the train, which came in just as she reached the platform, and then sailed across the bridge, watching the water dance to its own rhythm. *Peaceful.*

Excavating the memory had calmed her. She remembered something her mother used to say that had come from a book on the history of ballet and dance by Alexander Bland: that all of life was a dance, that everything could be reduced to a dance of some sort—music a movement of air, light a movement of waves. Abigail thought over the interaction with her father and Ginny now in this way: she had glided down the stairs, he'd called her in, they'd spoken softly and then more agitatedly, the tension had mounted—the music would have, too (her father should have realized this; he was a musician, after all, even if he only used his talent for commercial jingles now)—and then she'd run offstage, for the intermission. Only now did Abigail realize how atypical her role had been. *She'd* ended the scene, she'd exercised a bit of control, taken it in her hands to end the talk at that precise moment.

"Nick Gralnick," Abigail said to the front-desk attendant at Hayden Hall, Nick's dormitory. She'd met Nick just a few steps from here—on a bench in Washington Square Park. She'd been looking around, struggling to describe the trees, a certain flower, the scuffed shoe of a little boy. Nick mistakenly thought she'd been staring at him, checking him out and trying to look away before he noticed.

"Hey, saw you checking me out," he'd said, winking and smiling in a silly way.

Abigail laughed and laughed. And boy, had she needed that. Her mother had been in the hospital for over a month by then and she'd thought herself completely incapable of laughter. She'd gone and told her mother about Nick, about the funny way he'd approached her, and they'd both laughed about it. Her mother seemed to like him, or at least the idea of him.

"Nick, you've got a visitor here," the attendant said into the telephone now. "Oh, your name, miss?"

"Abigail," she said timidly. Geez, she'd only been here about a hundred times. You'd think this guy might recognize her.

A taller, black-haired girl approached the desk as Abigail moved off to the side to wait for Nick to come down.

"Ah, Cynthia!" the guard exclaimed, as if they were old friends. The girl said nothing, just ran her fingers through her impossibly straight hair.

This was Abigail's curse. She went unnoticed, unheard. She thought of the way she had walked out on her dad and wondered where she'd gotten the nerve.

"Hello, pretty girl," Nick said in his booming voice. He

bent down to kiss her hard and loud on the mouth. He wasn't a small guy. *Linebacker.* Ironically, he had baby-blond hair, which made him look like someone you could trust, someone nice. Randall had once called Nick his opposite, and she could see why. Randall was lean—his pants would slip right down if it weren't for the big "Texas" buckle and belt he wore to hold them up. And though they were both around the same height, Randall's black hair did make a huge contrast to Nick's fair coloring. She imagined them as a chess set—dueling it out on either side of the board.

"I see your beard is growing in," Abigail said with a smile. With such thin hair, he shouldn't have tried to cultivate whiskers, but all the same he'd been "growing" a goatee ever since they met. There was something quirky and endearingly human about the way he felt around the peach fuzz with his fingertips. People laughed but that was okay with Nick; he loved to make people laugh, often inviting them to with an open palm after delivering a joke.

"Hey, Abigail," a couple of Nick's roommates chorused from behind him. There was the tall one from Florida and the heavy one from New Jersey.

"Hey," she said.

As they all made their way across Washington Square Park, Abigail and Nick fell behind the other two.

"So, how are you feeling today?" Nick asked. Abigail was struck by this question. She could see why someone would ask it, but just yesterday Randall had said he wouldn't dare ask her that. He said he knew how difficult things were now—he understood she was operating in "the shadows of life," was how he put it. He said he knew she wouldn't feel good and would lie and say she did.

Even if there hadn't been that point of comparison, something was holding Abigail back from talking to Nick the way she talked with Randall. She felt bad about it, but she couldn't bring herself to change. She'd practiced the words in the mirror, stupidly. She'd said, "Well, Nick, I feel lost and hopeless and like I am incapable of exerting myself in any situation whatsoever." But she hadn't been able to exert herself in this situation, either, apparently.

"I'm doing fine," she said.

"Well, a little party is exactly what you need." Nick kissed her slowly and softly, affording a little tingle that at least proved she was still alive.

"I'm much better now that I'm with you."

"Well, this should be an awesome party. Zeta Psi always has great keggers. Frat party fun is just what you need."

Abigail heard Randall's voice mocking Nick in her head, but she told it to shut up.

It wasn't Nick's fault that he didn't realize this was the opposite of what she wanted. After all, she had been so closed off about her feelings that he couldn't possibly know anything about what she needed. Still, Abigail couldn't help thinking that if he'd understood her better, he would instinctively have comprehended.

"When my dog died last year, I made sure to fill up every waking second with some kind of activity. I got a new dog right away, too. It really helped."

I have a new dog, too, Abigail thought. Her name was Ginny, and if something didn't happen soon, Abigail would be living with her in Aspen. *Oh God.*

Nick pulled Abigail in tighter and kissed her again. "If I don't tell you enough how amazing you are, you should let me know," he said.

This did feel good . . . safe . . . warm.

A few blocks away, the party was too loud and too crowded. Someone slapped a plastic band around Abigail's wrist. Nick passed her a beer in a plastic cup.

"To getting loaded." He smiled.

"To getting loaded," she said, and emptied the entire contents of her beer cup down her throat. *When in Rome* . . . , she thought.

Three beers later, they were dancing to the new Madonna when the heavy one from New Jersey (Steve, she thought . . . or was it Stew?) tapped Nick on the shoulder and said, "Beer pong . . . far corner." He nodded in the direction of the long table for playing the Ping-Pong-ball-in-the-beer-cup game.

"Oh, I can't. I got my hands full right here," Nick said.

"Oh, go," Abigail said. "Please. I'd love to brag about my beer-pong champion."

"Well, if you insist." Nick kissed her on the forehead and sprinted off to defend his title.

Abigail closed her eyes and let the beat of the song overtake her. It was strange, but she started to feel bold. She normally held the wall up in such places, but now she danced to the rhythm of the music, to her own rhythm . . . it was there, somewhere, and it seemed to be calling out to her.

7

As if the fates were mocking him, Randall's instant messenger jingled his latest guitar riff, signaling he had a new message from none other than Abigail herself. He'd just put Abigail's poem back in its hiding spot, still with no song lyrics or melody to show for it.

Abbyroad: Hey, sexy . . .

Randell melted into a pile of grape jelly at the sight of that. He breathed deeply, rolled his chair over to the computer, and settled in for an evening of friendly torture.

Rantheman: Hi, gorgeous . . .

Abbyroad: How was the big Friday?

Rantheman: Ate some R-n-R, smoked a jay, you know . . .

Abbyroad: Ah, the life of a musician . . .

Rantheman: How was the party tonight?

Abbyroad: Average mainly, but . . .

Rantheman: But what?

He hated when she did that. Anything could follow those three dots, the worst possibilities being "I had amazing sex after," or "I finally experienced multiple orgasms." Of course, he could never picture Abigail saying those things, but that didn't stop him from fearing she could at any moment.

Abbyroad: My, my . . . we are curious, aren't we?

She had to know. She had to freaking know how he felt! Still, Randall knew he was reading too much into her words tonight. They'd always had this intimacy, but he'd never made a move because he was too much of a wuss, so how *could* she know?

Rantheman: Actually, no. Not interested in the least, actually. In fact, I was thinking of maybe going . . .

There. Two could play at that game.

Abbyroad: Nooooooo. Sorry. Don't go. ☹ I need you.

Could there be three better words than that? The day she realized she needed Randall—someone to walk beside her, rather than pull her along like that schmuck-o Nick with his "let's be happy!" bullshit and that poor excuse for a goatee—now *that* would be an un-freaking-believable day.

Rantheman: You know I'm here for you.

Abbyroad: Can I call?

Rantheman: Sure.

"Hey." Her voice was layered with a heaviness that few people would be able to recognize, but he noticed it right away. They'd spent all of yesterday together, and now this. It was devastating. It was intensifying his feelings and accelerating them, as if everything needed to change . . . *now.*

69

"What's up?"

"Well, it's hard to explain."

"Just jump in; that's always the best way," Randall said. Why did he sound like Jesse advising *him?* Maybe one of them would benefit from the wisdom.

"All right. Well, it all started yesterday, after I left your place. I thought of this day my mother took me to her studio. I could remember the way the floor felt, the sound of the tape she wrapped her toes in ripping from the roll, the smell in there—sweat and candles and chalk. I'd hardly thought of her like that since last year, when she stopped dancing because of the cancer. And now I can't shake it, she just keeps twirling and twirling there inside my head."

He thought he heard her sniffle. Something in his chest tightened up like a fist. "I think it's good . . . you thinking of this lovely memory, rather than all that hospital stuff you'd been bombarded with. Knowing your mom, maybe she's trying to tell you that." Abigail's mom had traded in dancing professionally for teaching it to children when she suffered a knee injury, and she'd always been around after that. In fact, she'd been there for Randall, too, when his mom had first left. He wouldn't put it past her to be there for Abigail even after her death. She was just that kind of person.

"I didn't think of it that way. Hmmm," Abigail said, sounding as if she was mulling this over in her head.

Randall let her enjoy the silence while he imagined her, hanging upside down off her bed, the way he knew she often did, her hair against the blue blanket like tall wild grass.

"You know, after I left the One Trick yesterday, where I saw Jesse, by the way—"

"Yeah, he mentioned it." *And gave me hell about how I'm torturing myself . . .*

". . . I couldn't stop thinking about her. It was kind of wonderful. This memory felt all mine, something I could have control over."

"That is amazing. It really is."

"Yeah, it is. But then tonight, I think my dad lost his mind. He'd told me Ginny was calling a family meeting, that we all needed to have a talk, and I thought maybe he was going to say *Ginny* thought I should try to take the SATs this year, but then he just bursts out with 'We're moving to Aspen . . . with *Ginny* . . . they like art there.' "

Randall's heart sank like a bowling ball in a plunge pool. Could she really leave without his ever having told her how he felt? He could just see an empty future playing video games with Jesse while Kate called them both losers but stuck around anyhow. There would be nothing left to motivate him. Abigail would be gone, off to forget about him and find some muscled skier or artist loser who wouldn't even recognize how special she was.

There was a knock at the door. It opened and his father poked his head in.

"Hey, can you hold on a second?" Randall asked Abigail, still reeling from the bomb she'd just dropped on him.

His father bopped his head to the music Randall had playing on the stereo.

"Sure," she said.

He pressed the Hold button on the telephone.

"What's up, Dad?"

"Just wanted to see what you thought of that program I e-mailed you."

"Oh, the musical note taker? It's cool."

His dad looked around Randall's room as if he were

visiting a new place. Mr. Gold rarely got off the couch these days so his little drop-by could only mean one thing. He must have been real lonely.

"All right, well, talk to you later," his dad said, taking his time leaving.

"Night, Dad," Randall called as the door latch clicked into place.

He picked up the phone and resumed his conversation. "So are you really moving?"

"Well, that's the thing. I was at the party and Nick went to play beer pong with his friends and I was dancing—"

"*You* were dancing?"

"Yeah, I know. I just got this weird feeling, like I wanted to. I didn't think of how I looked or anything. I was spinning around and around, getting all sweaty. Weird, right?"

Oh boy, that was all Randall needed—to picture Abigail dancing and sweaty. "You're losing me here. So what did the dance have to do with the move?"

"That's the crazy thing. As soon as the song stopped, there was Nick and he says, 'I just decided. I'm going to get an off-campus apartment. And I want you to move in with me. This way I can keep you right here with Nick where you belong. We can get you a little dog or something. Whaddya say, babe?' "

"You mean he talked about himself in the third person? You're right. That *is* crazy!" Randall didn't mean to minimize the situation. It was just so unbelievable, he didn't know what to say. His brain was spinning and spinning like an amusement park ride and that was where it had stopped.

"Randall," she scolded him gently.

"You're not really going to move in with Nick, are

72

you?" Randall was nearly screaming, but he couldn't help it. He considered himself lucky for not having thrown up yet. Aspen was bad enough, but having her this close and not being able to see her, having to deal with the fact that he'd missed his chance completely, only to have it swiped from right under his nose by Nick the Dick—that would be intolerable.

"You know what . . . it sounds crazy, but that it's better than living with revolting Ginny, drooling all over my dad and his platinum card. Besides, Nick has enough in his trust fund to support the both of us. And my dad probably wants me out of his hair."

This was his chance. He could say it right now. *I love you.* He could bust out of his room, fly down the steps, and run the seven blocks to her house. "You should . . . think about it" is what he said instead.

"Yeah, I'm done thinking. I'm just gonna do it," Abigail said, sounding, honestly, more decisive and confident than she had in a while. If only Randall could practice what he'd been preaching to her all these weeks, maybe he'd sound that way, too. He wondered where she got the nerve.

8

On Sunday morning, Kate found an old-fashioned easel-style chalkboard on the sidewalk in front of the One Trick Pony, and a few new cane chairs set up in pairs around four marble café tables. Now, *this* place had style. She walked up to the chalkboard to see what had been written on it: "I have measured out my life with coffee spoons.—T. S. Eliot."

And I've measured mine in disappointing relationships, she thought. And it was true—for every month of her life she could give you a failed connection, a person who had disappointed her. *Ah, but my friends never do,* Kate thought as she saw two of them there—Jesse, behind the counter, as he'd always been, and Randall, looking glum as hell, chatting awkwardly with a woman she didn't recognize.

"Ah, *chérie*," the woman singsonged, "you must be

Kate." She came up and grabbed both of Kate's hands in her own. "Let me get you *un café.*"

"I drink tea," Kate said, grabbing a stool at the counter next to Randall, across from Jesse. "Who's that?"

Randall leaned over and whispered, "Her name is Caroline. She bought the place."

"So how are you, Sarge?" Jesse asked, leaning against the back of the coffee bar, drying a cup with a blue-and-white-checked towel. He'd started calling her that because he accused her of always wanting everyone to do things her way.

"I got fired."

"Again?" Randall asked in disbelief. "What is this, the fourteenth time this year?"

"Third," Kate said with a sneer, pushing her stick-straight blond layers out of her eyes. "And I told Ken off in the taxi yesterday." She thought for a second and then added, "I hate everyone."

Caroline placed her signature cup in front of Kate.

Kate rolled her eyes. "I said I drink tea," she barked.

But Caroline only smiled. "I heard you. Now, you listen to me. This robusta coffee bean takes five years to be ready for picking. Now, *that* is patience . . . patience for time and for the natural course of things."

Kate opened her mouth to tell Caroline that coffee was bad for you and made you age prematurely, just like cigarettes, that it stunted your growth and gave you bad breath. But Jesse cut her off, didn't even give her a chance to get a syllable out.

"Did you know that Caroline says people banned coffee back in the day because they thought it was evil?"

Why is Jesse speaking to me like a kindergarten teacher? Kate thought.

She rolled her eyes. "That's because it *is* evil. It can cause heart palpitations and pre—"

"Caroline roasts her own." Jesse cut her off again, still using that crazy manner of speech.

"If she knows how to do all that by herself, then I'm sure she can speak for herself, too."

Jesse snapped the towel at Kate, and there it was, that smile of his. For a second she'd thought there was something really off with him.

"Get me an orange spice tea, towel boy."

"Just try it," Jesse whispered. Caroline was at a table only a few feet away.

"What do you care if I try it? I don't drink coffee. Hello, don't you know me? Your hottest, coolest, sexiest friend, Kate?"

"Hey, I thought *I* was your hottest, coolest, sexiest friend," Randall said.

They all laughed, easing the tension that had settled over them even before Kate had walked in the door that morning. Jesse shook his head and slid the cup of coffee from the space in front of Kate. He scooped out some tea from a plastic-lined tin and placed it in a silver tea ball, which he dropped into a mug and filled with hot water. "There. Happy now?"

"Thrilled." She took a sip and moaned exaggeratedly.

"Should I leave the two of you alone?" Randall asked, eyeing Kate and Jesse.

"Oh please, me and Mr. Shits on Girls for Kicks? Not in a million."

"Kate, we know you're pissed, but don't take it out on us. Why don't you go and learn how to keep a guy or a job and then come back, and maybe we'll listen to your buttinsky advice." Jesse hung three mugs on hooks and tossed the towel over his shoulder.

At that moment, Kate couldn't believe that she had once had a thing for Jesse; they'd kissed at one of Jesse's "parents away" parties and then messed around a few times after, but that was last year. Still, he'd been an excellent kisser, knew how to touch her hair, look at her in a way that made her feel like the only girl in the world. Jesse had an intensity, as if he felt things very deeply, split time into tiny fragments so that every last bit of enjoyment could be sucked from it. She could see it even now, though he did his best to hide it most of the time.

"You're right. I'm the bitch and you're completely innocent. I forgot my role for a second, but I think I've got it now." She winked at Randall.

"Hey, I wanna be the bitch," Randall countered as he finished off his enormous mug of coffee.

"You already are," Kate said.

"Hey, leave him alone. He's already all weepy," Jesse answered for Randall. "Abigail's moving in with Mr. Fun Guy."

"Jesus, Randall!" Kate was always pointing out to Randall how easy it would be to get Abigail if he would only tell her how he felt.

"I know. I know. A million times, I know. Believe me. You might not be aware of this, but it's not as easy for everyone as it is for you."

Randall looked frazzled, but Kate thought if she could

just push him a little more, maybe he'd actually do something. "You won't get all the chances in the world. One day you're going to run out of them."

"Wow, you know, I hadn't thought about that yet. Thanks, Kate. You're so smart." Randall's voice was heavy with sarcasm.

"Yeah, lay off, Sarge." Jesse defended Randall when he thought Kate got too pushy, which he almost always did.

"Why don't you teach me how to be sweet, Jesse?" She got in his face then. "Give me a private lesson."

"Wouldn't you like me to show you," he said smugly.

"All right, children, play nice," Randall said, "or I'm gonna have to separate you."

"Sorry," Kate and Jesse said at once, retreating into their own thoughts.

Caroline fluttered over. Her throwback shirtwaist dress elegantly swayed after her as she lit a couple of candles along the back wall. She disappeared through the door again.

"Hey." Kate broke the silence. "This Friday at nine p.m., Cabernet and Cash." She knew this band called Wayne was going to be amazing. Kate never steered them wrong when she put a party together, so she knew most everyone would show.

Caroline returned now with four plates and forks and a steaming pie with a flaky crust and what looked like a ring of tomato slices over the top. She placed the pie on a towel on the counter and grabbed a large knife.

"What's that?" Kate asked.

"It's a tomato pie. I went to the store yesterday and bought all the makings of it. And there was Jesse, like a knight in shining armor, to rescue me from having to carry it all back to my place."

"Anytime," Jesse said. At times like these, he usually took the opportunity to hit on a girl, which was why Kate was so perplexed at his response.

"Jesse, a knight? He doesn't *rescue* girls, he hooks up with them and then loses their telephone numbers. Right, Jess?" she joked, thinking he'd deliver the typical lines of their script: "I don't know what you're talking about," or "Jesse, who's this Jesse everyone keeps talking about?" But he just shot Kate a mean look that pissed her off. What the hell was going on here? Did Jesse actually have feelings for this coffee pusher? What was she—thirty years old? He must have been suffering from an absent-mother complex. It was actually kind of sad, when Kate thought about it. She'd have to talk some sense into him later.

Randall shifted in his seat and cleared his throat.

Caroline just continued. "My mother used to make this pie for me every fall. To me, it's not fall without a tomato pie. We used to sit at our long farm table in the kitchen— my feet cold on the tile floor—and listen to the big bands play on the radio while we ate tomato pie."

"Where was your father?" Kate asked.

"My father lived in Spain. My parents loved each other, but much more from afar." She said this as if it was a fact of life, and it bothered Kate that she felt admiration for this practical sentiment. Already Kate had it set in her mind that she wouldn't like Caroline. She certainly didn't trust anyone who dropped in out of nowhere and tried to be everyone's best friend. And Kate couldn't believe how consumed Randall and Jesse were with her romantic stories. Big deal.

Though the pie was rich—layered with cheese, fresh spices, and black pepper—Kate declared her distaste. "Yech, it's not for me," she said.

"Well, I think it's delicious." Jesse moved in closer to Caroline and bumped his hip against her as if they'd known each other forever.

"Seconds, please!" Randall said. Of course, he'd eat anything, since he never had any real food at home.

"It's been fabulous, folks, but I have to get going," Kate said, kissing Randall and then Jesse on the cheek and shaking Caroline's hand with a big fake grin on. She left twenty dollars for the tea and the pie and a hefty tip, to show that she could afford to. As she waltzed out the door, Kate realized that flashing that twenty was something her mother would do. A nasty aftertaste suddenly took over her mouth, and although she would have loved to, she knew that she couldn't blame it on Caroline's tomato pie.

9

Jesse wasn't scheduled to work on Friday, but he told everyone he was and therefore couldn't make it to Cabernet and Cash.

Why did he do that? He couldn't say precisely, but he needed to be at the One Trick; right now it was the only place he felt he belonged. The start of school earlier in the week had been uneventful. He'd been attending classes with the same people since kindergarten. There was the same combination of courses: math, science, English and history, gym and art. There was the same combination of instructors: the funny one, the awkward one, the witchy one, and the one who gave easy As. His parents were still in L.A. He was sick of takeout.

And if he met another girl he could figure out at a glance, he was going to throw in the towel for good, become a Buddhist monk or something. He could just picture himself telling his parents that. "Oh, okay, Jesse. Sorry we won't be able to get home to say goodbye, but go buy yourself a nice yoga mat. You've got the credit card."

Jesse spied Caroline through the window before he made his way through the front door. He'd spent the whole week with her and still didn't know very much about her. She kept her life pretty private, though she enticed everyone who came in to tell her every single detail about themselves. Already people were walking out the door, calling "See you tomorrow, Caroline" as if they were best friends.

She was leaning over the counter now, on the customers' side. Jesse noticed she barely ever stood behind it the way most proprietors did. The curve of her back reminded him of a flower stem. How, he wondered, did she get her skirt to stick out so stiffly like that at the bottom—was there some kind of undergarment that could push the hem out that way?

Jesse pushed the door open. There were about six occupied tables—one old couple, and the rest looked like college kids, some with books, but most in sociable groups, laughing and talking animatedly. In the week the café had been open, Jesse had watched the number of patrons grow day after day. There were even one or two customers who were regulars. But Caroline treated each one of them like family, which was why Jesse was drawn to her.

"Hi," he said, soft as a whisper.

Caroline lifted her head from her paperwork and darted her eyes in his direction. Smiling, she kissed him on both cheeks warmly.

"You're not working this evening, are you?"

"No. I just came in to hang out," he said.

"Hang out?" she repeated the words, holding the *g* too long in her singsongy accent so it sounded like a joke.

Though Jesse didn't know exactly what was funny about it, they both laughed.

A group got up and made their way over to the bar. They purchased some bulk coffee to go. Caroline had just roasted and ground some—the sweet smell of it was in the air—and she bagged it up, folded over the top, and then tied bakery string around the bag, the way she'd shown Jesse the other day. She placed her wax seal with her family symbol where the string crossed itself, and charged twelve dollars for it.

"Working on the bills?" he asked when the group had left.

"I've never been very good at it," she said. "In fact, I'm so bad I don't even bother using a computer."

"Well, I happen to be excellent at it. When I was a kid, my dad used to do his bills while he spent time with me— he's really into multitasking." Now, why had he gone and said something so personal like that?

"Multitasking. This is just the way to rush through life without enjoying. Where I come from, you quit work early and you spend the whole evening with the people you love, make a big meal, watch the sunset."

Jesse liked the way her lips moved when she talked. "I don't remember the last time I watched a sunset. I guess I just turn around and it's gone."

"We'll watch one together, then," she said.

Jesse restrained himself from yelling "When?" "That sounds great," he said, pulling his hat off and shoving it into his back pocket. He crossed his legs and leaned back against the counter so that he was facing her. He couldn't help noticing that a bit of her skirt brushed against his leg and that she was wearing a different perfume, one that made him think of a giant garden he'd seen once in Bermuda. "So can I help you with those?" He gestured to the stack of bills.

"I would love nothing more," Caroline said, putting the sheets of paper in his palm, her fingers brushing his ever so lightly.

Jesse pulled one of his new marbled notebooks from his messenger bag and placed it on the counter. "First of all, you have the basics—debits and credits, or what you pay out and what you take in. And the best way to keep track of those is to record them every single day, rather than saving them up like this." He patted the pile of papers with his lips pursed and a smile in his eyes.

Caroline shrugged and swung her gaze heavenward.

"Don't worry. It's never too late to do the right thing," he said, grinning.

Jesse showed her how to draw up a balance sheet with her assets and liabilities; how to compute her capital and compare her bank statements to her own figures for the month.

When they were done, she said, "And now let me do something for you."

Jesse turned red, but thankfully Caroline was already in the back. He shouldn't have been thinking those kinds of thoughts about Caroline, but the way she said it, the way her back teeth shone when she smiled, he couldn't help himself. He scratched at his nose to see if the aroma of her perfume had stuck to his shirtsleeve. It had.

"Can I pay my bill?" A guy in jeans cut off at his knees had come up behind him.

"Sure," Jesse said, taking the heavy torn paper square that Caroline used to write the checks on. He walked around the counter.

While he punched at the old register keys, the man said, "That's one amazing woman you've got there."

"I know." Even though he and Caroline weren't a couple, Jesse figured it couldn't hurt to imagine it for a fleeting moment.

Now Caroline came out with an arsenal of items on a carved wooden tray. There were two simple cups of coffee—none of her fancy ingredients—side by side, sending wisps of smoke up around her; a couple of spoons; and a tiny clay bowl with some wet coffee grounds mounded inside, a small scoop stuck in the middle.

"Oh no. What are you going to do to me?" Jesse put his hands over his face, which felt warm, probably from the fire. Before Jimmy the Dude owned the One Trick, the shop had been a residence, but because Jimmy was cheap, he never used the fireplace. Caroline, however, was always generous with eveything.

"Don't you trust me?" Caroline pulled his hands from his eyes and held them a second before letting them drop.

"I do." Jesse had no idea what she was about to do, but whatever it was, he couldn't wait for it to happen.

"Drink your coffee." She batted her eyes before looking away.

Jesse took his first sip and smiled. Caroline had put in one spoon of sugar, just the way he liked it. A warm sensation was spreading through his limbs. It felt so good that he wanted to draw it out as long as possible by taking very slow sips every so often.

"You're being such a tortoise," Caroline teased when her own cup was empty except for a few tiny drops at the bottom.

"I'm offended." Jesse pouted.

Caroline giggled as she used the scoop to add a pinch of grounds to her cup. She seemed to be concentrating hard as she fit the cup in her left hand, swirled the wet mixture around a few times, and then turned the cup over to allow the small amount of remaining liquid to drip to the saucer. She then turned the cup upright, showing the grounds lumped here and there along the sides and across the bottom.

Jesse had only one sip left when she stared at him curiously and then snatched his cup. As she repeated the same steps, he moved behind the counter so he could stand next to her, and of course, have a good reason to place his hands on her hips so he could squeeze by. A shiver crawled all over his body when he touched her—he'd never felt anything like that before.

"Are you putting a hex on me?" he joked. A part of him didn't want to let go of his old ways, staying comfortably numb in the arms of countless girls who didn't matter that much to him. But when his elbow touched Caroline's, the other part of him, the one consumed with emotions he couldn't put words to, took over.

"I'm going to read your coffee grounds," Caroline said softly. Her straight hair was loose and caught the light so that she appeared almost angelic.

"Read away," Jesse replied, spellbound.

"Let's look at the bits down the side of the cup—farthest from the rim. Those indicate events in the more distant past. What I see there is . . . a bath. Do you see it?" Caroline tilted the cup toward Jesse slightly, her gaze more enticing than he remembered it before.

Jesse leaned in and peered at the grounds. There was the distinct shape of an old-fashioned bathtub, curved over at the top, with curled feet—right in his coffee cup. His breath caught for reasons unknown as he pulled away and said, "Well, I'll be damned."

"What do you think it means?" Caroline's hand had drifted toward his forearm.

Jesse leaned his elbow on the coffee bar and cocked his head to the side to rest it on his palm. "I don't know," he said. "What?"

"It shows you have been disappointed."

Jesse's first reaction was to wave that idea away. His entire life felt like a disappointment, but he didn't like to dwell on anything negative. That wasn't his style. In many ways, he was lucky, and that was good enough.

"But you have been. Why don't you like to say?" she asked.

Nobody had ever asked Jesse that before. Why *didn't* he like to say? "Why should I complain? I have so much."

"There are many different ways to have," Caroline said mysteriously, her curious look transforming into something he couldn't quite figure out.

Jesse's cell phone rang. He pulled it out of his front pocket and looked at the caller ID but didn't answer it. It was Kate. She was probably pissed that he hadn't shown up at the club tonight. Jesse thought of how he would have spent the evening if he hadn't met Caroline—doing the same old things with the same old people. By now, some girl would be begging to go home with him, and he'd be obliging if she was cute enough. Amazingly, he didn't find this idea appealing in the least. Actually, it was becoming all too clear that for the last year or two he had been wading in the shallows of the ocean instead of swimming out into the unknown, where the current took hold.

As Caroline began her closing ritual, Jesse took his finger and ran it through the coffee grounds in his cup, wondering when he'd leave the shoreline of his life, and, more importantly, if a certain Frenchwoman would be holding his hand when he did.

10

Cabernet and Cash was decently attended for a Friday evening, considering there were ten million other options available in town. Abigail recognized some people from school and some from the neighborhood. She walked over to where Kate and Randall sat on a royal blue U-shaped sofa, topped with Moroccan leather pillows. The lights were off. Candles flickered here and there. Low carved tables were surrounded by rounded benches, pillows woven with golden thread strewn all over the place. *Cozy.*

Abigail had never been happier to see her friends. It had been a long first week back in school, with so much expected of her and so little energy to live up to it. And although she'd managed to avoid another "family meeting" with Ginny and her dad by setting up camp in the school library after classes were through, hoofing it to the One Trick after that and spending the night at Kate's one night and at Nick's another, she knew there'd be more talk about Aspen. Ginny had already left a not-so-subtle hint on Abigail's bed: a pile of new and incredibly tacky clothing with a cheerful note attached: *Some new clothes for your new start!* It made Abigail want to gag. So much so that the idea of moving in with Nick seemed like a genius plan. But if that were true, why hadn't she told anyone but Randall about it?

"Hey," Randall said as she leaned in to kiss him on the cheek. He was clutching a large to-go cup from the One Trick Pony in his hand, as if it were his guitar.

Kate squeezed her arm as Abigail leaned over to hug her and then sat down between them. Abigail noticed two empty drink glasses in front of Kate. She was sipping the last from a third.

"What are you drinking?" Abigail asked.

"Rum and Coke," Kate said. She looked around at the lounge, which was getting more crowded by the minute. Across the room, the bartender was juggling a couple of rum bottles while a group of girls swooned. "There are absolutely no cute guys here. Not one." Kate crossed her arms as if her entire reason for throwing the party had been foiled.

Randall cleared his throat.

"Except for you, of course," Kate said. "But you're not interested in *me*, are you?"

Randall's jaw visibly tightened. "Nah, demanding, brash, and spoiled chicks aren't really my speed."

Abigail's eyebrows rose. Something must be up. Randall

90

never spoke with hostility like that. "Okay, what's going on?" she asked. When nobody spoke, she continued, suddenly very curious. "Are you into someone, Randall? Who?" She couldn't believe he wouldn't tell her, of all people.

"No. Kate's just being her usual retarded self."

"Retarded . . . or ridiculously hot?" Kate asked, slurring the words slightly.

Randall ignored her question. "Our little friend here got pissed because she already dated that bartender and decided he was going nowhere and he's the only one she thought was cute."

Abigail thought maybe she should change the subject before this turned into an argument. She would talk to Randall later, alone. "So where's Jesse?"

"He said he had to work," Randall replied.

"Caroline seems pretty cool, doesn't she?"

Ever since Abigail had started slurping coffee at the new-and-improved One Trick Pony, she had been thinking of her mother wherever she went—in the library, on the street, and at Nick's place. There was a movie of her mother playing in Abigail's mind even now. She found this by turns off-putting and comforting. She wished she could ask her mother if she was doing the right thing, moving in with Nick, but in her interior feature film, her mother only danced—second position of the arms and feet, third position of the arms and feet, her eyes lined with kohl as if she were dancing a big show. Abigail imagined what her father's reaction might be: he'd sigh with great relief at giving up the burden of her, he'd be free at last to start completely anew with Ginny.

"I think Caroline's a little kooky," Randall said. "But

in a good way. And she definitely makes a stellar cup of joe."

"Well, I for one don't trust her," Kate said emphatically.

Given the source, Abigail and Randall laughed.

Kate shrugged. "Seriously. There's something off about her. I mean, at the very least, I think it's weird how much time she's spending with Jesse."

"You're just jealous that Jesse's all smitten with her," Randall said, challenging Kate again. "And the fact that he really might like someone this time threatens the hell out of you, doesn't it?"

Abigail was completely thrown by Randall's sharp tongue and Kate's sudden silence. It was as if they'd switched places all of a sudden.

But before Abigail could ponder this bizarre turn of events any longer, Nick arrived. He was wearing a striped button-down shirt that they'd picked out at a small shop on Broadway recently and he smelled of a crisp, spicy cologne. He shook hands with Randall, who seemed increasingly peeved, and then leaned in to kiss Kate on the cheek. When he sat down next to Abigail, Nick pulled her in close.

"What's everybody drinking?" he asked.

"Drinks," Randall answered.

Abigail shot him a stern glare.

Nick took it upon himself to call the waitress over. A girl in slim jeans and a white tank top stopped at their table and he said, "Four shots of tequila, please. We're celebrating."

The waitress wrote down the drink order and scurried away.

"Celebrating, huh?" Kate said in a shrill tone.

Abigail realized that Nick was going to announce they were moving in together. She squirmed a little at the thought of what crazy thing Kate might blurt out, especially because she'd be angry that Abigail hadn't told her. As for Randall, Abigail didn't dare look him in the eye now. She knew how he felt, and since he was acting all Kate-like, she was afraid of what he'd do next.

"Abby and I are getting a place together," Nick said, jutting his palm out, even though this wasn't a joke.

The waitress returned with filled shot glasses, a salt shaker, and some unfresh-looking lime wedges. One at a time, she unloaded each item onto the small table in front of them.

Nobody said a word, and then Kate broke the tension. "Are you sure that's a good idea, Abigail? You know, with everything that's happened? Maybe it's not the best time to be making decisions like that."

"Well, the decision was kind of made for her. Her dad said she'd be moving to Aspen otherwise. I wasn't gonna let her get away from me," Nick said, passing out the shot glasses and the lime wedges.

When Nick offered a glass to Randall, Randall just rolled his eyes and shook his head.

Nick shrugged and asked Abigail if she'd like another. Abigail accepted it happily. For some reason, she was feeling rather protective of Nick. He was only trying to help keep her from moving away, which she'd thought would please her friends—so why did they need to second-guess her?

Abigail, Nick, and Kate put salt at the base of their thumbs, licked the salt off, and clinked glasses.

"To moving in," Nick said before they all drank.

"To moving in," Abigail repeated.

"Excuse me." Randall got up in a huff and stormed outside.

Abigail couldn't help looking out the window at Randall as he paced back and forth on the sidewalk. This weird mood of his was really worrying her, so she took Nick's hand and gave it a quick squeeze.

"I'm just going to see if he's okay," she said.

"No problem. Kate'll keep me busy, I'm sure," Nick said with a wink.

When Abigail slipped through the front door and into the night, she saw Randall talking into his cell with such anger that he didn't even notice she was there. "I can't freaking take it anymore!" he said, gripping the phone so tightly his knuckles were turning white.

"Can't take what?" she asked.

It was obvious from the way Randall flinched that he hadn't expected anyone to hear what he'd said.

"I'll call you later," he said into the phone, and snapped it shut. Then he pushed it into his back pocket and looked at Abigail. "It's nothing, really."

"Randall," she said, her face close, her hand on his shoulder. "You know you can tell me anything."

"Yeah, I know." The somber sound of Randall's voice betrayed him. Abigail could tell he was holding something back. Something important.

"Does this have to do with your father? Is he okay?" Abigail's chest went cold just thinking about Randall having to endure the pain she had felt about her mom.

"He's fine. I'm fine. That was someone else." Randall didn't say who, though he didn't usually keep things like

94

that to himself. Perhaps it was a new girl? Abigail found herself imagining, for a second, the kind of girl Randall would go for. There'd been that tall, thin brunette from the record store he went out with a few times this past summer—Cecilia. But that had fizzled out when Abigail started leaning on him more.

Randall calmed himself with a few deep breaths. When he seemed more composed, he said, "Are you sure about this moving in with Nick thing?"

Abigail sat down on a bench against the brick façade. "Am I sure?" She looked across the sidewalk where a couple walked hand in hand. Even from where she stood she could see the glow in their eyes.

"Randall, Ginny is intolerable. I don't think I have any other choice." Abigail wanted to say something about how, on the way over here tonight, she'd imagined telling her father about her plans, only this time he said he was so sorry he'd been so stupid; he'd break it off with Ginny because there was nothing more important to him than his beloved daughter. But this fantasy seemed so foolish.

Randall sat next to her and took her hand in his. Abigail swallowed hard so she wouldn't cry.

"Why don't you just move in with *us*? My dad probably wouldn't even notice." Randall smiled big and they both laughed.

"Oh yeah, I'm sure Nick would love that." Even as Abigail dimissed Randall's offer, she couldn't help warming to the idea. She could cook for everyone and sit on Randall's bed as he played the guitar. At least there was beauty in that. She leaned into Randall as she sometimes did and relished the strength of his body.

Randall sighed in defeat. "Okay, enough moping around. Let's go have a good time in there. We deserve it."

Abigail loved that she could feel his chest rise and fall with each of his words. *Intimate.* She felt the heat of his whisper after she pulled away and they stood face to face. "We sure do," she said.

"One question." Randall tucked a stray hair behind Abigail's ear. "You don't really want to move in with him, do you?"

Abigail wasn't sure of her answer, so instead she pleaded with him. "Ran, I could really, *really* use some support here."

Randall leaned back on his heels and looked up at the flickering streetlight above them. "I'll support you, Abby," he said. "But I won't like it."

She smiled. There was the Randall she knew.

When they wandered back inside, Randall led Abigail through the packed crowd, holding her hand tightly and glancing over his shoulder every other second to make sure she was okay. When they arrived at the table, Kate popped up from her seat.

"Hey, watch this!" she shouted as she walked with her long denim-clad legs and cherry platform sandals right up to the bandstand and pulled the microphone from the singer.

"It ain't me-eeeee, babe, it ain't me you're lookin' for," Kate sang completely off-key, but enchantingly all the same. She pulled the singer in sexily and made it a duo. Kate didn't take her eyes off Randall the entire time, and Randall looked pissed off beyond belief.

"What is going on with you two?" Abigail asked.

Randall crossed his arms in front of his chest. "She's drunk. And looking for attention."

"Aren't we all?" Nick said, and kissed Abigail on the mouth.

Uncomfortable. The word surprised her, but what about the past week hadn't?

11

The following weekend, Abigail and Randall were at Abigail's house. "I can't believe it's just one month left until Dad moves to Aspen. Nick already found a place down on MacDougal Street."

"MacDougal Street? It's got to be loud as hell over there" was all Randall could think to say. *Dumb ass.* He'd been full of stupid responses lately when it came to Abigail. He was still cringing over the way she'd surprised him outside Cabernet and Cash, when he was in the middle of complaining to Jesse about Nick's kissing Abigail right in front of him. *Can't take what?* she'd asked. *Uh, duh, nothing,* he'd said, like a flaming moron.

"We're not a hundred years old, Ran." Abigail was wearing a T-shirt that read "We Don't Need Another Hero." She'd widened the neck hole so that one of her shoulders was bare, and Randall was trying hard not to stare at it.

"Sometimes it feels like we are," he said, giving himself five more seconds to look away from a pair of freckles on her soft skin. When he finally looked into her eyes, he noticed that she'd been aware of him staring. But instead of slapping him playfully and calling him a perv, which he expected her to do, she bit her bottom lip and changed the subject.

"So what's going on with that guy from Live Records? Have you called him? Please tell me you've called him."

"Soon," he said, thinking of the song he had been working on recently. He'd been playing with a riff for a while, but now all he could remember was the lyrics.

> *But life and the words. (3x)*
> *Kick and tuck and slide, yeah, yeah, yeah, you*
>   *can,*
> *though you don't think it, you can.*
> *You can, my baby, you and me.*
> *Together we can.*
> *Sway leaf and hail cab and sweep the floor. (2x)*

"I know you will, Randall. I do." He loved the way she didn't go on and on about "but you have to do it now!" like everyone else. Abigail was the only person who seemed to have real faith in him . . . *that* truly inspired him to keep on. And now Randall was actually building up to doing something about it. But what? Or how? And when?

They were in Abigail's second-floor family room. This area of the house was an ode to Mrs. Jones's career. There were black-and-white prints framed in slightly dulled chrome with wide cream mats. Stage after stage, some with elaborate backdrops—castles and weeping trees and thorny rosebushes. "New York City Ballet Presents *Carmen*," one poster read. There were old, yellowed pages of sheet music framed here and there.

Randall thought of what Abigail had said the other day, how she was thinking of her mother constantly. He caught her looking at a black-and-white photo, the one with dozens of girls in their stiff puffy skirts, none of them smiling. He wanted so badly to push that hair off Abigail's forehead, kiss her there, and tell her how much he loved her. But all he did was move closer to her side of the sofa.

When Abigail turned and saw him gaping at her, she seemed caught off guard. Immediately, Randall panicked. The last thing he wanted to do was screw up. "Want to go to the One Trick?" he asked. It was a Saturday and Jesse would be working. Hopefully, Kate wouldn't be there—she could ruin Randall's chances altogether.

"That sounds like a great idea," Abigail said. Together they walked the six blocks to the One Trick, enjoying the sunlight and the idea of the weekend lying in front of them.

Today the chalkboard read "The discovery of coffee has enlarged the realm of illusion and given more promise to hope.—Isidore Bourdon."

Jesse was grinding beans when they arrived. Randall could smell the fresh-roasted coffee. The place was bustling with people and all the tables were occupied. Caroline was chatting and laughing with a group of four older women who kept calling after her even when she returned to the counter. Today she wore slim black pants cropped a few inches above her ankles and a white blouse, with a silky red scarf around her neck.

When Jesse turned around from his grinding and saw Caroline, Randall thought there was something familiar about the way Jesse held his gaze a little too long, as if he was harboring strong feelings that couldn't be ignored or professed.

" *'Allo, 'allo,* " Caroline said, welcoming the two of them.

Randall had been to the One Trick Pony every day this week, the same way he'd done back when Jimmy the Dude was running the show. But the ambiance and the coffee were so much better now. From the size of the crowd, everyone in the neighborhood had obviously figured that out. Caroline had a way of making life seem easier and simpler. Yesterday she'd told a story about how her family had built their own home in the country. "We just worked on it every day until it was done," she'd said. It wasn't a revolutionary thing, really, but it struck a chord with him. Actually, the story had inspired him to go home and take a bite out of that song he was working on.

"Can I get another of those coffees you made me last time?" Abigail asked.

"I thought you might like that one," Caroline said. "Powerful, no?"

Abigail nodded knowingly.

"What's new?" Jesse asked while Caroline fixed the drinks.

"Abigail's changed her mind," Randall said.

"Oh yeah, about what?" she countered.

"She's gonna move in with me instead. We're gonna kick my dad out and make lots and lots of creative, intellectual, shy children and spend the summers in Woodstock with the last of the living hippies."

Jesse darted his eyes back and forth, and Randall knew exactly why. He was proud. On the other hand, Abigail's

cheeks became flushed. Randall figured she was embarrassed, but when he stopped to think about it, she hadn't
put the kibosh on the notion either time he'd mentioned it.
Maybe she could see the future the way he did—the two of
them lingering in bed in the mornings, unable to drag
themselves away from each other. For Randall, it was easy
to picture them going through life together, sharing all the
important things. There was no limit to what he could accomplish if he woke up next to that shoulder.

"I didn't know you thought of yourself as an intellectual" was all Abigail said, smiling widely.

Smiling, Randall thought, the way she used to.

Caroline brought the drinks, placing them delicately in
front of Abigail and Randall, watching them drink. Randall
admired the way Caroline could show people she cared for
them with a gentle look or the way she smiled. If only she
could teach him how to do that and more.

"Abigail," Caroline said after a minute or two of small
talk. "I want to hold an open-microphone night for artists
here—you know, poets and musicians—and I want to see if
maybe you can organize it for me. I love to find new talent,
but, I'm afraid, I don't know the area."

"Me?" Abigail asked, putting a hand over her heart.

"Yes, you. You are an artist, no? Who better to do it?"

Randall grinned as he watched Abigail's face brighten,
if somewhat hesitantly. "Okay," she said. "I'd love to."
Caroline gave Abigail a friendly hug.

"I think that is the perfect gig for you," Randall said.
"It'll be awesome."

"Thanks, Randall," Abigail said, her smile big but her
eyes serious.

They hung out for an hour more, drank their weight in

coffee, and then retreated again into the warmth of the daylight.

Neither of them felt like going home, for their own reasons, so they went for a long walk. When the sun finally set, they decided to see a band that Randall particularly liked at a small bar with a sawdust-covered floor over on Union Street. It was a regular four-piece band, except they also had a fiddle player.

"That's amazing," Abigail said, just as Randall was thinking it.

Randall noticed that over the course of the evening, during which neither of them drank, Abigail had shifted her chair closer to his, that her body had turned so that she was facing him. Something was definitely changing between them. No, wait, it was him. *He* was changing things, and that idea encouraged him to grab for those fingertips, with their tiny glittery blue fingernails, and hold them in his own on the walk home. He did his best not to think how many times Nick's hand had been there.

Later, Randall turned up all his amps and worked on his song until the sun came up. Maybe he was ready to play it for Abigail. In the safety of his room, it sounded really good.

After school on Tuesday, Randall went over to Abigail's house to help her with open-mike night preparations. Abigail brought him to her room nonchalantly, as if she hadn't been painting the ad posters for the past four days. Randall walked in and she had them propped against the back of her desk chair off in the corner of the room so that he might not even notice them. But he did, and he caught

103

his breath, thinking of how Abigail had used deep, dark colors, all of which seemed to suggest pain and hurt. Randall knew that she had probably sat on the floor of her room, with the canvas over her knees, and cried when no one was looking.

"Let's go get these fired up," Randall said. They were going into Manhattan to take them to his father's office, where there were dozens of professional-quality printers. They gently slid the canvas board into Abigail's leather portfolio and took the F train up to Jay Street, switched to the A, and got off at Canal. They walked the rest of the way to Reade Street.

"You know this is the original Duane Reade drugstore," he said to Abigail as they turned the corner.

"I didn't know that," she said, smiling.

"How's everything going with the move?" Randall asked. The idea of it had been torturing him.

"I'll have to talk to my dad about it pretty soon," she said. "I know he's going to be pissed."

"What do you wanna move in with Nick for?" he asked again.

"I don't want to talk about this now, Randall," she said.

He felt that their dynamic was changing already. Nick was off limits as a topic of conversation. Randall dared to hope the reason was that Abigail was recognizing her own feelings for him. They were silent as they approached the half-empty office, slid the iron gate of the elevator closed, and rose to the third floor. However he willed it not to, the time seemed to race by as they ran off the copies in a small room, the rhythmic hum of the machine making background music for their conversation.

Abigail spoke of many things as if they weren't going to

change, as if she would continue living right where she was—new curtains she was thinking of making, an easel she had her eye on—and Randall was thankful for that. Perhaps she was reconsidering, thinking of alternatives.

"Such strange weather right now, don't you think?" she said, looking toward the window.

It had been by turns gusty, stormy, fantastically sunny, and frosty cold.

"Funny you should say that. I thought I saw a tornado pass by my window last night," Randall teased.

"Randall." She went to smack his arm playfully, where it was crossed over his chest, but he grabbed her forearm before she could. He pulled her in close so that his T-shirt was touching hers. His hands tingled when he thought about her skin underneath the thin fabric. They stood that way for a while until Abigail finally stepped back, her chest rising and falling fast.

After that, they seesawed between being chatty and quiet, Abigail with her legs stretched out in front of her on the slate floor, Randall on the table with his sneakers scuffing the floor. He couldn't remember the last time his dad had worked here instead of at home. It was probably better that his company didn't see him depressed and disillusioned, but things were stalled here. Randall could see just by looking at the place—not much had changed, there was no one working on the weekend the way they used to. A company couldn't run itself, and if his father didn't return to the hands-on approach he'd used while growing the place, it could very well crash and burn. Randall could see how simple it would be to build it back up again, if his father did with the company what Caroline had done with the One Trick—take one day at a time and do it. But when

Randall looked down at Abigail and considered how long he'd been doing nothing with her, he realized just how similar his life's philosophy was to his dad's.

"I don't want to go home," Abigail said when they were done working. It was sweet music to Randall's ears.

"Perfect. Come over," he said. He could show her the song, or tell her the truth. Now he had more time.

On the subway ride back, a homeless man was singing "You are so beautiful to me." Usually, Randall barely acknowledged these unsolicited tunes, but tonight he folded a five-dollar bill into the man's paper cup.

12

As soon as Kate saw the letter from her guidance counselor in the mail by the door on Thursday, she knew her mother was going to pitch a fit.

"Kate, you should be running that place! How could you go and get yourself fired?" her mother wanted to know.

Her mother pushed and pushed; that was how she and Kate's father succeeded in the movie production business. "It's cutthroat out there, Kate!" She hadn't even given Kate a chance to answer, but she did manage to lower her voice to a calmer tone. "We had to work our asses off to get where we are today, to have all this! There is no room for weakness. None. I know it seems like a lot of pressure, but that's because it *is*. I don't want to delude you by telling you otherwise."

They were sitting together on the deep leather sofa

with the nail heads on the arms. Kate's mom gently put her arms around Kate and hugged her. Mrs. Foster had struggled—she'd been an orphan and had lived in squalor for many years before she earned a scholarship and met Kate's father at NYU. Kate knew that her mother didn't want her to have the same kinds of hardships, but at the same time, she wanted Kate to learn the meaning of determination, which was why she was so vigilant with her.

"Mom, everyone keeps saying I'm too aggressive," Kate explained.

"Those are middle-management thinkers," her mother said.

"Mom, she was the *president*. And she hated me." Kate knew it was a tiny little nothing company where Ellen Saneman could have titled herself the queen if she'd felt like it. Still, Kate was growing tired of the stress and expectations that came along with the quest to be number one. Sure, most of the time other people were wrong, but did that mean Kate had to make her mark at age sixteen?

"Everyone is threatened by you, Kate. That's all it is." Kate's mother put a comforting hand on her daughter's knee. "They know how smart you are and they're worried you're going to take their job. So they try to cut you down to size. But you can't let them. You must always stay strong. Understand?"

Kate nodded, but honestly, she wasn't so sure. What was she always being so strong for? Right now she felt vulnerable, as weak as a cheap, wet paper towel. What would be so bad about calling up one of her friends and saying "Look, I need some support right now"? Didn't they all do that to her? Well, all of them except for Jesse, but that was only because he, too, had issues with sharing his feelings—he didn't even know how to share them with himself.

"I'm only putting this pressure on you because that's how the real world is, but if you don't find another internship this week, you're going to have to forget about spending next semester in London."

Kate wanted to scream. Talk about threatening? Her mom practically invented the tactic. When Kate screwed up, her mom would "motivate" her with stunts like these. Although Kate admired and looked up to her mother for all her accomplishments, these moments always made her blood boil. But she knew better than to throw a temper tantrum—the only option here was to give in.

"Okay, I'll do my best."

Her mother raked her hands through Kate's hair. "I know you will, my beautiful genius daughter."

Back up in her room, the words in Kate's SAT book swirled around in her head. She sat cross-legged on her African carved bed, the swirled spires reaching high up toward the ceiling. The softest cashmere throw blanket was draped over her shoulders; she played with its soft nubs. She had her childhood plush bunny, Mr. Hops, in her left hand. What could she say? It was her one weakness. Her parents joked, but they got a kick out of it. They smiled each time they saw Mr. Hops; it probably brought them back to when she was a perfect little girl who amazed them daily with her knowledge of Spanish and fractions and the metric system.

When had things become so complicated?

Kate lay back and pulled the blanket over herself. As she snuggled with Mr. Hops, she tried to think of the moment when her life had started to feel a bit out of control. Surprisingly, her thoughts turned to Jesse and all the hours he was putting in at the One Trick. He obviously had a thing for Caroline. Normally, Jesse tried out a different girl every couple of days or so—he certainly didn't follow them around and drool over their coffee beans. What was so great about Caroline, anyway? Kate really didn't get it. So she had an accent. Big deal. Plenty of people in the five boroughs had accents, and Kate never followed any of them around like a lost puppy. Besides, what did anyone know about Caroline? She could be some crazy French ax murderer out for blood. In fact, now that Kate thought about it, after Caroline showed up things had started shifting, and the balance of her universe felt off. She'd have to think of a way to get back on track, and for some reason, keeping Jesse out of Caroline's clutches seemed like a good place to start.

Mrs. Karpo's internship office was just about the most dismal place in the school, with powder blue cinder-block walls and floor tiles that probably contained asbestos. Kate nearly laughed out loud at the plaque on Mrs. Karpo's desk that said "School of Excellence."

Please.

"Well, Kate, I'm sorry to tell you there are no more internships in marketing and publicity. None. So I guess you'll have to do one next semester."

Kate's eyes narrowed to slits. When she woke up this

morning, she'd shifted herself into determination over-drive. She was going to find a way to study in London next semester, even if she had to take Mrs. Karpo down. Kate had a thing for British guys and their understated sophistication, and although some of them were living in New York, she figured she might as well travel to where her favorite breed roamed free.

"Karpo, let's level here."

Mrs. Karpo leaned back and crossed her arms slowly and dramatically over her chest. "I can't wait to hear what comes next."

Kate had been in Mrs. Karpo's advisorial care at the Martin Hall School since the sixth grade, so they had a certain rapport. "Give me twenty-four hours to come up with a new internship, something outside the program."

Mrs. Karpo brushed her fluffy canary-colored hair away from her face, moved her lips around like she was chewing fatty meat, and then finally agreed. "You've got twenty-four hours. To the second. Starting"—she looked at her watch—"now." Her smile gave her soft spot away. "And don't abuse my cell phone number either. Just use it to call me when you've got something else lined up."

Karpo handed Kate a business card as they both stood.

"Will do," Kate said, walking to the door and closing it behind her.

Kate left the meeting with a newfound zest. She loved a challenge—it was just what she needed to get over this horrible hump she'd hit. Two periods later she met Abigail for lunch at the delicatessen around the corner from the school. Over a small container of pasta salad, she explained the predicament. "I'm going to head over to Fifth Avenue and I'm just going to knock on every door until I get somewhere," she said.

"You're not serious?" Abigail responded. She'd been mixing some vegetable soup around in a cardboard takeout bowl without actually eating any of it.

Kate had noticed that her friend's appetite had been diminished for months now. "Completely serious. Now try some of this pasta salad. It is fabulous," she instructed.

Abigail tried a bite and said, "That's pretty good, I guess." She did it just to get Kate off her back. That was the way she usually handled Kate. Just do what she suggested and move on. Kate could sense that. She'd never realized it before, but it was precisely the way she did things with her mother. But at least, she figured, she got Abigail to try. And that had to mean something. Her mother probably told herself the very same thing about the pressure she'd put on Kate last night.

"What's going on with Nick? Are you really moving in with him?"

"Why does everyone keep asking me that?" Abigail dropped her plastic spoon into the soup and smacked her hands on the table.

"Well, because we're in high school, for one. And also because you're going through a really hard time right now. We don't want you to make decisions for the wrong reasons."

Kate regarded Abigail as she watched people come in and go out of the busy delicatessen.

"What decisions have I been able to make for myself, really? I didn't want my mother to die, I didn't want my father to be my sole parent, and I certainly didn't want Ginny in my life."

112

"You've got more power than you realize," Kate reasoned.

"That's what I've been figuring out lately. And it is precisely why I'm moving in with Nick."

"All I'm saying is, you probably have other options you haven't explored."

"Like what?" Abigail cocked her head. Abigail was a lot more aggressive than Kate ever remembered her being.

"For one, you haven't asked me or Jesse or Randall if you could stay with us."

"That's too much of an imposition. I would never ask—"

"Well, you're not asking. I'm offering."

"It's really nice of you, Kate, but moving in with Nick . . . it's like starting my own life, whereas moving in with a friend is more like putting my life on hold and giving the power over to someone else."

"You don't think you're giving Nick any power by moving in with him?"

Abigail looked as if she was going to say something but then changed her mind and took a different tack. "Kate, you know what? I really appreciate your concern, but I don't want anyone's advice on this."

Kate felt as if she'd been stabbed. Abigail always listened to Kate's advice. This had been the basis of their friendship all these years. She was wounded, so she jabbed back. "Sure, you're free to make your own mistakes. Whatever." She turned to her pasta salad, finishing up the last couple of corkscrew noodles and a sliver of carrot.

"Kate, not everything is about you," Abigail said sternly.

Even though Kate figured that Abigail was just misdirecting some of her anger, she still felt as if she were under attack. But instead of verbally sparring with her friend, Kate tried to keep her cool. "Let's not argue." She sipped her peppermint tea. It was getting cold for mid-September, and the tea helped to warm her. "Tell me what else is new."

"Let's see. Well, Randall and I made lots of copies of the poster for open-mike night at the One Trick."

Abigail had briefly mentioned the project to Kate on the phone the other day. "So how else are you promoting it?"

"I put a sign-up sheet in the hallway at school."

"That's it?" Kate's wheels were spinning already. They could take out a little ad in *Time Out New York*, or the *Voice*. Maybe a radio spot . . . "Hey, Abigail, I've got an idea."

Abigail rolled her eyes. "Uh-oh."

Kate grimaced. Here was a little spark of their former friendship. "No, no, it's great—really great."

"What?"

"I need an internship, you need a genius marketing and public relations mind on your project to free you up to be creative instead of worrying over all the details. . . ."

"Yeah?"

"So . . . why don't I make *this* my internship?"

"Well, I guess, as long as Caroline doesn't object." Abigail shrugged.

Oh, Caroline. She hadn't thought of the fact that she'd be working for Caroline. It wasn't exactly appealing. Although it would give Kate a chance to find out what Caroline was really up to and warn Jesse. Plus, Abigail seemed excited about the event, and even if it was a passing goal of Abigail's that she could lose interest in at any moment, Kate was going to grab the chance to see her friend

114

come back to life. She extended her hand and Abigail took it in hers.

"All right, then, since you begged me," Kate teased, fluttering her lashes.

Abigail shook her head in dismay.

"Oh, fine, I'll be serious. We have a deal, Miss Abigail." Kate smiled, letting go of her friend's hand and reaching into her pocket for Karpo's business card.

And then the nicest thing happened. Abigail smiled, too.

13

Jesse arrived early at work on Saturday morning, just a tad shy of six o'clock. He had to check expiration dates on the milk, roast the beans, prepare the blended beverages, but he also had a secret agenda. There was something he'd been wondering about, and he saw that now was his chance to satisfy his curiosity.

Jesse knew that Caroline wouldn't come down from her apartment above the café until around eight-thirty. So he tended to all the rituals of coffee preparation, listened during the roasting for the first crack and then the second, not rushing—Caroline had said it wasn't a thing to be rushed, because during this time she would get lost in her thoughts. Jesse really liked the idea of that.

However, the things Jesse normally thought about seemed to have taken a vacation. He'd been fine, and then he'd gone on that date with Cammie and everything had gone wrong and now he wasn't fine. Maybe he was sick? Jesse could die and his parents wouldn't even know about it. They had gone from L.A. straight to Texas, instead of stopping at home first, because the screenwriter had decided the ending should now happen in the Lone Star State. God forbid they should make an L.A. set look like Texas so they could come home and hang out with their son.

The reason Jesse had originally decided to go downstairs wasn't because he wanted to snoop. Sure, he'd wondered about Caroline and that guy in the picture since the moment he'd laid eyes on it. But really he was low on raw sugar and needed to go down there to fill up the huge tin canister in which Caroline stored the packets.

It was already eight o'clock, and if Jesse was going to look at that box—the one the picture had fallen from—he should have done it an hour ago when he had all the time in the world. But he kept thinking it was wrong to invade her privacy like that. Still, there was this feeling inside him that he couldn't ignore, something that made him want to forget logic and sense and embrace curiosity and passion.

Jesse set the canister down and listened to the furnace click on in the opposite corner of the basement. Even in his T-shirt and jeans, he felt hot. His chest heaved a little as he pulled up one flap of the box and then the other. His breathing became shallow now as he saw that the picture had been moved. He was right! It *was* something she looked at regularly. He'd known from the start that the

117

photo was something important, monumental. In fact, he thought the whole box was probably precious to her.

On the top was a package wrapped in brown butcher paper, tied with the bakery string Caroline used to wrap purchases for customers. And her seal—the enchanting little candle on its holder—was stuck at the crossing of the strings. A candle! She'd said it was the symbol of the flame inside everyone, that "each of us needs someone else to kindle our flame." Was there a chance Caroline had meant that as an invitation? Jesse suddenly felt faint just thinking about it. Jesse, who'd once juggled three dates in one evening. How could these little things affect him so much?

He studied the package from several angles. His main concern was that he wouldn't be able to rewrap it properly; Caroline had shown him how to press the little wax seal, but could he do it as precisely as she had? He stared and stared, fingering the raised design of the candle; it would be so easy to pull it right up. Jesse glanced at his expensive souvenir watch, which read 8:11 a.m. He was running out of time.

Jesse placed the package gently to the side of the box and shuffled around to see what was beneath it. He found a couple of rumpled napkins with the words "Café Parisienne, Villette" printed in gold. He brought them to his face and inhaled. He'd recognize Caroline's lavender scent anywhere. When he put the napkins to the side, he spied a couple of little matchboxes with other café names on the front, their contents shifting inside. It was obvious from the tiny scratches along the edges that they'd been used. Suddenly, Jesse felt so odd—how could he feel so close to Caroline in such a short time and yet not know some of the basics, like whether or not she smoked?

Frantically now, he pushed aside a floppy felt hat with a band of red ribbon, a Chinese paper fan, and a couple of smaller packages, wrapped as the larger one had been. The photo was lying at the bottom. Jesse curled his fingers around one edge of it and pulled it toward him. Again, he checked his watch: 8:15 a.m. He knew he'd better put this stuff back and get back upstairs quick.

Instead, he dug further, his body temperature on the rise. He found a tiny soap in the shape of a shell, wrapped in foil and sealed with a sticker bearing the name L'Hôtel Fontaine. There were other mementos from the hotel—a couple of receipts with different dates, a sheet of notepaper, another soap that was open at the back. Jesse couldn't bear to think about Caroline and that guy at a hotel. The kisses they must have shared, among many other things that he'd only dreamed of doing with her.

All of a sudden, Jesse reached again for that package, circled the stamp with his finger once, twice, and then pulled up so it would give way. He reached into his pocket for his Swiss Army knife—a gift from his parents' trip to Chicago—and cut the string. His heart was racing, and yet time was standing still. He waited a second before turning the paper over. When he pulled the panels of paper apart, his chest went numb, his mind wild with images sprung from what he held in his hands—a piece of ivory lace lingerie—with its silky string straps and its tie beneath where her breasts would have been. His breath caught in his throat and he choked, letting one side of the lingerie fall as

119

he struggled to cover his mouth and leaned on the table behind him.

"Jesse!"

Caroline yanked the garment out of his hand.

Jesse turned to look at her. He wanted to say something, but he was absolutely speechless—and that was something that had never happened before.

Caroline was looking at him angrily. He couldn't blame her. It was a horrible thing he'd done, invading her privacy like that. He was angry at himself, too. So much so that he didn't even want to defend himself. And in a way, he couldn't. There weren't words to describe the feelings that had made him do something so unconscionable.

Finally, Caroline broke the ice between them with a shrill yell. "How dare you? Go upstairs, now! And don't ever look in here again!"

Jesse went cold with fear. By the look in her eyes, Caroline might not forgive him for this. Terrified, he climbed the stairs slowly, watching his sneakers kick up dust as they did every day.

Caroline didn't speak to Jesse much during his shift, apart from telling him an order was ready for a table or clarifying the size of a drink. A few times he tried to lighten things up between them by saying something funny, but it never turned out right. Rather than laughing at what he'd said, Caroline tightened up her eyes and her mouth, as if he'd confused her. It was all wrong. Very wrong.

Still, at six p.m., when they closed the shop, she hadn't fired him. For now, he'd have to take that.

*   *   *

120

An hour later, Jesse got a call from Kate, who wanted to meet for dinner.

"I feel like we haven't hung out in a while," she said.

Jesse hadn't thought far enough ahead to plan for dinner, since he'd been sitting on the couch going over and over the scene where Caroline caught him holding her underwear, trying to find a way to explain it to her later so he didn't look like a psycho pervert.

"Let's go to Carbone's on Smith," Kate suggested. "I'll see you there in fifteen minutes."

Carbone's was all about low-key dining. Red-checked vinyl tablecloths covered the small square tables running along either wall and stuffed in the tiny loft up a set of rickety stairs in back, where Kate and Jesse sat. The waiter placed ice-filled glasses of water in front of them and wandered away into the crowd.

"What the hell is wrong with you?" Kate asked brusquely. "You look like crap, and I'm being nice." She brushed his bangs out of his eyes and he slapped her hand away.

"We can't all be as hot as you, Kate," he said snidely.

"Oh, but you usually are," she said. "Which is why I'm concerned."

Jesse let out a loud breath. He could appreciate Kate's directness from time to time, but honestly, she was a bit much to take. He used to be able to tune her out by remembering one of their many make-out sessions—the only time Kate was actually quiet—but now when he looked at her, all he saw were the million ways she wasn't Caroline. "To tell you the truth, I need some advice."

"Tell Miss Kate everything. She grabbed for his hand

and patted it for a few seconds before pulling away and lifting her glass to her lips.

A waiter came up to them and set his hungry eyes on Kate. "What can I get you?" Jesse could tell by the look on the guy's face that he was thinking of very, very bad things.

"I'll have the chicken parm," Jesse said, shooting the waiter an icy glare.

"I'll have the pasta primavera with whole-wheat fettuccine, please," Kate replied, smirking.

"You got it, beautiful," the waiter said. He was tall and had the kind of muscles that required hours a day at the gym, grunting. His tight white T-shirt ensured that people would see that.

"I don't like that guy," Jesse said as he grabbed a roll from the basket.

Kate laughed. "You don't have to be jealous, Jesse, there's enough Kate to go around."

One of the long fluorescent light tubes overhead buzzed.

"First of all, get over yourself, and second of all, I'm not jealous. It's just that the guy has no idea what our relationship is and he flirts with you. It's tacky. But hey, if you go for that sort of thing, don't let me stand in your way." Jesse had a hunch that his words were falling on deaf ears. His relationship with Kate had always been complicated. They'd had a hot, short fling over a year ago, but they'd both known they were better as friends, or at least that was what Jesse had thought. Although lately he'd wondered what kind of friendship they had, considering that most of it was made up of scathing comments and sarcasm.

"Speaking of tacky, how's Caroline?" Kate's tone had never had more bite.

Jesse's spine shot with heat and he sat up very straight. "What the hell did you say something mean like that for?"

"Um . . . because I don't like her."

"You don't like anyone," Jesse said with a scowl.

"I like *you*. That's why I tease you so much," she said, winking.

Soon Jesse found himself grinning back at Kate. It was just like her to enrage him one minute and then completely disarm him the next.

Fifteen minutes later, their meals arrived—large white plates piled with heaping portions. Jesse's came with a side bowl of spaghetti in marinara sauce.

"So you never told me what you needed advice about," Kate said, twirling her fork around the pasta.

"Oh, right." Jesse sawed a piece of chicken off with his knife. A long string of cheese stretched up to his fork and finally snapped.

"Well, what is it?"

Jesse told her what had happened in the basement that morning, going through each detail, all of them fresh in his mind. His heart sped up the way it had when Caroline found him down there, holding her silky lingerie. He felt the same shame and embarrassment telling the story as he had when it had actually happened. "I don't think she'll ever trust me again," he said finally.

Kate stabbed a carrot with her fork a little too forcefully. "What I haven't heard you ask is . . . why did she have all that stuff? Why was something so personal stored with the extra coffee supplies? Maybe that guy is her husband or something and she ran off with all his money. Who knows what kind of trouble she could be in?"

Jesse hadn't thought that Caroline could be married. She didn't wear a ring, as far as he remembered. Jesse had looked at her delicate hands so many times, but now he couldn't say for sure if he'd ever seen a wedding band on her ring finger.

Kate kept poking at the food on her plate. "Anyway, why should you care what she thinks of you? You never worried about that before."

"I don't know. She's just . . ." Jesse stopped himself from opening his heart to Kate. This was too private, and guessing from her demeanor up to this point, Kate was not interested in consoling him.

"My advice is don't get involved with her. She seems like she's hiding something sketchy, so don't waste your time."

An anger rose inside Jesse's chest, and suddenly his voice was stern. "Kate, I'm gonna tell you once: don't talk about Caroline that way."

Kate's head jerked back in surprise. "Don't tell me what to do, Jesse," she said.

"Why shouldn't I? Oh, wait, because you've got all the bases covered when it comes to ordering people around." Jesse couldn't help lashing out at her. He'd needed someone to lean on and Kate was falling short on her friendship duties by a mile.

"Fine, here's an order, then." Kate's cheeks were red with hostility. "Go to a therapist and deal with your abandonment issues instead of boinking someone who could be old enough to be your mother."

Jesse was too pissed off to back down. "She's freaking

twenty-two, Kate. Like you never dated anyone that age. Why don't you stop walking around thinking you know what's best for everyone all the time and deal with your own inadequacies for once?"

Kate threw her napkin down on the table and grabbed her coat off the back of her chair. "Sorry, I just lost my appetite," she said harshly before bolting out the front door.

Great, Jesse thought as he ate the rest of his meal alone. *Now two girls are mad at me.* Where, he wondered, had his simple floating-by lifestyle gone?

14

On Sunday night, Abigail sat in her room with her eyes fixed on the poetry criticism section of her English textbook. She was reading about the New Critics, who had been popular in the 1940s. They believed that no reading of a poem could ever reveal every bit of its meaning. This was precisely what she loved about poetry. Even when she thought she understood a piece of symbolism or could identify some unique imagery, she would come to the same poem a day or week later and see something completely different within the same stanza.

"Dinner, Abracadabra!" Ginny yelled up the stairs.

Abigail felt a gnawing sensation in her stomach, and she was sure it wasn't from the three cups of coffee she'd ingested at the One Trick that afternoon. Abracadabra was the nickname her mom had thought up for her when she was little and walked around with a plastic toy magic wand for an entire year. Hearing that term of endearment come from Ginny's tight-lipped mouth, and knowing that her father had probably encouraged her to use it, made Abigail cringe.

Abigail got up from her bed and looked in the mirror over her dresser. As she fussed with her bangs, she couldn't help thinking that maybe, just maybe, she was starting to look like herself again. Or perhaps even someone different. Lately, she'd been surprising herself with a supply of fortitude she hadn't known she had, but there were complications to that, too. She seemed to be hurting people's feelings more, and there were more tense moments between her and those she'd come to rely on. Still, ever since that day when she had that transfixing memory of her mom, Abigail had felt more alive than she had in a long time. So she tried to keep that in mind as she headed for her bedroom door, down the steps, and into the dining room.

Her father and Ginny were already sitting side by side, so close their chairs were actually touching. Ginny had her dark hair pulled back, and Abigail noticed the big diamond studs decorating her earlobes. Most likely a generous gift from her dad, not that Ginny deserved it.

"I'm so glad you were able to clear your schedule for this Sunday family dinner," Ginny said, clinging to Mr. Jones's hand tightly.

Abigail grunted as she took her seat. Her mother had started the Sunday family dinner tradition back when she was dancing. Mr. and Mrs. Jones had performances five nights a week at least. They'd made Sunday-night dinners seem so special that Abigail looked forward to them each week, dressing up in her prettiest clothes (often the same pink taffeta dress, which belonged to her mother—it gaped and flowed all over, since it was about three feet too long and at least ten inches too wide). Abigail's father would wear a suit and her mother a chiffon cocktail dress with a delicate flounce at the hem. They'd eat something very grown-up, like chicken cordon bleu (before Abigail's vegetarian days) with asparagus spears.

Now Abigail was choking back the strong smell of fish. As Ginny lifted the glass cover from the serving plate (Abigail's parents' wedding china), Ginny announced: "Grouper! It's loaded with minerals and vitamins." She winked at Abigail.

Abigail pinched her lips together and reminded herself that soon enough she'd be living with Nick and this would all be ancient history. Ginny spooned out one piece, swimming in a white sauce, for each of them. Abigail covered her mouth with her hand—the fish smelled like it belonged in the trash, not on her plate.

After a few tense minutes at the table, her father started some small talk. "I looked into the schools over in Aspen today, and it seems like they offer extensive creative writing courses—some even have courses that give college credits."

Abigail thought she should probably say something now about moving in with Nick. But despite how fired up she felt, she couldn't bring herself to say anything. Of course, there were lots of four-letter words swimming around in her head, but they wouldn't make their way to her tongue. She thought of how her mother used to stick up for her. How she'd say to Abigail's dad, "Martin, she doesn't have to eat meat. She's smart enough to know whether she wants to be a vegetarian or not."

One of her mom's favorite prints was hung above the side of the table where Ginny and her father sat, the two of them glued together as if they couldn't handle eating on different ends of the table. It was the Patrick Thurston photo of Margot Fonteyn and Rudolf Nureyev. Abigail thought how striking the differences in the two couples were—her father and Ginny with their forks moving mechanically to their mouths, and the two dancers with their blur of movement and curved bodies, passion glowing on their faces. In Abigail's mind, her mom and dad used to be that dancing couple.

It was just too painful and difficult to put into words the feelings that made Abigail seek such drastic measures as moving in with Nick. Where would she begin?

"So how did you like those clothes Ginny bought for you, Abigail?" her father asked.

"They were . . . something," Abigail said with the enormous fake smile she was using to mask the incredible discomfort and hurt she was feeling. Somewhere, deep, deep down, she was able to find the words, "Thank you, Ginny."

But maybe she shouldn't have tried so hard to please. Maybe she should have mustered the courage to get it all out, to say, "I'm moving in with Nick instead of moving to Aspen." Because then Abigail might not have surprised them so greatly when she was asked, "Why aren't you eating your fish?" and she blurted out, "Because it is unbearable, just like the two of you sitting here, acting like Mom never existed and expecting me to go along with it. Excuse me!"

With shaking hands, Abigail pushed her chair out and rushed up the stairs to her bedroom, slamming the door behind her. She grabbed the notebook on her desk and turned to a fresh page. When she uncapped her pen, the words flowed and so did her tears.

> *They speak and speak*
> *. . . and she silent*
>
> *They stamp and stamp*
> *. . . and she silent.*
> *And behind, beyond, the beauty*
> *Unreachable.*
> *And the silence brings it further.*
> *And she SILENT.*

She added one final line.

> *Finale: THE SCREAM*

When she'd finished writing, Abigail wiped at her eyes and stared awhile at her old-fashioned coil-cord phone. After dialing Randall's number, she twisted the stretched-out length of cord around her fingers.

"Hey, Abigail," he answered. Everyone had caller ID these days, but it still surprised her.

"Are you busy?" she asked, her voice uneven. She was calling him more often than usual lately because, honestly, she needed to—in a way she hadn't needed to before.

"Just playing around with this song. Are you okay? You sound upset."

"Oh, I'm fine," Abigail said, not wanting to rehash the

whole scene. She just wanted to hear Randall's voice and get lost in their world. "Let's hear your song."

Randall hesitated for a second, as though he was considering it, but then said, "Nah, some other time."

"Come on, Ran. I'd really like to hear it." Abigail thought of how he'd held her hand and how he'd surprised her by pulling her toward him at his dad's office. Her neck and chest became very warm.

"It's not finished yet. I haven't worked all the kinks out." These were Randall's signature excuses.

But Abigail knew what he needed to hear. "You can trust me, you know."

"Okay, hold on." Randall clicked his phone into speaker mode and then started the play-by-play of what he was doing on the other end. "Now I'm plugging in the amp. Now I'm tuning a couple of strings."

Abigail laughed at the way he was talking. It was kind of poetic, in a way, and made her forget about her outburst at dinner. Not that she was feeling guilty about what she'd said, or about how good she was feeling right now listening to Randall tune his guitar.

Randall cleared his throat. "All right. You ready?"

After making herself comfortable on her bed, Abigail sighed and said, "Yeah, go."

And then he sang:

> "Today it is the end.
> Today it is the end.
> They say it is the e-end.
> I hear a car fly by,
> and then I turn to say,
> 'Your love is all I got

and that's all I got
and that's way ok-a-ay.
So come here close, baby,
and just kiss me now.
We're gonna make it, baby,
or we'll die trying.'"

"That was . . . unbelievable, Randall. I mean, *you* are . . . really amazing." Abigail was so moved she could barely string words together and form a meaningful sentence.

"Stop." Randall was always so modest, especially when it came to his music. Abigail wished he'd acknowledge how talented he was, but she understood why he didn't—she'd never fully recognized her prowess at writing poetry, either.

"Seriously, Ran. You need to record this one."

"I'm thinking of laying some tracks down," he said nonchalantly. "Like I said, it's not quite there yet."

"So, who's it about?" Abigail asked as she picked at some dry skin on her elbow.

"Who's what about?" From his tone, Randall didn't seem to like where this conversation was headed.

But Abigail had to heed the voice inside her head, telling her to press on. "Which girl do you want to 'kiss you now'?"

"No one you know," he mumbled.

"Really?" Abigail searched her brain for any clue to who Randall might have been writing about, but no one came to mind. Their group of friends did all their socializing together. Of course, she'd spent a significant amount of time with Nick over the past year. Had she missed someone he'd met? Abigail secretly hoped it wasn't anyone from school. There wasn't a girl there who would be right for Randall. He needed someone . . . more . . . like him. Sensitive and creative, in touch with her feelings. Someone like . . . well . . . her.

"She doesn't seem too into me. So I'm not sure if we'll ever be together."

"Unrequited love, huh?" Abigail said wistfully. "That's pretty romantic."

"I'd describe it more as extremely painful." Randall sounded nasal, as though someone were pinching his nose. "You get just so close and then . . . nothing. It's like chasing your own tail."

Although she could tell he was not in the mood to talk about this, Abigail couldn't resist. "Just tell me who it is, Randall. Please?"

"So how come you're not with Nick tonight?"

There he goes again, changing the subject, she thought.

"Well, we have a big date lined up for tomorrow. It's our anniversary."

Randall coughed a few times. "One year, huh? Wow, when you two first got together, I didn't think it would last more than a month. Go figure."

"Okay, that was uncalled for," Abigail said, growing defensive.

"Interesting. I thought that comment was long overdue," he said snidely.

"God, what is your problem?" Abigail was half furious, half confused. Why the hell was Randall turning on her like this, and where did he get off judging her relationship with Nick when he, Randall, was sitting around writing songs about a girl who didn't even like him?

"My problem is that you're afraid," Randall shot back.

133

"Me? Afraid! That's like the pot calling the kettle black, now isn't it, Ran?"

"It's so clear Nick is all wrong for you, and I wish you'd just see it already. Everyone else does. You just don't want to take risks because you're afraid of what might happen!" Randall's voice was trembling. Abigail didn't think she'd ever heard him speak this way before.

Her cell phone buzzed and the screen flashed "NICK . . . NICK . . . NICK." She wasn't about to admit to herself that she preferred to let it go and finish this conversation with Randall.

"Well, I'm glad to know how you really feel," she said, deflated. Here she'd wanted to lean on Randall and now they were at each other's throats. Why did it seem that lately there was so much bubbling under the surface where they were concerned? "I have to go. Nick is calling my cell phone."

"See ya," Randall said harshly before hanging up.

The phone danced around on her end table. "NICK . . . NICK . . . NICK." Abigail flopped back into the stack of vintage linen-covered pillows on her bed and blindly reached for it. "Hey," she said.

"I'm around the corner, thought I'd surprise you." Nick's voice was breathy, probably from the cold air.

She dropped the heel of her hand onto her forehead and closed her eyes. She didn't want to see *anyone* at the moment—she was still too raw from what had happened at dinner, and then her fight with Randall. But what was she supposed to do, turn Nick away after he'd come this far? "Are you at my block yet?"

"I've just got ten steps left—nine, eight, seven, six, five, four, three, two—*aaaaaaannnnnnnnnd*—here I am."

Abigail sat up, pushed her feet into the sneakers next to her bed, her heels crushing down the backs, and opened the door of her bedroom. The sun was down and the hallway and stairway lights weren't yet illuminated. As she walked toward the stairs and down them, she could almost convince herself things were as they used to be. There was the soft cushion of the hallway runner—its intricate, exotic pattern twisting and turning—and the dozens of framed photos, the romantically worn ballet posters. She walked slowly and then picked up her pace, racing down the stairs the way she used to. All of a sudden the desire to hide out in her room alone was replaced by this warm, inviting feeling that kept telling her it was okay to seek comfort wherever she could find it.

She pulled open the front door, hopped down the six steps, and pushed open the iron gate. There was Nick, just a few feet away, gorgeous as ever. His light hair was desperately feathery despite the gel, and his cheeks were pink with windburn. Suddenly Abigail was thankful that Ginny and her dad had retreated to the living room, and that there was a lock on her door.

"Hey, you," he said, engulfing her in a big hug, his soft corduroy jacket tickling her arms. He kissed her sweetly on the mouth and then gave her a peck on the forehead.

"My, my. Your beard is very sexy." Abigail pinched his chin playfully.

"I was hoping you'd say that." Nick ran the back of his hand alongside her face.

Within minutes, they were messing around in Abigail's bedroom, rumpling the old log cabin quilt on her bed and yanking on each other's clothes. She thought this might be a nice escape from the myriad conflicting feelings she had been experiencing throughout the day, but once Nick had rolled onto his back and brought her close so that her head was lying on his chest, she felt empty.

"Just think," Nick whispered, his breath tickling her ear. "Pretty soon we'll be able to do this every night."

Abigail just lay there, motionless and speechless.

"We've got an appointment on Monday to see the place I told you about. If you like it, it's ours. The guy who owns it is a friend of my dad's."

Abigail tried to picture herself waking up in his arms and making him Caroline's special blend of coffee, but she couldn't. There was a pulling sensation roped around her heart, and she wanted so much to give in to it. Yet at the same time, she didn't think she was ready.

"Have you told your dad and Ginny yet?" Nick stroked her back gently, the slow rhythm almost putting Abigail to sleep.

"Not exactly." She hated the way she always told half-truths to Nick.

"Well, why don't we go downstairs now and I'll tell them with you? It'll be a lot easier if you don't have to do it all alone."

"You'd do that?" she asked, surprised at how grounded and mature he was being.

"Of course. I'd do anything for you, Abby. I love you."

She should have said it back right away, she knew that. But the words got lodged in her throat and Abigail didn't force them to come. Instead she let the pulling sensation inside take control and steer her toward her father.

"Okay, let's go talk to him," she replied.

When they reached the foot of the stairs, Nick squeezed her hand and nodded in the direction of the living room, where her father and Ginny had been watching television. They were sitting on the opposite side of the couch as if they'd had an argument. Ginny's eyebrows were high in anticipation. Most likely she was waiting for an apology. Her father looked tired, as if he'd been getting the business for a while now and was looking for someone to take it out on.

"Hello, Mr. Jones, Ginny," Nick said politely.

"How are you, Nick?" her father asked.

"I'm doing very well, Mr. J. How about you?"

"We're okay," Abigail's father said unconvincingly.

There were two candles flickering on the table in front of them, constantly changing the shadows on their faces.

Nick was about to speak and say all the things that Abigail was too afraid to say herself. In an instant, an avalanche of memories covered her from head to toe. There were flashes of picnics with her mother, concerts with her father, games of tag with Kate, used bookstores with Jesse, and smooth coffee with Caroline. But what stood out the most was every moment spent with Randall, especially their phone call tonight, when he said she was afraid to take risks.

It was then that Abigail surrendered to the pulling around her heart, told her father that she was moving in with Nick, and faced the fear of what might be as the image of her mother twirling ran on repeat inside her mind.

15

"You waited too long. What did you expect?" Kate said, sipping her tea slowly.

Randall knew she was right. It was Monday after school at the One Trick Pony—the start of another week, and he still hadn't revealed his feelings to Abigail. Did he imagine he'd be able to hold his tongue forever? It was no wonder he'd exploded last night. When Randall had gotten off the phone with Abigail, he'd been so upset that he threw his king-size to-go cup of coffee from the One Trick against his wall, spraying half its contents onto his four-track. It had definitely been one of the worst days of his life.

"Kate, I've been trying. I really have. I have gone beyond anywhere I'd gone just a couple of weeks ago. I've said things and done things I never would have been able to before," Randall said as he fingered the handle of his mug.

Kate spooned more sugar into her tea. "Yeah, well, I guess it's not enough. You have to step things up, Randall. She's gonna move in with Nick. Do you understand? *Move in with him!* After that, there's no turning back."

"Thanks for clearing that up, Kate. I hadn't considered it," Randall said sarcastically.

They were sitting at the bar in two tall cane bucket chairs that twisted back and forth, the noisy crowd shifting and chatting all around them. Jesse surfaced from the basement with a few boxes of paper cups. When he set them down on the floor behind the bar, he wiped the sweat from his brow with the sleeve of his shirt.

"You okay, dude?" Randall asked.

"Yeah, why?" Jesse tried to sound cool as always, but Randall could tell something wasn't quite right. Jesse wasn't radiating his usual easygoing vibe.

"You look like you've just seen a ghost," Kate said.

Jesse rolled his eyes. "Yeah, well, maybe there's something in the coffee that's made you both paranoid."

"You're forgetting: I don't drink coffee," Kate said.

"God, you're annoying," Jesse said. He began removing long sleeves of cups and lids, sliding each into designated slots behind the bar.

Randall took another gulp of his coffee and thought of the first time he'd come through the new One Trick Pony's doors. He could almost taste the licorice or spice or whatever it was in that first batch of brew Caroline had given him. So much had happened since then. Abigail preparing to move, that time he'd held her hand along seventeen city blocks, the song he'd started, the embrace, the fight they'd had. It seemed as if more had happened in the past few weeks than had happened in the rest of his lifetime.

"*I'm* annoying? You're obviously still talking out of your ass," Kate said roughly.

Jesse just ignored her and kept on working.

"Hey, are you guys in a fight or something?" Randall had picked up on the tension between them, but that wasn't strange at all. What was different was how little Jesse was fighting back. When Jesse took lip from someone without a fight, Randall knew he was particularly pissed off.

"Why don't we get back to how you need to get off your butt and do something?" Kate said as she licked a few particles of sugar off her spoon.

"Do something about what?" Caroline asked, flitting over.

"About how Randall is a 'fraidy cat," Kate said, picking up her cup again.

"Oh, I can't believe that. What have you to be afraid of, Randall?" Caroline slid behind the counter, next to Jesse, who immediately shoved his hands in his pockets.

"That's what I'd like to know. . . . He's a talented musician but won't do anything about it, and he's in love with Abigail—whom he's perfect for—but he won't do anything about that, either," Kate went on.

It was official. Randall wanted to pull Kate's hair so hard she screamed. In his head, he yanked it back and forth a few times and then stuck his gum in there and got it really matted up. This made him smile.

Caroline picked up on his lightened expression. "Randall, you know who else I've made that drink for?"

Jesse's head swiveled quickly toward her, his eyebrows arching.

"Who's that?" Randall liked all the different stories she had to tell.

"For a powerful, passionate musician from Villette, where I lived before—Georges Peridot. He played the saxophone like the devil."

Randall noticed Jesse's Adam's apple bobbing up and down.

"Are you okay, Jesse?" Caroline asked, her hand moving to his shoulder.

"Of course. It's just, don't you mean he played the saxophone like an *angel*?" he said quickly, crossing his arms over his chest.

"Oh no. You'd have to be the devil to be like this man—so amazingly gifted. Anyway," Caroline continued, "when I gave him this drink once, he came back for it always. He became the most famous saxophone player in all of France." A lock of her hair fell into her eye, and Jesse nearly went to push it behind her ear. Randall saw him jam his hand into his back pocket to stop himself.

When she walked away, Kate said, "Do you actually buy that bull?"

Jesse was quiet. He turned to the machine so his back was to them.

"I don't know," Randall replied. "I mean, Jesse said he thought there might be something in these drinks." He smiled big and then pulled out the card from Jonathan Sizemore. "If it worked for Georges Peridot, maybe it'll work for me," he said, tipping his cup back and emptying the remainder of the contents into his mouth. Wouldn't it be nice, he thought, if a drink could change all the things he disliked about himself?

Randall held the card between two fingers. From here, it looked so easy. There was a number on the card, and all he had to do was call it, right? Now it seemed silly that he'd hesitated. Wasn't he decently happy with the track from Abigail's poem, and at least seven other songs? He was close to doing it now, to picking up the phone and—

"Hey!" he yelled at Caroline as she pulled the card from his hands.

His friends turned to stare. Randall wasn't a screamer. "Sorry," he said. "Please give that back."

The door opened and closed, letting in a stream of cold air and the sound of a city bus droning by.

Caroline turned to Jesse. She wore a black dress that tied at the waist, and her hair was in a low ponytail that made her look about fifteen years old. "What's this card?"

Jesse looked to Randall, and Randall shook his head. Jesse stood there, looking very uncomfortable and unlike himself, his hands fidgeting at his shirt hem.

Kate looked Randall directly in the eyes and then said, "It's the record producer who told Randall to call him six months ago to listen to his demo."

Was the entire world ganging up on him? Why didn't they all stand around and pelt Kate on account of her bossiness?

Caroline picked up the cordless telephone that hung on the wall and started to dial immediately. As each pressed number gave off a tinny beep, Randall's heart skipped a beat.

"Caroline, please don't." Randall was halfway over the bar now, his torso pressing into a sugar bowl. It would have been very easy for him to jump over and pull the phone from her hand. But maybe deep down he was thrilled that someone would force him against a wall, put him in a predicament that was now or never.

" 'Allo," Caroline sang into the phone, and winked at

Randall. "Dees issss Randall Gold's secretary, Caroline, and I am calling to schedule his session with Monsieur Sizemore for one month from today. Ah, *oui?* He'll be back from L.A. then? *Parfait! D'accord,* so the demo tape . . . we will bring it on that day. À *bientôt.*"

Randall's mouth fell open so wide that all of Brooklyn could have been parked in it. Even Kate was stunned into silence.

"Whoa," Jesse said when at last he spoke.

"Oh my God. Caroline! Do you know what you've just done?" Randall finally exclaimed. Now that this was real, he was terrified. What would he do when his entire career was smashed to bits before he even graduated from high school? He sat back on the stool and put his hand over his heart, which felt as if it were being pulled in ten different directions.

"Hey, she's trying to help you, buddy," Jesse said. "It's a good thing."

Kate didn't say anything, just sat back in her chair with her legs crossed, wearing a smirk.

"Don't stop him, Jesse. Yell, Randall! Yell! Get it out! Be angry. Be fired up! Hate me! Go and use that passion! Harness it and create a record you can be proud of, a song of yourself, from your soul," Caroline urged.

"You think you know everything, Caroline. But you don't. I can't do this! I'm . . . oh, screw it!" He grabbed his messenger bag off the back of his chair and stormed out of the café without looking back.

"Congratulations," he heard Jesse say to Caroline as he walked out. "I think you were able to do what we haven't been capable of since kindergarten. You lit a fire under his ass."

Oh, I'll light a fire under someone's ass, Randall thought. And though seconds before, there had seemed to be so many people whose asses deserved some burning, the only person he could think of now was himself.

Randall strode quickly to his house, angry but energized. He saw something now. He saw a clear path from A to B. It was all geometry. Just like he'd shown to Abigail. It was a simple equation to get from here to Jonathan Sizemore's office. The complicated part was the risk. The risk was more difficult to calculate, but it didn't change what he'd have to do now. At least, for once, that was clear.

If there was one person who'd understand, it was Abigail. Kate had been right about one thing: he needed to speed things up. To start with, at least he could go and apologize to her. And then he could tell her what had just happened.

He huffed up the hilly five blocks, walking his bike, his light jacket not doing much to keep him warm. The streets seemed too full, loud, alive. He waited for a light at which a preschool group and two adults held hands and sang "Row, row, row your boat." A couple of guys rode by on long skateboards, with a stereo playing rap music he vaguely recognized.

Had there always been this much going on? Was it possible that Randall was just noticing this for the first time? Maybe. Maybe he was waking up and making things happen. *Call me Diablo,* he joked to himself. As he reached Abigail's house, he swung the gate open, a huge wave of warmth and desire washing over him. Things were possible, it seemed. For once, he saw that though there was risk, he had more control than he'd realized. He didn't have to take the path that would lead him where his father had gone.

As Randall pressed the doorbell, his right foot bounced up and down in anticipation. *I'm sorry. And the only reason I said those things is because I'm in love with you.* That was it, all he needed to say. He'd pull Abigail in like the other night, the way his heart was being pulled on now, but this time he'd kiss her, he'd give it everything he'd had pent up inside all these months, and then she'd know. Finally, she'd know.

"Oh, hey, man." It was Nick. And his hair was undeniably rumpled.

Randall's heart sank. He heard Abigail pad down the stairs.

"Randall?" She cocked her head when she saw him. He thought he noticed a smile forming, but he'd already turned and retreated down the front steps, grabbed his bike, and opened the gate.

"Randall! Where are you going?"

He wouldn't turn around. He wouldn't look back and take that again. What if Kate was right? What if he'd waited too long? What if he'd missed his last chance?

16

As she padded down the stairs for school the next day, in a new pair of gray skinny jeans and a black sweater vest over a slim white satin blouse, Kate was sluggish and annoyed and went so far as to ask Selma to feel her head to see whether she had a fever.

"You crazy?" Selma asked. "Ice cold. You're a frozen margarita!" She shook her head—her tight black bun didn't move a centimeter—and walked toward the kitchen, her generous silhouette shrinking with each soundless step. But she didn't walk away without offering a bit of insight. "Look inside, Kate, inside you'll find the problem." Her dark eyes were serious.

Selma was always saying that kind of hokey greeting-card crap, so why did it bother Kate so much today? She turned to the mirror mosaic to watch herself shrug her coat over her shoulders. The hundreds of triangular shards around the border of the mirror distorted her beyond be-lief. Kate was practically unrecognizable to herself—her nose off to the side, just one eye, wavy lines in place of her perfectly straight ones—but then right in the middle, where the mirror was an ordinary mirror, Kate was as she'd always been.

It was around third period, in English class, when Justin Singleton made that asinine comment about Jay Gatsby, calling him a disgusting criminal and such, that Kate realized why Selma's comment bothered her so much and why she raised her hand and said, "When you find someone you love, any means of attaining him can be justi-fied." Because *she* wasn't the problem! She *had* looked in-side. She had ended relationship after relationship because she could see that down the road it would never work out. Kate had done all that, and still she found herself stuck in the same loop—with no one to call her own. She wanted to risk everything for someone and see what that felt like.

Normally this pathetic pattern of hers didn't bother her so much. But seeing Jesse transform so dramatically had done something to her. It made her doubt herself. She couldn't help wondering what was it about Caroline that Jesse liked so damn much that he could change his ways—and why hadn't Jesse seen that in her? The thing was, there had been one time when she hadn't called things off . . . and that time was with Jesse. It was Jesse who'd glossed over the whole thing a few days later. He'd been the one to say, "I'm so glad we're not the kind of people to let this ruin our friendship. I'm so glad we're so much alike, Kate."

Sure, she'd agreed and got herself to the point where she barely thought about it anymore. But what other choice did she have? He'd made his point, and she knew what kind of guy he'd been all along.

Still, Kate decided to mend fences and stopped by Jesse's locker before fifth period. He had one ear bud in; the other hung down his navy T-shirt, which he'd worn over a long-sleeved white shirt. Was there something different about him? He didn't appear to have a new haircut or any new clothes or cologne.

"Hey," he said to her.

Ah. There it was. The change. Hadn't he always addressed her as "Hey, sexy"? She wasn't going to let that bother her. He was just Jesse. Her friend. What did she care that he had a thing for Caroline? It was laughable, was what it was. He was going to make a fool out of himself and possibly get very badly hurt. But she certainly wasn't jealous.

She leaned in close. "No, 'Hey sexy'?" Okay, maybe she *was* jealous—a teeny, tiny bit.

"Oh . . . hey, sexy." Jesse was distracted and it didn't seem as if he really meant it. He turned to his locker and rummaged around on the overhead shelf, pulled out a book, shoved it into his bag, and took another book out, placing it on the locker shelf.

Kate recognized the lavender scent from the One Trick, and just as Jesse was about to close the locker door, she stuck her hand in and pulled out a tiny sachet, tied with a ribbon and sealed with that candle thing Caroline had on all the cups. "What is this?" Kate held it up by the ribbon, laughing wildly.

"Give me that," he said, trying to snatch it from her hand.

But Kate was too quick for him. She took a step away and clutched it behind her back. "Caroline has you keeping potpourri in your locker?" She shook her head. "Jesse Majors has gone soft. No one's gonna believe this."

"So. What's the big freaking deal?" he said, his face close to hers.

She stuffed the tiny mesh bag into his warm palm. "Like I said the other night, I'm just worried about you, Jesse. Do you even recognize yourself these days? If there's one thing no one should ever compromise, it's their identity."

He slouched forward as if something heavy had been placed on his shoulders. "Yeah, well, you've got a funny way of showing you care, Kate. I swear, sometimes I don't know what the hell is wrong with you. Didn't we just have a fight the other night? And now you're starting on me again?"

Well, if I'd have gotten some kind of reaction from you, then maybe we wouldn't be in this situation again. "You aren't listening, Jesse," she said. "And honestly, it's infuriating. I'm not gonna sit here and watch my friend get hurt."

He took a few steps away from her, then swiveled back around. "Kate, I'm going to ask you one more time. Please stay out of this."

"Okay, fine," she said, appeasing him for now.

But I'm not giving up entirely, Jesse Majors, not by a long shot.

The next day Kate had arranged to meet Abigail at the One Trick after school. The place was crawling with customers, more so than last time. But Kate was too distracted with work to notice. She had invested a lot of time in preparations since she'd cleared the internship with Caroline yesterday (stopping by the One Trick and seeing Jesse trailing after Caroline like a little kid with a crush had been more painful that she'd expected), and she hoped that Abigail would be impressed with all the work she'd done.

Kate had made a mood-board collage with magazine clippings and some pictures she'd found on the Internet, which depicted the inspiration for her ideas. She went through them, pointing out the related pictures as she described her plans for open-mike night. "So I think we should arrange a huge 'old Hollywood' stage with lots of red velvet and lacquer furnishings and huge white flowers. We'll serve Polynesian cocktails with kitschy umbrellas poking out. And we'll have all the performers wear sequined dresses and tuxedos." Kate sat back, took a sip of her favorite tea, and waited for Abigail to tell her she was a genius.

Instead, Abigail gulped some coffee and shifted around in her seat. "Hmmmm. While that sounds amazing— truly—I was envisioning something more low-key, intimate, unprofessional-looking. You know, something that would be a welcoming amateur-night environment for us ambivalent artist types to participate in. As if it were someone's garage or backyard. Know what I mean?"

Kate didn't speak right away. Here she'd come into a completely new situation, and she found herself in the exact same predicament as before. Why did everyone have to think so small? How did they ever expect to get anywhere? People seemed to think they had all the time in the world to take little teeny, tiny baby steps to wherever it was they wanted to go.

Abigail continued. "I figured if we get people to feel

comfortable performing here, then maybe we can build it up a little more professional the next time."

Kate gripped her cup tightly. "In theory, that sounds like a very nice idea, but do you really think it's a good idea to coddle people that way? When they get into the music industry, or the art industry or whatever, they'll be eaten alive." She knew this was a little bold, but at the same time, she felt as though Abigail could benefit from hearing it.

"I see what you're saying," Abigail said sympathetically. "And ideally, you're right, but we're just not at that stage now."

The record Caroline had been playing ended and there was a bit of static until Jesse ran over to change it. Kate tried not to get caught watching his fingers carefully slide the record off the spindle and slip it back into the jacket. She shook her head and tried to focus on the matter at hand, which was honestly getting on her nerves. "Abigail, I really don't know what has gotten into you. You're being so difficult!"

Abigail had always followed Kate's advice, and Kate had never steered her wrong. She'd done a ton of things for her friend and she didn't see why their dynamic should shift now, when Abigail needed Kate's guidance most. Did Abigail really think this was the best time for her to start making decisions on her own?

Abigail's normally easygoing expression hardened. "I didn't expect that you'd understand." She sounded quite wounded. Maybe Kate shouldn't have been so blunt.

"I just want what's best for you." Kate put her hand on Abigail's. "I mean, you seem to be making some questionable moves lately, especially with Nick."

"Well, some of us can't be perfect like you, Kate. And

here's a news flash. Some of us don't even want to be!"
Abigail gritted her teeth. "All I know is I've only got myself
to depend on and if I don't trust my own decisions, then
I've got nothing. So lay off!"

Kate was blown away, speechless. She'd never seen
Abigail freak out like this before. She had to find a way to
get things back onto their regular course. "You do have
other people to depend on. You've got me, and Randall,
and Jesse. We're all here for you."

Abigail took a deep breath and sighed. "You're the
publicist and I know this is your job. But let's try it my way
for the time being. If it really isn't working, we'll see what
changes we need to make."

Even though Abigail was suddenly being diplomatic, it
didn't change the fact that Kate felt as if the entire world
was against her. Everything she'd gotten used to in her life
was being turned on its head, and the people closest to her
were changing into people who had sudden emotional outbursts and passionate crushes. It was all too much.

Abigail pulled out a pen and paper and started writing
some things down, but Kate was so overwhelmed that she
lashed out. "Maybe you should realize that when it comes
to style and success, I know what I'm talking about."

Abigail stood, grabbed her stuff, and said, loudly
enough to be perfectly understood over the piano music,
with an authority that was new for her, "Why don't we quit
for the day and come back tomorrow when you've thought
about it?" Before Kate realized she'd just had another
meeting abruptly closed on her, Abigail was out the door.

Kate felt horrible that she'd upset Abigail, but when she
looked up and realized that Jesse had witnessed the whole
thing, she felt much, much worse.

"Don't you know that staring is rude?" she yelled at Jesse, ignoring his concerned look as she gathered her things. She pulled her jacket over her shoulders, tied the belt tight at her waist, and turned to go—then tripped over her own foot and wound up in a heap on the floor. Along with her knees, her face burned red. Trying to keep everything intact, trying to hold on to the way things were, was proving one hell of a difficult job.

"I'm fine!" Kate barked when Jesse ran over. But she didn't even believe it herself.

17

As he walked to his locker after fifth period, Jesse counted fifteen girls he'd hooked up with in the past four years or so. It was Friday and he would normally have at least two dates lined up for the weekend. But here he was— no dates, no plans for dates, no desire for plans for dates. Weird.

And to make matters worse, Caroline had forced him to take the night off, even though his name was written right there in her own handwriting on the schedule over the butcher-block counter in the back room. If there was a bigger sign that she was still pissed at him over the snooping incident, he couldn't imagine what it would be.

Ever since then, Caroline had been hot and cold with Jesse, allowing him to think she was over it and then growing quiet and distant, which only intrigued him more. Then he'd say the most ridiculous things to get her attention. Like on Wednesday when Jesse had asked her to come over and smell the beans to make sure they were all right, but all he wanted to do was be close to her. When she got there, though, he didn't know what to do. So she smelled the beans, gave him a funny look, and went back to what she was doing without saying a word.

"Hi, Jesse," Larissa (number seven out of fifteen) said, waving flirtatiously.

Jesse tried to force a smile but it wouldn't come. "Hey there."

"What are you doing tonight?" She stopped in front of his locker, a denim binder snuggled to her chest.

"Working," he lied.

"Well, maybe I'll stop by." Larissa swept her severe bangs aside with a single finger and then turned dramatically—to make sure he watched her—as she retreated down the hallway.

Jesse was amazed. This pretty girl was knocking on his door and he couldn't even bring himself to care. It was treachery, this feeling. And he was sure it had something to do with whatever had been going on in Caroline's photo—it had gotten under his skin and wouldn't let him be.

He dragged himself to the cafeteria, got a slice of pizza and a Coke, and sat down at a metal table where Randall, Kate, and Abigail were already gathered.

"What's up?" Randall asked.

"Not much, you?" he answered.

Abigail was writing something in her notebook while Kate inspected her hot tea as if it were the most interesting thing in the room.

"Working tonight, Jesse?" Randall picked at his burger mindlessly.

"Nah, Caroline gave me the night off." Jesse's gaze shifted to Kate. He was waiting for her to pounce on him at any second with another reason why he should stay away from Caroline.

But instead Kate did something rather surprising. She looked up from her tea, dug into her huge brown leather tote, and pulled two concert tickets from an inside pocket. She held them out in front of Jesse. "Since you're free, want to go with me to see Leonard J?" That was a local DJ who was following in Moby's tracks, and Jesse definitely respected him an as artist.

Still, he was skeptical about Kate's motives. What if this was some kind of intervention and all she was planning on doing was kidnapping him and using torture to convince him to forget Caroline and return to his old player ways? On the other hand, maybe this was Kate's idea of a peace offering. Sure, Kate could be bitchy, but whenever she realized that she might have crossed a line, she was always racing over with some chicken noodle soup when he had a cold, or inviting him to Christmas dinner when his parents were stuck on some movie set in Morocco. He figured he could give her the benefit of the doubt.

"Sure," Jesse said. "That sounds cool."

Kate offered him a warm smile, her equivalent of an apology—or as much of an apology as one would ever get from her.

Jesse looked around the lunchroom at the framed canvases hanging above the wood chair rail that bordered the lofty room with its peaked, carved-oak ceiling and crossbeams. These were art projects by classmates and Martin Hall graduates. There was one deep-hued painting with lots of flowing chocolate, maroon, and forest green movement in the brushstrokes; in the foreground rose a long dining table with eight chairs, all empty but for one occupied by a woman in jeans. This was Abigail's work. He knew the model had been Abigail's mother. He thought Abigail must feel as if she couldn't escape the pain wherever she went.

"So what's going on with you, Abigail?" he asked, kicking her foot playfully under the table.

Abigail dragged a fork around the inside of her salad bowl, pushing the last pieces of lettuce to the left and right. "Nick and I are going to check out an apartment on MacDougal Street tomorrow."

Jesse could see that Abigail was ignoring Randall. That was a bad sign. Maybe they hadn't made up after their blow-out. "That's cool," he said, smirking. "But kind of far from all of us, no?" Even though he felt sometimes as if he didn't have parents, with them being gone so much, he knew there was a massive difference between his situation and Abigail's—he did have them both, safe and sound, and there was always the hope that one day they might wake up and realize they needed to spend more time with their son. To have lost her mother, who was the mother of the century for sure—Jesse couldn't begin to imagine Abigail's sense of loss.

Abigail leaned her chin on her palm. "Well, it's closer than Aspen."

Jesse noticed that Randall had caught Abigail's gaze and she didn't look away.

"I'm really sorry," Randall whispered to her.

"That's okay," Abigail whispered back.

"Oh, get a room, would you?" Kate said.

"Okay, freaks. You can cut the tension at this table with

a knife," Jesse said, remembering the scene between Abigail and Kate the other day at the One Trick. "Can't we all just play nice?"

They all smiled and shook their heads and tossed balled-up napkins his way, but nothing else was said on the subject. His pizza had gone cold and was a little on the mushy side. He didn't have much of an appetite, so he took a few bites and dropped the rest back on his plate. He sucked down the soda so he'd have some energy at least.

Before they parted ways, Kate grabbed hold of Jesse's arm. "All right, why don't you come to my place at seven, so we can take my mom's car service over to the concert?"

"Sounds cool," Jesse said, returning Kate's smile. He was glad that a familiar note had sounded in the song of confusion that had been his life lately.

As he rode his bike home a few hours later, Jesse realized that it was truly fall now. The leaves were red like fire and rustling through a heavy breeze that smacked his jacket loudly when he changed directions on his bike. Though it was only five-thirty p.m., the sky looked grayer and smaller; not bright and endless as it had a few weeks earlier.

Jesse passed Copper, the restaurant where he'd had that terrible date with Cammie. Everything had gone downhill from there. He thought about the leaves changing colors, and how he had, too, the moment he laid eyes on Caroline, drank her unique coffee, and saw that mysterious photo. There had to be something behind this metamorphosis, just as there was behind the changing of the seasons, and if he didn't find out what that something was, he felt sure he'd go mad.

Jesse turned his bike into the alley alongside the One Trick Pony, looking left and right to make sure no one would see him. He felt the loose gravel crunch beneath his tire and listened to the popping sound of them grinding against the ground beneath him. When Jesse heard a lilting voice, he hopped off the bike and walked it quietly along the length of the brick building. He leaned against the end of the wall and craned his neck around the corner, trying to catch a glimpse of Caroline.

She was on the telephone, standing close to the brick pile on the near side of the outside staircase that led down into the basement. She had the phone cradled between her shoulder and cheek, her head tilted in such a way that he could see just how elongated and beautiful her neck was. One of her hands was tucked into her apron pocket and the other was pressed against her forehead in distress as if she was crying.

The oddest thing about all this was that it seemed as though the front door of the One Trick was shut and the Closed sign was up. This was Caroline's busiest time of day, when all the neighborhood kids would stop by and commuters dropped in to decompress. Something serious had to be going on to interfere with her serving her patrons.

Jesse pulled his head back and slumped down against the side of the building. His breath caught in his throat. He had to know what was bothering Caroline. But when he glanced at his watch, he saw that he didn't have much time to waste. He had to meet Kate in an hour or so. He had to act now.

As soon as Jesse's black canvas sneakers and the tires of his bike hit the sidewalk in front of the One Trick, a man whizzed past him and started banging on the café door. "Caroline! Fire! Someone call nine-one-one!"

Jesse knew it would look bad that he was there—desperate, really—but he made a split-second decision to do the right thing anyway. It wasn't a choice as much as the only clear path he could see. He dropped his bike, used his key to open the door, and ran into the coffee shop. Caroline appeared a second later, charging through the back, in front of the orange tongues of flame, the dark, dense smoke already flowering, and by then Jesse was using a towel to smother the flames, which had spread through the front of the fireplace and onto the floor a few inches in front. He smacked and smacked at the lowermost flames—the ones that threatened to catch the tables and chairs beyond. He kicked the furniture legs out of the way, amazed by his ability to think so clearly in this terrifying situation.

For the first time in his life, Jesse really cared about something and someone; his heart was filled with so much love right now, nothing could stop him from risking his life for either of them.

Even in the clouds of smoke, Jesse noticed how Caroline's pretty red dress stood out like a flower in the desert. She pulled more towels off the counter as Jesse continued through the blistering heat, ignoring the burning sensation he could feel on his hands and forearms. "Grab the extinguisher!" he shouted.

Within seconds Caroline was back with the red extinguisher and then ran to fill a metal bucket with water. Jesse aimed the hose at the base of the fire, and it made a sizzling noise, which created extra smoke but appeared to put out some of the flames. The smell of burning was everywhere when Jesse heard the engines screaming down the street; a moment later the firefighters came running in, carrying a huge hose, ready to spray the fire that still burned just outside the fireplace.

Jesse stepped out of the way and escorted Caroline out the back of the building, holding her hand protectively. Their breathing was heavy and labored as they stood silently in the back lot. He was still clinging to Caroline's hand tightly, and when he looked at her, he could see her chest rising and falling, her eyes still glassy from the emotional conversation she'd been having just moments ago, before the fire had erupted. He closed his eyes; his head inched closer, closer; he was ready to take the chance and kiss her.

"The fire's out, folks," a husky voice called out.

When Jesse's eyes sprang open, Caroline's beautiful, full lips were just inches from his own. But she was already gaping at the firefighter and Jesse had no way of knowing if she'd realized that he was about to kiss her—and if she did, if she would have let him.

The firefighter took off his helmet, and soot sprinkled onto his face. "You'll have to have someone take a look at the tiles inside the chimney. Looks like some of them might be loose, which could have meant a really devastating fire creeping inside the walls. But whoever contained it saved you from that."

Jessie's heart plummeted and rose in such great leaps, he had to hold on to the banister. He was immensely relieved that everything was safe once again, yet the fear of something happening to Caroline and the One Trick had intensified his emotions tenfold.

As Caroline filled out paperwork with the fire marshal, Jesse started cleaning up so that Caroline wouldn't have to do it all herself after such a frightening experience. When all the firefighters had left, Caroline joined Jesse and they scrubbed the black from the brick with heavy wire brushes and a solvent cleaner until they were so exhausted neither could move an inch. That was when Jesse realized he'd forgotten all about Kate.

So much for her peace offering, he thought.

He ran to his bag to retrieve his cell phone, which was still on vibrate mode from school. There were four missed calls. He dialed Kate's number and waited for her to pick up, though he had a feeling she wouldn't. Kate had a thing about how people should act, and leaving her flat was certainly not acceptable to her, regardless of the reason. He didn't want to hurt her, certainly not this way, but it seemed he couldn't win with her lately no matter what he did. For some reason she was giving him the hardest time about Caroline and everything else, and he wondered if it was simply that she was jealous that she hadn't found the same kind of person for herself.

As Jesse suspected, Kate didn't pick up the phone. Her voice mail message played. "I can't take your call right now. Leave a message, and if you're lucky, I'll get back to you."

"Kate, listen, I'm really sorry about tonight. I really wanted to go to the concert with you. But there was a fire at the One Trick, and we just finished cleaning up the mess. The concert completely slipped my mind in the midst of it all. Let's talk tomorrow, okay? Bye, sexy."

Jesse hung up, knowing right away he shouldn't have

said that the concert had slipped his mind. If there was one thing Kate didn't like, it was attention being diverted from her. It looked as though he would be putting out flames tomorrow, too.

"Everything okay?" Caroline asked. She sat on one of the bar stools looking adorably droopy, her limbs loose and her eyes red. She'd pulled her hair up into a tight bun, and all Jesse could think of was how smooth and silky her neck was.

"Oh, that was just one of my many lady friends." Jesse nearly collapsed after he said that. It sounded so fake. Caroline had to have seen through his bravado.

She smiled, shaking her head. "I'm sure a hero like you can get any girl he wants."

Hero? Jesse was practically beaming. He felt emboldened and decided to seize this opportunity. "Hey, why don't we get out of here for a little while and eat some Chinese takeout at my house? Nobody's there and we'll have the whole place to ourselves."

"Where are your parents?" Caroline's eyebrows rose with concern.

Jesse didn't like the tone she'd used. Hero or not, it seemed as though Caroline still thought of him as a kid. "They're in Texas." He tried to act as if this were nothing big. He shrugged.

She was quiet a second and then hopped off her chair and stood next to him. "I'd love to have dinner with a friend tonight."

Friend? Why did she have to use that depressing word? Even though it deflated his ego, Jesse hoped he could change her mind. "Great. Let's go," he said, walking behind the counter and pouring room-temperature coffee into a paper cup, intending to drink it along the way.

After they'd walked the few blocks to President Street and had ridden the glass elevator of the industrial-building-turned-loft complex, Jesse was in shock at the sight of Caroline on his family's angular leather couch, her flowery purse sitting on the bean-shaped glass coffee table. She looked like a stranger in a strange land, and suddenly he was embarrassed by the expensive modern style of his home. The décor was so different from the style of Caroline's One Trick Pony. In fact, looking around the walls at the pricy modern art, he realized for the first time that he hadn't a clue as to what any of it meant: the black canvas with the purple dot; the orange, green, and yellow squiggly stripes; the white steel egg hovering on the far wall. None of it felt like a true reflection of him. There was no warmth, there were no cozy lines and fluffy pillows, the things he connected to through Caroline. It made him want to shift closer to her, pull her in, and kiss her so deeply that he became one with her.

They ordered a couple of dishes and some soup, and when the delivery guy arrived, Jesse refused Caroline's offer of money. "But I owe you," she said. "If it weren't for you . . . well, who knows, there might not be a One Trick anymore."

"It was my pleasure, Caroline," he replied. "So let me buy you dinner and finish off this night properly."

As they began to lift the food to their mouths with the chopsticks, Jesse felt the urge to bring up the basement incident that had been the cause of so much tension. He wanted to ignore this feeling so badly—why reopen that can of worms? But no matter how he tried to resist this pulling sensation around his heart, he couldn't.

"So, are you still upset with me about what happened in the basement?" he asked as he fiddled with a fried wonton.

Caroline's slightly stiff posture softened and she put her hand on his shoulder. "No, I'm not. All is forgiven."

Although Jesse was glad to hear that, more questions still begged to be asked. Just the other day, he'd been finishing the backlog of accounting for Caroline, trying to make sense of her receipts and register tapes from the little coffee shop she had owned in France before coming to the States. He'd tapped all the figures into the calculator, but then something strange had happened. He'd noticed that her income had ceased completely in the middle of April. Surely this couldn't be correct.

"Caroline, are you missing some of your April tapes?" he asked now, as if he were just making casual conversation.

She stalled by shoving part of an egg roll into her mouth. When she'd finished chewing, she said, "I guess they must have gotten lost in the move."

But Jesse had looked on through May, June, and July, and there was only a nominal amount here and there—the price of a single coffee. "You're sure you're not missing anything?"

"Can you ever be sure of anything?" Caroline asked. "You just have to make do with whatever you've got on hand and live with the mystery of the rest of it."

Jesse had a feeling there was more to this mystery.

What could have happened back in France? Why did Caroline's business slow down and why did she move here, of all places?

As if reading his thoughts, Caroline gently placed her chopsticks along the edge of her plate and leaned back, as far back as the straight sofa would allow, and sighed deeply. "Jesse, I feel very close to you, especially after everything that happened tonight."

Were his dreams coming true?

"I would love to confide in you, to entrust you with these things that weigh so heavy on me. To be honest, you are the only person here in Brooklyn I feel I truly know." She toyed with a button on her dress.

"You can tell me anything, Caroline. Anything at all," he said urgently.

"Well, that box you were snooping in . . . ," she began, her eyes narrowed, but in a playful way.

Jesse was glad to see she had a light tone about it now, after she'd been so angry with him, but his cheeks flushed with embarrassment all the same.

"Well, those things represent a time in my life that . . . a time with someone I loved very deeply. Georges and I . . ." A tear slipped down the side of her nose, making her skin glisten in the light cast from the round chandelier that hung from the high ceiling.

Jesse reached out and softly swept the tear away with his finger. "Tell me what happened."

But instead of letting Jesse into her past as he'd hoped she would, Caroline jumped up from the couch and moved away from him. "I've said too much already. I've allowed it to go too far."

She gathered her coat and purse and headed for the door.

"Don't go, Caroline. Please don't go." Jesse knew he sounded as if he were begging, but he didn't care at all about hurting his pride. "I want to help you, to be there for you, like you are for me."

Caroline hesitated for a moment, her hand squeezing the doorknob and her back to Jesse. "I can't go through this again. I just can't."

And in a flash, the spot on sofa that had felt so warm and alive was once again cold and empty.

18

Abigail was glad the weekend was finally over. Though they'd made up in the cafeteria on Friday, she and Randall hadn't spoken since—she'd felt too weird to call, and also half hoped that he'd be the one to make the move toward getting them back on track.

After the initial sting of what he'd said had worn off, Abigail had realized that even Randall's blowup offered more insightful advice than the careful, delicate words of anyone else she knew. She'd wanted to forgive him right away, but she wasn't sure. On the one hand, she felt she would be betraying Nick if she wasn't angrier over the mean things Randall said about him. On the other hand, she couldn't help feeling that there was some truth in Randall's comments. Ultimately, though, Abigail decided that she'd gone through enough changes for an entire life-time in the past few months, and she wasn't ready to pack up and leave New York, even if it meant moving in with Nick and cutting ties with her father, who had barely spoken to her in recent days.

As Abigail made her way to the first-floor study lounge on Monday afternoon, she thought about how her father had reacted when he'd heard the big news. Secretly she'd been hoping he'd shoot up from his seat on the sofa, toss the business section of the *Times* aside (maybe even accidentally smacking Ginny in the face in the process), push Nick out of the way, embrace her, and say over and over, "I'm so sorry, Abigail, I'm so sorry. I love you. You're the most important thing in my life."

When he'd done nothing of the sort, Abigail's heart had plummeted. The sight of him quietly going back to watching TV with Ginny at his side would probably be etched into her mind forever, although she would do anything in her power to get rid of it.

Abigail walked into the study lounge and headed straight to the sign-up sheet she'd posted for open-mike night. *This will be a good distraction,* she thought. She counted fifteen names on the form (see *that,* Kate!) before she came to one that shocked the hell out of her. *Randall* had signed up! Since when did he have the nerve to perform in front of strangers? He could barely get up the courage to play her a song over the phone.

Abigail stood for a second, feeling more drawn to Randall than she'd care to admit. It was inspiring, seeing his messy scrawl on the poster. Randall was facing down a big phobia of his, and Abigail was so impressed and elated that she burst out of the lounge running.

She picked up her pace even more, smiling at familiar faces as she darted by. The bell rang out shrilly, which

169

meant she'd be late to her next class, but she had to see Randall right now or else she might burst. Her heart was racing by the time she got to the end of the hallway, her huge fabric tote bag weighing heavy on her shoulder, her thermos slipping out of her loosening grip.

Abigail turned left, and when she didn't find Randall at his locker she tried to remember what class he had now. Her mind was jerking in so many directions, she could barely see straight. *Music!* He had band in a room down this very hallway. Abigail continued, all the classroom doors closing now. Her teacher would be starting without her. She came to a stop outside the double-doored band room, stray notes of music already seeping through the crack under the door. Abigail tried to catch her breath as she peered through the glass window in the door of room 108. Randall was sitting with his guitar lying faceup on his lap. He was wearing a navy sweatshirt and brown corduroy pants and joking around with the saxophone player, Lenny Singer.

As Abigail watched, Lenny threw his head back in laughter while Randall smiled. She couldn't figure out what she was supposed to do now. Walk in there and tell Randall in front of a gawking audience how proud she was of him? Wave him out into the hallway and ask how he'd found the strength to do something so brave, sharing his music with people he didn't know? She just stood there frozen, wishing for some sort of sign.

She was ready to turn on her heel and leave when Randall looked up and caught her eye. Abigail could feel her cheeks becoming pink. She must have looked crazy standing like that, gazing at him so starry-eyed.

"What's wrong?" he mouthed to her.

Abigail furrowed her brow in confusion, then shook

her head. "Nothing," she mouthed back before bolting down the hall even faster than she had come. It was those words—"what's wrong?"—that had set her off. In her head she answered, "Everything." But the pulling around her heart was happening again, tugging so hard that she had to bend to its will. Instead of going to class, she found herself back in the study lounge, standing before the sign-up sheet. Without thinking, she finished off the contents of her thermos, shoved it into her bag, and grabbed the blue Bic that was tied to a string and tacked to the bulletin board.

It wasn't until she'd signed her name under Randall's that everything felt right.

When school let out, Abigail sprinted out the front doors and walked the bustling, leafless-tree-lined street to the main thoroughfare, Smith Street. She wanted to stop by the One Trick to refill her thermos before she met up with Nick. She passed an elderly woman walking a cocker spaniel and stopped to pet the dog. *Spunky.* Abigail loved fall—its rich colors, and the lively way people decorated their front doors. There were wreaths and garlands of autumn-hued leaves around windows. Baskets of gourds and tiny pumpkins topped stoops, and giant jack-o'-lanterns watched over tiny patches of lawn.

She turned right onto Smith Street and passed the few shops on the way to the One Trick—the Laundromat, the pizzeria, and the expensive jewelry boutique with its twisty silver pieces and dangling charms. When she arrived at the café, the quotation Caroline had written on the blackboard easel caught her eye: "The basic need of the human heart in nearly every great crisis—a good hot cup of coffee.—Alexander King."

Abigail found the place looking a bit scarred. She'd heard at lunch about Jesse's heroics and was thankful that no one had gotten hurt. Abigail knew she wouldn't have been able to handle losing someone else close to her. Which was why she wandered into the One Trick so often these days. Just being there made her feel like a part of a loving family. Abigail was also getting used to Caroline's easygoing yet spirited demeanor, and the way she always knew what kind of coffee Abigail wanted to drink without having to ask.

That especially reminded Abigail of her mother.

"How was your day?" Caroline inquired once Abigail had settled in at the bar. Caroline was making small talk with throngs of customers while she whirled around the machines, but for some reason, Abigail felt as though Caroline was speaking just with her.

"Pretty good," Abigail replied, swinging her legs back and forth as she sat on her stool. "How are you holding up after the fire?"

"Thanks to Jesse, it's just a little mess to clean up," Caroline said, smiling genuinely.

"Well, I'm glad both of you are okay." Abigail shuddered briefly when she glanced at the charred brick near the fireplace.

"We must all live with these frightening things," Caroline said as she filled another customer's cup to the brim. "It's what makes us see who we really are."

Abigail couldn't help wondering what kinds of experiences led Caroline to say these things.

"Do you miss your family back home, Caroline?" She remembered Caroline mentioning that her father was a wanderer, but she didn't know anything about Caroline's mother.

There was a break in the flow of coffee buyers and Caroline gave Abigail her full attention. "I do. It was very difficult to leave, as my mother, she is my dearest friend. I miss her very much."

Abigail swallowed hard. She was envious of Caroline, who could hop on a plane and be in her mother's arms again whenever it pleased her. The feeling overtook her, threatening to make her cry.

"And I know you miss yours, too," Caroline said, placing a warm hand on Abigail's forearm as she passed her the full thermos. "But don't forget that you have many gifts, and losing one of them often strengthens your tie to the rest . . . if only you know where to look."

Abigail thanked Caroline, paid her three dollars, and made her way to Manhattan on the F train. She could have sat there with Caroline all day, listening to her stories and her vague riddles. Abigail chuckled to herself when she thought of how much Kate hated that trait of Caroline's. But when Abigail sipped at the piping-hot coffee in her thermos, she suddenly turned serious. It seemed apparent to everyone but Kate that the reason Kate didn't like Caroline was that she was threatened by Caroline's presence. Could Abigail deny that some of her anger toward Ginny had the same cause? Sure, Ginny was nowhere near as wonderful as her mother, but even if she had been, would Abigail have welcomed her with open arms? It was doubtful.

Outside 24 MacDougal Street, at the top of the narrow iron staircase with its peeling handrail, Nick was sitting, waiting for her. To the left of the stoop was a dry cleaner, and just next to that a Middle Eastern restaurant. The fragrance of exotic spices was everywhere on the street; there were at least five other Middle Eastern restaurants, with their giant rotisserie meats slowly rotating in the windows she'd passed on the way.

Abigail liked the way the neighborhood was crammed with college students, who always seemed to be hurrying off to the library to study for exams or to the bar to celebrate a passing grade. She'd just seen a few of them paying for cigarettes at the small newsstand, with its colorful rows of candy and chewing gum and hanging latticework of lottery scratch-off tickets. Soon Abigail would be one of these students, and while such a realization should have brought her comfort, all it did was make her nauseated.

Nick whistled at her as she came down the street. "Are you ready to get a look at our future?" he asked, taking her free hand in his and kissing her ring finger delicately.

Abigail yanked her hand away and Nick flinched. "Sorry. I'm a little jumpy."

Nick gestured to her thermos. "Coming down off a caffeine high?"

"You could say that," Abigail replied, although she could never easily categorize how she felt after having some of Caroline's delicious brew.

Nick led her inside the run-down building. A foot-trampled blue carpet lined the hallway and extended up the stairs. There were a couple of apartments on each floor, marked with gold numbers and letters on black-painted doors. The old plaster walls were painted a rich red color over peeling layers of previous paint, and in spots those old colors poked through—a hospital green and a sickly yellow.

Abigail knew that ordinarily she'd look at this place as a true fixer-upper and see all the home improvement opportunities as her chance at being on *Extreme Makeover: Home Edition*. But right now all she saw was the immense challenge of trying to fix something up that was just too broken down, or attempting to make something real out of something that fell short of that.

At the third floor, Nick turned to the apartment across the landing—3B—and rummaged around in his coat pocket for the key.

Abigail sipped her coffee and imagined a space beyond that black door where a square wood table stood, one blue chair and one red one beside it. She put herself on the blue one, sitting Indian style with her head resting on her arms, listening to Randall playing one of his new songs while he perched on the red chair.

She shook the image from her head just as Nick scooped her up and carried her over their threshold. She begged him to put her down, and when he did, she glanced around and noticed that the apartment had been modestly renovated; the ornate moldings looked new and the wood floors gleamed.

"So, what do you think?" Nick asked.

"It's . . . nice," she said. And it was. Nice. Not unbelievably amazing, couldn't be more perfect, everything she could have dreamed of. Just nice.

Together they took a peek at the small bathroom with its white tub and out-of-date sink fixtures, then checked out the kitchen with its new compact refrigerator. In each room, Randall's face kept popping up and Abigail had to blink it away forcefully.

"Have you spoken with your dad again about the

move?" Nick asked, leaning against a post that supported a cutout wall that peeked into the kitchen.

"Not exactly," she said, fidgeting with the shoulder strap of her bag. "Obviously he doesn't care too much, if he hasn't said anything since."

"I'm sure he does care. He's just scared of losing you, and I know how that feels."

A wave of guilt crashed against Abigail. Why couldn't she be more excited about building a future here with Nick, who was just so . . . *nice?* Saying that word in her head made her skin crawl, but she wondered why she hadn't had this reaction before. What was so bad about nice? Look at the light, easy back-and-forth they had here. Didn't that count for anything? Abigail had always believed it did, but as she took another hit from her thermos, all the niceness seemed weightless. When her mom had died, she really craved that weightlessness, but feeling it now with Nick standing in the kitchen made her feel hollow.

Nick closed in on Abigail and wrapped his arms around her. "I could definitely get used to this," he said, kissing her on the forehead. "As a matter of fact, there's one very important room I haven't shown you yet."

As they made their way toward the bedroom, Abigail stiffened. Nick was chock-full of excitement, though, as he pointed to the spot where their full-size bed would sit.

"Isn't it great?" Nick asked sweetly, nuzzling her neck.

That was when Abigail spotted the view from the bedroom window—a redbrick wall.

Futility.

It was the most accurate word she could think of.

* * *

When Abigail got home, there was peace and quiet. No one was there, thank God. She took her thermos with her into the family room and tossed Tchaikovsky's *The Sleeping Beauty* onto the stereo, or "the hi-fi," as her mother had always called it. Abigail listened and remembered the part when Aurora pricked her finger and danced as she passed into the infamous sleep—a frantic dance, and terrifying, around and around until *thump!* She was out cold.

Abigail took a sip from the last few drops of coffee, staring at the poster of the ballerina Anna Pavlova in her frilled white costume. Again, Abigail's memories seemed to stand up and march around like dancers themselves, a long string of them, and she needed only to sit and enjoy.

After a few minutes of delightful procrastination, Abigail pulled out the reading homework she had for American history. They'd been given a handout from *The Living Past of America* by Cornelius Vanderbilt, Jr. The subject was a beautiful old mansion, the Colonel Black Mansion in Ellsworth, Maine. She began to read, "The original furniture, much of it priceless antiques at the time the house was built, may be seen. Among the notable features are a beautiful circular staircase, a French girandole mirror, a German hand organ, and a Dutch wing-back chair which may be lengthened into a bed, as well as Waterford and Sandwich glass."

There were photos, but it was the unimportant items she wouldn't be tested on that stood out for her—the tarnished cups and the worn-out arm of a chair, the stubby pencils with bite marks. There was poetry hiding in things like that. Before long, she was jarred by the sounds of her father and Ginny at the door. Abigail grabbed her schoolbooks, ran into her bedroom, and locked herself inside until she heard Ginny call, "Dinner's ready, dear," a couple of hours later.

Abigail dragged herself down to the dining room only after her dad called for her, too.

"Ginny made tofu stir-fry for you," her father said when she sat down at the neatly set dining room table.

"Mmmm," Abigail said sarcastically. The brown saucy concoction in the bowl in front of her looked less than appetizing.

Ginny's eyes widened, as if Abigail had insulted her—and that was when Abigail noticed it. That poster behind them, her mother's beautiful poster—it was gone!

Her dad misread Abigail's horrified expression. "It's not that bad, is it, Abby?"

But the pulling on her heart was so fierce, all she could do was yell, "Where's the poster?"

"What?" Her dad was completely clueless.

"Where. Is. The. Poster?" Abigail shouted, and pushed her chair back from the table.

"Well, honey, we . . ." He looked to Ginny for support, but she rolled her eyes. "We thought it would be good for all of us to update the place."

Abigail glared at Ginny. "You know what? If my mother were here, she would wipe that expression off your face!"

Ginny gasped but then steadied herself. "Well, she's *not* here, so . . ."

"So I'm going to move in with Nick as soon as humanly possible." Abigail no longer cared about the recent uneasiness she'd felt about her boyfriend—in comparison, being with him was way better than living like this.

"Abigail, you honestly didn't think I'd let you move

in with your boyfriend, did you?" Her father's voice was gravelly and concerned. "You're only sixteen years old, and I'm your guardian, so you have to listen to me on this."

This was only a shred of the attention Abigail had been yearning for, and it wasn't enough. "Maybe I would listen if you had the decency to wait until my mother's body was cold before you started removing every last shred of her from my life."

And with that, Abigail charged out the door and galloped down to the street without even grabbing a jacket. Words were popping into her mind with every object that she saw; the cold chill in the air didn't even register. A flower growing out of a sidewalk crack was *bloody*. An orange T-shirt was *on fire*. A scraggly tree looked *furious*. Abigail had never felt upset and powerful and lost and liberated all at the same time. She couldn't really understand any of it, but she knew someone who might.

Fifteen minutes later, Abigail was standing at Randall's front door.

"Hi, Jeff. Is Randall here?" She hated to call Mr. Gold by his first name, but he always made a big deal about it if she didn't.

"He's at Platinum Record Studios, cutting an album." Mr. Gold was munching on a burger while the television bellowed in the background.

Randall was at the studio? This was huge. He had made so many excuses not to make a demo, but now he was actually doing it. Abigail swelled with pride. "Went out for some burgers this evening?" she asked his father.

"Nah, Ran bought me this, oh, I don't know, a few days ago."

"Gross," she said, making a face.

Mr. Gold's laugh sounded just like Randall's, and that made the pulling around her heart even tighter.

Abigail booked it over to the studio, sprinting at intervals to keep herself warm. When she finally made it to the building and then the sound booth, she saw that Randall was in the middle of a song. She was enchanted by the way his head gently rocked back and forth, how his eyes were tightly closed and his foot tapped against the bottom rung of the red chair he was sitting on. In front of her was a guy in a flannel shirt who was working the levers up and down on the long sound board. He didn't notice her, either, that was how mesmerized he was by Randall's music.

When Randall finished the song with a long, slow strum on the guitar strings, the sound reverberating a long time, he glanced up and waved her into the glass-walled studio. Then he reached down to the floor next to the chair and grabbed a large paper cup that had definitely come from the One Trick Pony.

Abigail never remembered him looking so confident, or herself feeling so strongly that she couldn't live without him.

19

Randall sipped at his coffee as Abigail made her way through the studio door. Frankly, he couldn't believe either one of them was here. If someone had asked him months ago if he'd be recording a real demo for a record producer and Abigail would show up out of the blue just to stare at him—all in one day, no less—Randall would have told that someone they were out of their mind.

"Wow," Abigail said, so softly it was almost a whisper. Her cheeks were a dark shade of pink, as if she'd run to Manhattan and back.

But that wasn't the only thing Randall noticed. In fact, his senses were in overdrive and all he could see, hear, and smell were the little details, like the way her voice lilted, and how the undone belt of her black jacket hung around her waist, and the scent of the vanilla hand lotion that she used religiously. Everything about her was just . . . magical.

Abigail took a few more steps toward him, but Randall couldn't wait another second to touch her. He put his cup on his chair and sprinted over to her, pulling her in as tight as his heart commanded him to, his hands tangling in her hair. Instantly he could tell that this was no ordinary hug. Abigail was clinging to him for dear life, pressing her face into his chest as if she were trying to hide from something. Randall knew that feeling all too well, but over the past couple of weeks, it was becoming more and more foreign to him, as if a recurring bad dream were being weeded out from his subconscious.

"I have to say, I'm surprised to see you here after I blew up at you the other day," he said, rubbing his hands up and down her back.

He felt Abigail's shoulders shake as she laughed. "Me too," she said.

"I'm sorry if I hurt you." Randall wanted to say more, but a couple of the tech guys came into the room to check on his equipment, prompting Abigail to break free from his embrace.

They stood there silently for a while as the men worked around them. When the crew left, Abigail closed in on him again, wringing her hands nervously. "You didn't hurt me. You just . . . shocked me."

Randall liked how that sounded, so much so that a wide smile formed on his face. But then he remembered that she'd been with Nick looking at an apartment on MacDougal Street today, and his heart felt as though it had been pierced by broken glass. "I don't like being apart from you, Abby. I don't like it one bit."

"I know what you mean." Abigail took his hand

tentatively, as if she were testing the boundaries of this unfamiliar ground.

Randall ran his thumb along her palm. "Was there something you wanted to talk about?" He figured something must have happened for Abigail to go through all the trouble of finding him here.

Abigail slipped away from Randall's grasp and then pulled herself atop a huge speaker, her legs dangling a few inches above the floor. "Where do I start?"

Randall hopped up next to her and nudged her gently with his elbow. "At the beginning."

It was just the invitation Abigail needed to open up. She dove into a long, winding story about the apartment not feeling quite right (thank God), and blowing up at Ginny and her father during dinner.

"And the funny thing is," she said, after she'd caught Randall up on everything that had transpired. "I don't know why I'm always coming to you instead of Nick about these things."

Randall could think of a few reasons! "Because we understand each other," he said confidently.

Abigail grinned and looked Randall directly in the eyes. "Yeah, I guess we do."

When she was silent for a moment, Randall asked, "Are you feeling a little bit better now?"

Abigail nodded.

"Good, because I just happen to be looking for a backup singer."

"*Me?*"

"You," he said, hoping that shocking Abigail was the way into her heart.

The next day, Randall had to double-check somehow that he'd actually experienced what he thought he had the night before. Because without proof, it would have been impossible to believe that he'd laid down half a record; had Abigail sing a couple of backup tracks; listened with his own ears as Abigail lied to Nick the Dick on the telephone, saying she didn't feel well and would unfortunately have to break their plans for the evening.

When he got home from school around three-thirty, Randall popped in the CD he'd burned. This was proof enough. Sitting at his computer desk, Randall closed his eyes and listened to all the tracks through his headphones. He was amazed, mostly because he'd actually gone and done this at all, but also because he liked how everything sounded. And there was Abigail's angelic voice. *So come here close, baby, and just kiss me now.*

Suddenly Randall's phone rang, scaring him out of a particularly intense fantasy about Abigail's tender lips. He looked at the caller ID: Jesse.

Randall barely got out a hello before Jesse started babbling frantically. "Dude, you have to come over, like now!"

"Hey, man, are you okay? How come you weren't at school?"

Jesse answered very fast, as if he'd been drinking Caroline's coffee through a funnel. "Well, first there was this box, right? A photo—Caroline, a guy; I'm thinking possibly that Diablo dude. And it fell on the floor and I saw it and went kind of crazy. It was possessed or something, I think—"

"Whoa, whoa! Get ahold of yourself, Jesse. I'm on my way over."

Randall threw on some clothes, snapped the demo CD into his old Walkman, and rode his bike to Jesse's place.

Jesse answered the door in pajama pants and a ratty T-shirt that Randall recognized from their childhood summer camp.

"Okay, follow me," Jesse said, leading Randall up the stairs. The house was kind of a mess; takeout food containers were all over the place and magazines littered the floor. Cindy, their maid, must have been on vacation.

It didn't look much better in Jesse's bedroom. There were clothes all over the unmade queen-size platform bed. Atop the black lacquer dresser lay stacks of computer printouts. The red leather chair was barely visible beneath more clothes, a couple of newspapers, and a cardboard box with Styrofoam peanuts flowing over the top.

"Where are your parents?" Randall asked.

"Texas," Jesse said as he sat down at his Macintosh desktop.

Randall rolled another chair over to the computer desk to see what Jesse was looking at. There were at least a dozen Internet windows open, and Jesse enlarged the first one, which contained an article translated from French. It was in faulty English, and Randall had difficulty understanding the sentences. *Villette, France,* the article began. *Café proprietor Caroline Deneuve has finally had to close doors business.*

"Our Caroline?" Randall asked, stunned.

Jesse shook his head, his eyes wild.

You will remember our coverage of this story amazing from two month ago.

Randall squinted and furrowed his brow. "Two month ago?"

Jesse pointed at the screen. "Look, here's what it says:

185

Caroline owned a famous shop. People in the town loved the coffee, came in every day . . . just like they do here. Customers claimed that the coffee was so powerful that it made them do crazy things and that Caroline must have spiked it with some poison or drug."

"Oh, come on! That's absurd."

"But wait!" Jesse clapped his hands in front of Randall's face. "There's more. Caroline had an affair—with a married man—and the wife hired a lawyer to sue Caroline for putting a love spell on her husband. Then Caroline fled the country to avoid prosecution."

Randall rolled his eyes. "This is insane, Jesse. If there were such a thing as a love spell, I would have put one on Abigail years ago."

"I know, that's what I thought at first. But then I started to notice things. I started to have—well—feelings for Caroline. I wasn't hungry. I haven't been out on a date in *three* weeks! The last date I went on was a disaster. I can't seem to do anything right. I don't know how to talk to Caroline. I'm dropping things all the time. And then somehow I have the superhuman strength to fight a fire all by myself. How do you explain all that?" Jesse blurted all this out without even taking a breath.

"Um, dude, I hate to tell you this . . ." Randall laughed as he patted his friend on the shoulder. "But first of all, you need a shower, and second of all, I think you're in love and it has nothing to do with a spell."

Jesse flung himself on his bed and covered his face with a pillow. "But what about that time I said there might be something in the coffee that was making everyone weird?" he mumbled. "It would explain a lot, including why she left France."

"I don't think any of us were serious, Jesse." Randall wasn't so sure, though. There had been some remarkable changes in all of them recently—Abigail telling off her dad, lying to Nick, and showing some real interest in Randall; not to mention the things Randall himself had been able to accomplish. But that was crazy, wasn't it? How could coffee make people do things? This wasn't an M. Night Shyamalan movie. It was real life. Fairy tales didn't happen in places like Brooklyn.

"You're not so sure, are you?" Jesse said, throwing the pillow at Jesse.

Randall tossed it on Jesse's bed. "No, I am sure." He sat down next to his friend. "It had to happen to you sooner or later, man. A girl has finally captured your heart. And she's amazing, too. Why don't you just leave it at that and go for it?"

"She doesn't have feelings for me." Jesse frowned.

"You know what, maybe there *was* something in that coffee. I can't believe what I'm hearing from you! Whatever happened to, and I quote, 'Every woman loves the Jess-ter'?"

"She's not like a regular girl, dude. She's . . . different."

"How so?" Randall asked.

"For one thing, she knows things—and not just any random thing, but things that matter to me, things that make me a better person. Oh my God, that sounded like freaking nonsense. I'm hopeless."

Randall smirked. "Actually, I think I know what you mean. Abigail always encourages me in just the right way, like she knows instinctively how to relate to me. She's like the candle on Caroline's coffee cups—totally illuminating. And maybe that's what Caroline is to you, too."

Jesse chuckled. "Also, she smells so good, and when she smiles, it's like someone is tearing my chest open and ripping out my heart. Know what I mean?"

Randall glanced down at his and Jesse's feet. There were at least ten empty coffee cups scattered on the floor next to them. Randall picked one up and held it to his nose, the invigorating aroma still lingering in the air. "I know exactly what you mean," he replied.

Randall called Abigail as soon he left Jesse's place and told her about Jesse's bizarre allegations as he rode his bike back home. Of course, he'd made a pit stop at the One Trick Pony and had a quick cup of Caroline's new French roast blend, just so he could see for himself if there was anything out of the ordinary. So far, all he felt was a little buzzed.

"Well, I believe him," Abigail said, quite seriously. "The coffee sure seems magical to me."

Randall loved that Abigail was a girl who believed in magic, no questions asked.

"I knew you would." He jerked his bike to the left to avoid a heap of leaves in his path.

"You know, Rupert Brooke once wrote, 'Safe in the magic of my woods / I lay, and watched the dying light.' He could hear the voice of his dead wife. Most people thought he was crazy, but he believed it was magic," she said. "It's all about perspective."

"And faith that love will heal you," Randall blurted out. His stomach twisted into a knot as he waited for Abigail's reply, but when she hurried off the phone with a quick goodbye, he had to get off his bike and walk it because his legs had become very wobbly.

Instead of going home, Randall went toward the park and circled a couple of big trees until he reached the dog run. He leaned his bike against a bench and sat down across from the fenced-in area. A golden retriever and a Labrador tore a ball apart with their teeth. A couple of white puffballs barked and chased each other.

Randall's mind drifted from this scene to the words he'd just said to Abigail: "And faith that love will heal you." It was the closest he'd ever come to telling her how he felt about her, and even though he felt sick with worry, he was also relieved—happy, even. He'd taken another step, and regardless of how Abigail reacted, he felt as though the only thing he had to fear was inaction.

Whether it was the result of magic or just a simple change in perspective, as Abigail had suggested, Randall could see that doing nothing was the equivalent of throwing your future away. He thought of his dad sitting at home, heating up a frozen pepperoni pizza for dinner and spending hours in front of the TV. Soon that pulling sensation was back again, yanking Randall off the park bench and onto his bike. He rode home to his father. Mr. Gold was already asleep on the couch, oblivious to what his life would be like if he met a special Frenchwoman and drank a cup of her coffee.

As for Randall, he was wide awake all night.

20

On Wednesday morning, Kate lay in bed for a long time, thinking about the way Jesse had completely blown her off for Caroline on the evening of the concert. She could still hear the nonchalant message he'd left. "Sorry, Kate. It slipped my mind." How insulting! It was no wonder she barely believed him about the fire at the One Trick. There'd probably been too many crumbs in the toaster and a tiny flame had poked up. The bottom line was that Jesse would always pick Caroline over her. While he'd been with other girls, Kate knew that his relationship with Caroline was something much more serious, and she couldn't seem to handle it.

Kate remembered the curt message she had left on his cell phone. She was so mortified that she pulled the covers right over her head.

"Oh, well, I suppose this is just another example of how

Caroline is such a fabulous influence on you." Kate recalled how cold her tone had been. "But no worries, Jesse. It's not a big deal. I went to the concert with Thomas Jensen—you know, that great-looking guy I dated over the summer? Anyway, we had an excellent time that night, and through the morning, too, actually. Much better than I would have had with you, I'm sure."

Kate tried to remind herself that she'd said these things because she was hurt, and that when she'd apologized to Jesse for it, he'd said he'd already deleted the message and forgotten about it. But the truth was that she hadn't gone to the concert at all. She had stayed home with Selma and baked an apple pie, wondering why the people in her life were acting so strangely toward her.

While Kate took a shower, she tried to focus on more positive things, like how hard she'd been working on the open-mike night preparations. On Tuesday, she had sat up all night long, trying to put together a proposal that would blow everyone away. The only disappointing thing was that Abigail's ideas had gotten thrown overboard in the process. From Kate's perspective, concerts and shows were all about grand spectacles and creating a setting where the players could be larger than life. If the artists themselves couldn't understand this, then they either shouldn't be there or needed to suck it up.

As she lathered expensive shampoo onto her head, Kate ran through all her plans. She would order the red carpet from the stage supply store in TriBeCa and get a bunch of potted palms from the store in the Flower District her mother used. The lacquer furniture could come from the rental company that Ellen Saneman had used for that last event at Armani, and the Polynesian cocktail accoutrements she could pick up in Chinatown. Yes, Abigail would see, when it was all put together, that Kate was doing the right thing.

In fact, the more Kate thought about it, the more she realized that this huge, dramatic push might shake some sense into Abigail. If her friend continued on the road she was currently taking, she'd soon be living with Nick and telling all her opportunities goodbye. But if Kate got her way, and she almost always did, she would be the one who got everyone back to normal—especially Abigail.

After school, Kate sat at the One Trick Pony in her cozy snow-white sweater with the huge turtleneck, black skinny jeans, and flats, waiting for Abigail to come and see the promotional pieces she'd had made. Instead of making lame plastic lapel buttons, she'd had rhinestone rings made up. The gold-toned, generous cocktail ring shape had the One Trick's candle symbol across the front and "OPEN-MIKE NIGHT, OCTOBER 2007" inscribed beneath it in elegant cursive. Kate had definitely outdone herself. And by agreeing to hand out "look books" of the jeweler's work, and allowing the designer to hold a minishop on the night of the event, she'd gotten it done at no charge. Surely Abigail would change her opinion when she heard all that.

When Jesse arrived for his shift, he gave Kate a half-hearted "Hey" and hurried behind the counter without even meeting her eye. He made a beeline for Caroline, and within minutes, she had Jesse doing things for her. It made Kate sick to see how quick Jesse was to please Caroline, who definitely seemed to enjoy all the attention. Kate really hated how much this bothered her, and no matter how hard she tried to turn these feelings off, they only grew stronger.

Just relax and have your tea, she told herself as she blew into her mug before tipping it up to her mouth for a sip. Thankfully, Abigail came shuffling through the door holding a huge navy binder with rainbow-colored tabs sticking out the side. Now Kate had something to distract her from Jesse.

"Hey, girl," Kate said as Abigail approached.

"Hey." Abigail placed the binder on the table and shrugged her denim jacket from her shoulders. Like clockwork, Caroline drifted by their table and placed a cup of coffee in front of Abigail, who took a big gulp before getting down to business.

As soon as Caroline sauntered away, Kate immediately shoved her hand very close to Abigail's face so she could show off the ring. Abigail stared at the rhinestones and the engraving; then her mouth went slack.

It was then that Kate noticed a button on Abigail's collar that read, I PERFORMED AT THE ONE TRICK AND LIVED TO TELL. The black letters looked hand-painted, with a drippy effect.

"Your button is cool," Kate said, bringing her hand back and taking the ring off her finger. "Maybe we can use it for a future event." She didn't realize how snotty that sounded until Abigail crossed her arms over her chest angrily. Kate tried to reason with her. "Sorry, Abigail, I've already had these rings made up—two hundred of them, to be exact—and the designer has donated them, and—"

Abigail cut her off. "So do you think Randall is going to wear that ring?"

Kate blinked rapidly. *"Randall* is performing at open-mike night?" This was preposterous. Sure, Kate wanted him to get off his ass and do something, but she'd never ever thought he actually would.

"Yeah, he is. And I think he'd rather wear a button, like *most guys* would," Abigail said, her voice suddenly husky. "Didn't you even think that our promo stuff should be gender neutral?"

Kate hadn't even thought of that. And it was a damn good point. But instead of telling Abigail she was right, she kept her mouth shut and her gaze lowered to her tea.

Abigail huffed and pushed her chair out. "Why don't you just do whatever you want, okay, Kate? Since you always know best." Then she threw her jacket on again and stormed out of the café.

Kate bowed her head and covered her face with her hands. The last thing she wanted to do was upset Abigail. On the contrary, she wanted to convince her that bigger was the better way to go. Usually, Abigail saw the light and took Kate's advice. But ever since they'd started coming to the One Trick again, it was as if they were all becoming strangers to each other. At least, that was how it looked from the seat Kate was sitting in. However, there was a hint of realization penetrating Kate's thoughts—this open-mike night meant so much more to Abigail, and she had practically taken that away from her. Same thing with Jesse— Caroline had become the be-all-end-all person in his life, and Kate was trying to interfere with that, too, with her concert tickets and impromptu stops at the One Trick.

What the hell is wrong with me? Kate asked herself.

She wasn't ready to answer such a frightening question. Instead, she took her hands away from her face and noticed that Abigail had left her binder behind. Kate spun the book around, turned back the cover, and began to sort through her friend's plans. After she'd read every page, Kate felt even worse than she had earlier. As Kate had suspected, Abigail had obviously put tons of work and energy into this project, which seemed more important to her than anything else had since her mother died. But Kate had been too selfish to let Abigail have this wonderful thing of her own.

When Kate left the One Trick Pony, she didn't feel like going home, especially because she'd just witnessed Jesse and Caroline having some sort of laughing fit that had all the customers chuckling, too. She'd missed whatever it was that was so funny, and honestly, she didn't want to know. Besides, even if Kate was in on the joke, she'd still be on the outside of Jesse and Caroline's cozy little duo.

Once Kate was outside, she noticed that all sounds seemed to be set at a higher volume. There was none of the calm of the One Trick, which seemed ironic to Kate, since everything had gone so haywire in there, and out here she could actually breathe again. She walked to the park and took a seat in front of the dog run. She had always wanted a little dog she could tote around in her favorite Pucci bag, but her mother couldn't have animals in the house.

"They are cute," her mother had said to Kate when she was little, "but they make tiny little scratches in the wood floors." She'd bent down on her hands and knees to show Kate that the floor had polyurethane on top of it, but that could only protect it so much. Little Kate had thought it was normal to consider such things, but now, as she looked at these furry creatures dashing around happy and excited, she wondered whether her mom ever stopped to think about how important being right and successful was if you didn't have anything or anyone special to make you smile.

"Hey, Kate," she heard someone shout from behind her. She looked over her shoulder and saw Randall approaching on his bike. He pulled an ear bud from his right ear and nodded his chin in her direction.

Kate was very glad to see him. She couldn't remember needing to speak with a friend so badly.

"Where are you off to?" she asked.

"I was just heading home to play for a while." He leaned his bike slightly to the side and set one foot on the ground. He was looking a lot more confident these days. A little cocky, almost. It worked for him, actually. His dark hair was dipping into his eyes, which made him look kind of like a rock star.

She patted the space next to her. "Do you have a little while to hang out? I feel like complaining."

"Well, how could I resist an offer like that?" Randall smiled, lifted his leg over the bike, and walked it over to the bench. He pulled the strap of his messenger bag from across his chest and let it rest on his lap when he sat down. "So, what's up? Do you still hate everyone?"

She giggled as she recrossed her legs and pulled her coat in tighter for warmth. "Well, I wanted to see if you thought there might be something wrong with Abby. I mean, she seems to be withdrawing from me."

Randall rubbed his bare hands together. "To tell you the truth, the last few evenings we spent together, I'd say she's really been coming along. I would almost say that she's finally finding a way to move on and figure out who she is without her mother."

Kate shook her head. "That's not how it feels when we're together."

"How does it feel?" Randall asked with genuine concern.

"I don't know . . . awkward, I guess. Like she's challenging me all the time." Kate tried to stop her teeth from chattering, but it was no use.

A flurry of leaves fell from the branch above them all at once, scattering at their feet. Randall picked one out of Kate's hair and began to tear it apart. "I hate to break it to you, Kate, but you can be a little . . . bossy," he said, shrinking back and covering his face as if she might smack him.

Kate laughed. "Come on, Randall, I only want what's best for everyone. Including you."

"But maybe what's best for Abigail right now is to test people and see what they're made of, especially herself," Randall said as he put his arm around Kate and gave her a good squeeze.

Kate sent Randall a crooked look. "You're in a weird mood. Are you on drugs or something?"

Randall chuckled. "Let's just say I think Abigail and I are finally making some headway."

Kate sat up as straight as a board. "You mean you guys kissed?"

"Well, let's not get crazy here . . . this is me we're talking about."

Kate rolled her eyes.

"You know what I've been learning lately, though?" Randall asked.

Kate leaned her head on his shoulder. "What's that?"

"You're not altogether wrong, Kate. There does come

a time when you've got to make a move before it's too late, when you've got to say, 'Well, maybe it's not going to be perfect, but I'm gonna give it a shot anyway.'"

"Wow, you really are on drugs," Kate said, pinching him on the arm.

As they both laughed, a couple walked by, holding hands.

"Why can't I have that?" Kate blurted out. She couldn't believe how candid she was being with Randall, but at the same time, it felt really good to lean on him.

"Are we talking about anyone in particular?" Randall asked.

Kate bit her lip. "There's no one, I'm sad to say."

"So there's no truth to that rumor that you're getting a little jealous of a certain someone falling in love with a certain Frenchwoman?"

Kate was all ready to deny the accusation nonchalantly, as if she couldn't care less. But then she heard it. That word. "He's in *love* with her? Jesse?"

"Awww, you really do care, don't you?" Randall teased.

"Shut up," Kate said as she poked him in the stomach. "I just didn't think Jesse *could* fall in love, that's all."

"You could, too, you know," Randall said. "You just need to let your imperial guard down."

"Whatever," Kate snorted. "So *really,* Jesse's in love with Caroline?"

Randall chuckled again and went on to tell Kate some pathetic story about how Jesse was basically stalking Caroline, delving into her past, snooping through her things. The Jesse that Kate used to know was way too proud to do anything like that. Add this odd occurrence to

Randall's being confident and Abigail's being willful, and Kate's whole world had come undone.

And for some reason, Kate felt deep in her bones that there was only one person to blame for it. A woman she had to protect her friends from at all costs.

Especially Jesse Majors.

21

"Jesse, I know Cindy's been off for a week, but we didn't expect the house to be such a mess," his mother said with a tight frown. She was drinking a mimosa when he emerged from his room on Saturday morning and found her on one of the bar stools at the black granite kitchen counter.

But Jesse was too exhausted from tossing and turning all night to respond. Last night at the One Trick, Caroline had come so close to opening up to him when again she'd stopped herself at the last minute. Jesse had wanted to admit to her that he knew about the "love spell" scandal, but he'd known that wouldn't be the right way to approach it. She had to feel comfortable enough to come to him. But would that ever happen?

"We had to call Cindy to cut her vacation short *and* come in on a weekend," his mother added.

Sometimes Jesse didn't know how his mother found

the nerve. They'd only been home for a few hours and she was already on his back.

"Nice to see you, too, Mom," he mumbled.

"Your father went to that café you work at and brought us back some coffee." She nodded at a white paper cup with a domed plastic lid. A napkin was taped to the side with his name written on it in Caroline's handwriting. He could only imagine what she'd thought of his father. It was somehow strange to think he'd spoken with her.

"Why didn't you tell us you saved the owner's life when we had our last family conference call?" his mother said in an almost perturbed voice. "Your father was very embarrassed that he didn't know what she was talking about."

"Oh, give it a rest, Grace," his father said as he walked out of their bedroom in a pair of light-blue jeans and a black button-down shirt. "Your new boss is a real looker, huh?" He raised his eyebrows twice, which drew attention to the deep lines that had settled into his forehead.

"Robert," his mother admonished him.

"Sorry, couldn't help noticing. I drank my cup on the way home too. She's got a gold mine there, believe me." As his dad rattled around in the kitchen, Jesse noticed how much older he looked. His dark hair had more gray flecks in it than Jesse remembered. But he was still tall and carried himself with the esteem of a top executive. He hugged Jesse. "Missed you, son. I did."

Jesse knew that was true, but it was also true that his parents had choices, and that they didn't have to leave him alone nearly as much as they did. How many piles of money did a human being actually need?

On the countertop, once again pristine, was a box wrapped in red, yellow, and blue plaid paper, with a wide gold bow. Jesse recognized the look of a five-star hotel gift shop wrapping. This time they hadn't even mustered the effort to leave their hotel to buy him something. He knew he shouldn't expect anything more, and it was the expecting that could really hurt him if he let it. Usually it didn't, but this morning, everything seemed much more difficult.

"Go ahead, open it," his mother said, whipping her head to the side and sending her bleached-blond hair flying.

Jesse picked up the box and opened it. Inside was a gray sweater with a slight V-neck. He pulled it up by both shoulders and let it fall open. "Very nice" was all he was able to say.

"It's one-hundred-percent cashmere," his mom said as she reached over and ran her hand over the fabric.

"Thanks," Jesse said flatly, "it means a lot." He tossed the sweater back into the box. "So how long you guys home for?"

"Actually, Jesse," his mother said, smoothing out her black dress pants, "we've only got a couple of days before we have to head back. But we really wanted to see you for the weekend. We feel like we've missed the entire beginning of your school year. We want you to fill us in on everything we missed. Get us up to speed."

Jesse choked back a sudden burst of anger. How dare she assume they could make up for lost time in just two days? *Calm down,* he told himself. *You'll be fine. You always are.* "I can't, Mom. I've got plans with Abigail and Randall tomorrow night."

"Here, Caroline said she made this coffee just for you," his dad said, passing the cup with the napkin taped on. Jesse looked at the way she'd written his name with the black marker—the one she kept tied to the register with bakery

202

string. He pictured how she grasped the marker with her delicate hands and it made him smile, if only for a second.

Jesse took a sip and let the drink energize him. He peeled the napkin gently from the cup. Then he unfolded it and found that she'd written something on the inside: "'Tisn't life that matters! 'Tis the courage you bring to it.—Sir Hugh Walpole."

All of a sudden the pull around his heart moved up to his throat. He couldn't just sit by and watch this situation continue. He needed to tell his parents how he felt, and in his head, the words that had seemed so impossible to find in the past lined up in the perfect order.

"Dad?"

"Yeah, Jess?" His father moved to the chair next to Jesse's after he handed Jesse's mom a mug filled with coffee. Jesse was still in his pajama pants and a One Trick T-shirt from the Jimmy the Dude days. His father leaned back, and even that rubbed Jesse the wrong way—even when they sat next to each other, he and his parents were still too far apart.

"Why don't we go to the summer house this weekend? I can cancel my plans."

His dad sighed and looked at Jesse's mother over on the stool, gulping down Caroline's unique brew. "I wish we could, Jesse, but the truth is we don't have enough time. We had to agree to a phone conference tomorrow morning in order to get today off. And we have a dinner meeting in the city." He spoke clearly and slowly as if it all made perfect sense.

"Mom, can you come and sit over here?" Jesse asked calmly.

"Okaaaaay," she said, almost seeming to mock him.

But Jesse didn't let that stop him. He was going to take a deep breath and let it all out. "I don't know why I never say anything, but it makes me incredibly angry that you're never home. Please, *please* find somebody else to finish this project. I just don't want to grow up and leave for college and realize that I have nothing to come back to."

They were both silent, staring at him and then at each other.

"Is this how you really feel?" his mother said, as she swished the last few drops of coffee around in her mug.

"It is, and I know I should have said something a long time ago."

Jesse and his mom looked at his father, who was fiddling with his wedding ring. "Well, in your defense, we haven't been around to listen," his dad said.

"I feel so terrible, honey," his mother put in. "We had no idea this was bothering you so much."

"We hope you know that we do love you, more than anything," his father added while putting his hand on Jesse's shoulder. "I'll try to reshuffle our plans, okay?"

Jesse let out a great sigh of relief. He'd gotten his feelings out in the open, and his parents seemed to be listening. He hadn't expected them to be so agreeable and nice. Immediately he began thinking about Caroline. Maybe if he confessed to her how he truly felt, she'd respond in kind. Sure, there was risk involved, but look at how calmly and understandingly his parents had reacted when he'd come to them with his heart in his hands. He had to cling to that hope. He just had to.

"Guys, I'm sorry to have to do this now, but I've got to leave for a little while," he said as he leaped up.

But his parents didn't say a word. They just grinned as if they were looking at their son for the very first time.

Twenty minutes later, Jesse hopped on his bike and listened to Randall's demo on his MP3 player. After the first song, Jesse had a hard time catching his breath. Randall's voice was amazing, and all the lead guitar parts were damn near perfect. He couldn't believe that Randall had faced his fears and done something this incredible. Jesse wanted Randall's achievment to inspire greatness in him, too, but when he reached the One Trick, he circled the block twice, unsure of what he'd do or say once he was inches away from Caroline and her luminous smile.

Finally, Jesse rode through the alley around to the back. He leaned his bike against the fence and locked it. Soon he was rounding the front of the café and there was no more time for hesitation. The new gypsy bells Caroline put up a day after the fire tinkled as he pushed the door open, but he doubted anyone would hear them—as usual, the crowd was big and loud. His heart was pounding so hard that he could feel it in his temples. When he scanned the room, he saw Caroline sitting with Abigail. Caroline looked like a porcelain doll today, delicate and as smooth as alabaster. She wore a pair of plaid pants that flared at the bottom and a tight turtleneck sweater, tucked in.

Caroline turned and faced him when Abigail waved hello. Jesse nearly clutched at his heart after Caroline said his name. He couldn't talk to her when he was feeling this . . . uncontrollable. God knew what he'd do. He decided he had to wait until after the café closed for the day, when his mind would be quieter and they'd be alone.

Thankfully, Abigail was there to distract him as she drank her cup of coffee. For hours, she went on about the apartment and Nick, complaining about all the things that were wrong with it—the warped wood planks on the floor, the view of the brick wall outside their bedroom window. Jesse couldn't help feeling strongly connected to Abigail right now. She was struggling with her emotions, trying to make sense of her life in a way she hadn't been able to do in the past.

"So when are you moving?" Caroline asked as Jesse rang up a customer who wanted a latte to go.

Abigail fidgeted a little with her hair, brushing a few stray strands from her eyes. "I'm not sure when exactly," she said. "I have to iron out some details first."

A crooked grin appeared on Caroline's face. "How come you've never brought Nick in here?"

"I don't know." Abigail bowed her head and breathed in the steam floating up from her mug.

"Randall was in earlier," Caroline said, stacking a couple of dirty cups from the counter in the sink just below.

Abigail's head snapped back up, her eyes wide. "Did he give you a copy of the CD?"

Jesse almost gave the customer the wrong change—Caroline's smile was that enchanting.

"Your voices bring out the best in each other," Caroline said, leaning over the counter and rubbing Abigail's arm. "I wouldn't be surprised if you two were meant for more than what you already are."

Abigail blushed so deeply her skin looked as though she

had a rash. Then she made up some excuse to leave and bolted out the door.

The next few hours were the longest of Jesse's life. He couldn't take his eyes off Caroline, and when she locked the front door at eleven that night, he was still watching her every move. She drew the curtains closed and put a few chairs upside down over the tables as Jesse swept and mopped the floor. At the end of their ritual, they sat down at the bar with two coffees steaming in front of them.

"Long night," Jesse said, biting his lower lip so he wouldn't say too much too soon.

"Very," Caroline agreed, kicking one of her shoes off and rubbing her other calf with her stockinged foot.

This last subtle movement of hers was enough to send Jesse over the edge. He took her hand. She seemed surprised, especially when he got down off his chair and onto his knees, right in front of her.

Take a chance! Jesse had said that to Randall how many times? And now it seemed his own life depended on it. He looked at Caroline, studying all the beautiful details of her face—her magnificent eyes, her darling nose, her succulent lips. "Caroline," he said, trembling.

"Yes, Jesse?"

He moved closer, his finger reaching up to tuck a lock of hair behind her ear, the thing he'd been wanting to do for forty-five minutes, ever since it had sprung loose from her ponytail. She looked at him, not recoiling, but thoughtfully, though he wasn't sure what about. He didn't wait to find out. Instead, he took her by surprise and kissed her with all the feeling in his heart. Caroline tasted so much better than he'd ever imagined—like decadent white chocolate—and her lips were as soft as a flower petal. Jesse didn't want to stop, but before he could move his hands to her waist and then up the front of her turtleneck, she broke away from him.

"Jesse!" she shouted as she sprang up from her seat. She put her open palm where his lips had been.

"I love you."

The words escaped so easily from Jesse's mouth. Although there was much more he wanted to say, he stood up and waited for her to respond, hopefully as well as his parents had earlier that day.

Caroline closed her eyes and smiled, as if she were imagining the two of them together, but when she reopened them, she appeared stunned and aghast. A shock of fear pinched Jesse's chest. What if he'd just ruined everything?

Caroline reached out and held him gently by his hand. She ran her thumb over all his fingers, feeling the class ring his parents had bought for him at the end of the past school year—the biggest, most expensive one in the catalog. "Jesse, my sweet boy—"

He cut her off because he was too afraid of what would come next. "I am *not* a boy."

Caroline let go of his hand and took a few steps away from him. "I really am sorry, Jesse. I know the pain of falling for the wrong person."

"But you are not the wrong person," Jesse said urgently. "You've shown me how to really live."

Caroline tried to say something, but her eyes welled up with tears and she turned her back to him.

Jesse closed in on her and ran his hand down her arm. "Caroline, if you tell me you have no feelings for me, I promise I will leave you alone."

Caroline moved away from Jesse and then spun to face him again. "I care for you greatly, Jesse, and in many ways I believe we were meant to meet, but my heart belongs to someone else." She looked so sad then, as if she'd just found out that someone she loved had died. "And if he were here right now, he would tell you that I only end up hurting the people I love."

Jesse's stomach twisted into a knot. "Like the man in the photograph?" He hated the way his voice sounded, so weak and jealous.

"Yes," she said, breaking into a subdued sob. "But no matter how much I love him, he and I will never be together."

Jesse knew that if he didn't help her to see that she had a second chance at love, he would become intimately acquainted with the same situation.

"You should go," Caroline said, choking back more tears.

"Wait, you haven't heard me out," Jesse pleaded. "And you haven't even told me what happened between you and—"

"No." Caroline shook her head and marched over to the door. She unlocked it and yanked it open, then covered her face with her free hand. "Just leave."

Jesse walked out of the One Trick Pony without saying anything else, and as he pedaled ferociously through the streets of Brooklyn, he cursed the day he had ever set eyes on Caroline and drunk her stupid coffee.

22

On Sunday morning, Abigail was woken up by a soft knock at the door. She rubbed her eyes and craned her neck so she could see the glowing numbers on her alarm clock, which read 8 a.m.

"Come in," she said, her voice raw and raspy. She sat up, reached over to her nightstand for an old paper coffee cup from the One Trick, and drank the cold contents. Even then, Caroline's brew tasted so good.

The door opened and her father poked his head in. They hadn't exactly been on speaking terms as of late, so his appearance came as a surprise to Abigail.

"Can we talk?" he asked simply.

Abigail pulled her covers tightly around her, as if her blanket could protect her from the argument she was about to have. "Okay."

Her father sat down on the corner of the bed and

pulled on the belt of his navy blue terry-cloth bathrobe, which her mom had given him three years ago for his birthday. Abigail loved the way it brought out the green flecks in his eyes. "I know the last family dinner didn't go very well," he began.

"That's an understatement," she said, rolling her eyes.

"I was just hoping you could try a little harder and be more welcoming to Ginny." He paused to take a breath. "And to me."

Abigail was stunned. *This* is what he'd wanted to talk about?

"Wait, you want *me* to change my behavior? After everything *you've* done?"

Her father's posture became rigid. "All I know, Abigail, is that your temper tantrums are growing tiresome. And you think you're entitled to make the decisions around here, *and* move in with your boyfriend. But I'm your father, and *I'm* going to decide what is best for you."

Abigail crossed her arms over her chest and fumed. How dare her father refer to her outbursts as temper tantrums? For the first time in her life, she was being vocal about her wants and needs; sure, it was coming out rather pointed and charged in certain situations, but she didn't have a choice in the matter. Abigail was angry as hell—about her mom dying, about her dad shacking up with Ginny, about *everything*—and her father would just have to deal.

"We'll see about that," she barked.

Her dad got up and shoved his hands into the pockets of his robe. "What do you mean?"

"I mean Nick and I already picked out a place together." Abigail winced when she said this, but she pushed on. "Once I'm there, you won't be able to flaunt Ginny in front of my face anymore."

"Abigail, I really don't know what to do with you anymore." Her dad's gaze was fixed on a picture on her dresser, the one from her eighth-grade graduation, when everything was relatively normal. Not too long after that, it had begun to fall apart. "I don't remember you acting like this when your mother was here."

"I didn't have to—she understood me. You never will," Abigail muttered, her lips quivering. She had thought she'd feel better if her father protested about her moving in with Nick, that it would be a sign that he truly cared about her, but it didn't have that effect at all.

When her father silently left the room and closed the door behind him, Abigail fell back into her pillows and pulled the blankets over herself until she was finished crying.

In the early afternoon, Abigail called Randall as she braved the harsh winds while walking to the subway. After everything that had happened with her father, Randall was still the only person she really wanted to talk to, though she pretended she was calling for no reason at all.

"Randall, I found some more everyday magic for you," she said instead of "Hello."

"Whaddya got?" he replied as strums from his guitar echoed in the background.

Abigail's purple scarf came undone and she twirled it back around her neck. In twenty minutes, she'd be helping Nick pack up his dorm room and cart his stuff over to the apartment, with no intention of mentioning that she was having second thoughts about moving in. Yet considering the way she'd spoken to her father a couple of hours ago, maybe it was something she had to do out of principle. By any count, there was still a possibility that next week they would be living together, and right now all she could think about was how it would affect her relationship with Randall. When had that become a factor in her decision?

Abigail pulled a scrap of paper from her pocket and cleared her throat before reading. " 'This Is Just to Say': I have eaten / the plums / that were in / the icebox / and which / you were probably / saving / for breakfast / Forgive me / they were delicious / so sweet / and so cold."

"It's beautiful. Is that one of yours?" Randall asked.

"Of course not! It's William Carlos Williams."

Randall laughed. "Well, you're right. It is everyday magic, pure and simple." A few more notes from the guitar rang out. "Is there something else you wanted to talk about? It sounds like you have a lot on your mind."

God, he knows me so well, Abigail thought. Soon she was telling him everything that had happened with her father and how harshly she'd treated him. It was so easy to do, especially because Randall never interrupted. He just listened to each word she said, and even though they were on the phone, Abigail could feel his presence so strongly that she had to stop on a street corner and catch her breath.

Finally Randall spoke up. "He's your father, Abigail. He knows you're going through a tough time."

Her eyes began to water. "It's just . . . he's not my mom, you know?"

"Well, he's never going to be, Abby. But, hey, don't think you're alone. You've always got me. . . ."

It was funny; when Nick said things like that, Abigail felt even lonelier, but when Randall said it, she felt almost as good as when her mom tucked her in at night and read her Shel Silverstein poems by the glow of her night-light.

"Why does everything have to be so hard, Ran?"

"Just think how boring it would be if everything was simple. We'd be just as hollow as your boyfriend."

Abigail rolled her eyes as she always did when Randall slammed Nick, but now she was beginning to recognize the truth in it, too. What did she and Nick have in common? They never had conversations like this, that was for sure. Their relationship's pattern was more like: (1) Abigail explains the general outline of her problems; (2) Nick provides advice that Abigail would never follow, but holds her and kisses her, which feels comforting in a way; (3) Abigail says, "Thank you, that's such good advice," though this couldn't be further from the truth; and (4) Nick walks away knowing absolutely nothing about Abigail's true feelings.

"Is simple really so bad?" Abigail said against the wind, which was picking up.

"Not if you're ready to throw in the towel at age sixteen. In that case, it's fine. But that's not you, now is it, Abigail? People like you and me require a little nudging; I'll give you that. But in the end we know we can't fight who we are."

"Thanks, Randall." Abigail sighed as she arrived at the subway entrance. The colored circles that denoted the trains resembled warning signs, and she didn't want to go to meet Nick. "Listen, I'm on my way into the city—"

"Okay," Randall interjected curtly. "Talk to you later, then."

A few minutes later, the sliding doors on the train closed, and Abigail held on to the pole as tightly as she could. At the moment, nothing else could prevent her from falling.

When Abigail arrived at Nick's dorm suite, she was surprised to see his place practically bare and boxes in every corner. *This is really happening,* she thought as she wove her way through the cardboard box maze and found Nick in the kitchen, where he was emptying the refrigerator.

"Wow, you got a lot done," Abigail said as she took off her coat.

Nick looked over his shoulder and smiled. Then he threw an old head of lettuce in the trash bin without hitting the rim. "Yeah, well, I'm excited to move in with you."

"Me too." The second she said it, Abigail knew she was lying, but at the same time, she couldn't get up the courage to say what was in her heart: that this didn't feel right to her at all.

The next five hours were a whirlwind. Abigail and Nick wheeled his belongings from the dorm to the apartment in the gray carts they'd borrowed from the dormitory front desk. Three of his friends helped, all the while predicting the fun they'd have at Nick's without having to worry about resident advisers who'd get them in trouble for having alcohol in their rooms. "We can get a kegerator!" one of them shouted. Abigail hadn't felt so out of her element since dinner with Ginny.

After the three had left, Nick inflated the air mattress in their new living room and gently pulled Abigail down onto it. As she lay on top of him and felt his hands moving all over her body, she didn't feel even a suspicion of the rush she used to feel when they fooled around. It wasn't long before she rolled off Nick and turned her head to the side so she wasn't looking at him. What surprised her the most was that Nick didn't even ask her what was wrong. He just lay there silently, as if he were waiting for her to get back in the mood. But she couldn't, because she was thinking of Randall and what it would be like to lie next to him like this.

"Do you believe in magic?" she blurted out.

Nick took her hand and kissed her sweetly on her pinky finger. "I do if you do."

Abigail's heart plummeted. From what he'd just said, it was so incredibly clear that no matter how much she played house with Nick, she would always be pretending with him.

She sat up and straightened her sweater, which Nick had tangled up. "I think I need to go home."

"But you are home, sweetie," Nick said, rubbing a hand up and down her back.

"Well, I don't have any of my stuff with me, and tomorrow is open-mike night." Abigail grabbed her jacket, which was lying on the floor, and sprang up quickly to shove her arms into the thick sleeves.

"All right, then. I'll come help you pack," Nick said, bounding up from the air mattress and stretching his arms toward the ceiling. "Then I can bring some of your stuff back here and you can stay over tomorrow."

But when Abigail walked out the door with Nick trailing behind her, she wished that tomorrow would never come.

23

At about seven on Sunday evening, Randall called it quits at the studio. When he pressed the intercom button and said, "I think that's a wrap, Cheeto," the blond, chunky guy who always wore retro concert T-shirts and operated the sound board replied, "Dude, did you ever see that movie *Ring of Fire?*"

Randall pressed the button and answered, "Yeah?" Where was Cheeto going with this?

"Remember the scene where Cash goes to the studio and blows the producer dude away? That is exactly what you reminded me of tonight," Cheeto said. "Just promise me you won't forget the little people," he added with a wink.

Usually, when Randall was paid a compliment, he would tell the person praising him to shut the hell up. But not tonight. For some reason, saying "Thanks" came so naturally. Maybe that was because he had an inkling Cheeto might be right, that this was a big turning point for him.

Randall packed his bag and zipped his guitars back into their cases—the old acoustic and the Fender Stratocaster his father had bought for him three Chanukahs ago. On the walk home in the mild weather, with a soft breeze whistling through the half-bare trees, he thought of that Chanukah. It was their last one as a family. Randall had been thirteen years old, a freshman in high school.

He'd been in awe of his father then. The Web company he'd built was in the newspaper every other day. They'd moved from their tiny apartment above the Italian bakery to this amazing home in the up-and-coming neighborhood of Cobble Hill. And it wasn't the money or the fame that had inspired Randall—it was the hard work his father had put in to get there. His father's energy had captivated everyone. Just being in the same room with him, Randall used to feel that anything was possible. And Randall had seen that spirit in himself recently, too—finishing this record, finally taking steps with Abigail. But he couldn't help worrying that if his father could lose that will, that confidence, after all he'd achieved, couldn't Randall lose it, too?

Of course, things could change at any time, and it would be the simplest thing in the world to give in to the self-doubt and blame. Randall knew that. But he'd learned, the hard way, that you had to persevere despite the doubts and question marks, that the most important thing was to remember who you were, to be confident about that, and eventually the good times and good vibes would return.

There was his house, looking so much like the others on the block of row houses that dominated this part of

Brooklyn. But Randall knew that inside, the inhabitants were all different—everyone had problems, and now that they were getting older, they had to find ways to deal with them, or they'd get left behind. You could see the reminders of people like that all over Brooklyn, too—there were six homeless people Randall knew on a first-name basis in this neighborhood. And no two of them were there for the same reason. The trick was to learn from these things, not to let them scare you stiff so that you couldn't move forward.

Now he passed Jonesy, the homeless guy known for his vintage ShopRite cart and his bottle of Jim Beam. Jonesy was on a bench at a bus stop, though he'd never get on and go anywhere. "Hey, Jonesy," Randall said, putting a five in his palm. "Why don't you switch things up and go somewhere new?"

Jonesy looked at him blank-faced, as he always had, but Randall didn't regret his effort. He felt filled with energy tonight, and he wanted to spread it around. He crossed the street and skipped up the six steps to his home.

He could hear the television from the entryway. He hung his coat on the rack, which was piled high with so many jackets, sweaters, and coats that it looked as if it might topple over at any moment. He carried his guitars in either hand and made his way to the sofa, where his father was in his usual position.

Randall set the cases down and sat next to his father, who was mesmerized by a Giants versus Jets football game. "How's it going?"

"Okay," his father said, not taking his eyes off the screen. "You just finished at the studio?"

"Yup."

"Well, hey, throw it on the stereo. Let's see what you got." His father picked up the remote and turned the television off.

Randall walked over to the stereo rack—it was a beautiful system, all chrome, with neon lights that crackled along with the sound waves. His parents used to play so much music that the flickering light of it had nearly blinded all of them. Lord knows they had tons of CDs and old records to choose from. They lined the room here, the way Abigail's house was filled with books. But his father hadn't listened to music in so long.

As Randall slipped the disk onto the tray and pressed the button to slide it closed, he thought about the power of music and hoped this might make an impression on his father now. For an hour they sat, listening to each song. Here and there, Randall explained the inspiration for a song. When it was over his father shook his head and brushed a couple of tears from his eyes.

"Whoa, Randall." He swallowed hard. "I . . . I know I haven't been much of a father since your mom left. And I want to apologize for that, son. But I also want to tell you how proud I am of you. The fact that you've managed to come into your own and achieve all this. It—well, it blows me away."

"That means a lot to me, Dad." Randall hugged his father tight.

"Thank you for sticking by me through this. I hate to think of all the time I've wasted, lying around like this."

"I know it's hard to get started sometimes."

"Yeah, I suppose," his dad muttered.

Suddenly Randall's eyes lit up. "Hey, can I see your wallet for a sec?"

His father shot him a confused look. "Do you need some money?"

"Nah, nothing like that. I just need to see it for a second."

His dad reached into a basket on the bottom tier of the coffee table, pulled the wallet out, and handed it over. Randall went straight for the billfold, took everything out—the cash and a wad of papers and cards—and started to flip through them. Soon he found what he was looking for: Carol Simmons's business card. She was the woman his dad had met and never called.

"One day, Dad, you'll thank me for this." Randall picked up the phone and dialed the number. On the third ring, her voice mail message played, and when it was over, Randall waited for the beep and said, "Carol, this is Jeff Gold. We met in the park a while ago. I've been away on business, but I'm back and I would love to take you out to dinner. How's Tuesday? Give me a ring when you get this."

When he'd hung up the phone, Randall recognized the shocked expression on his father's face. It was like looking in a mirror. But for once, Randall was pretty content with what he saw there.

After the talk with his dad, Randall showered, pulled on some new jeans and a gray sweater with blue stripes, sprayed on some cologne, grabbed his coat, and headed for Abigail's. He couldn't wait to play the finished demo for her. Every time he heard her voice on that backup part, his whole body went completely numb. This could be the night for them. Randall could feel it in his bones.

After stopping by the One Trick for a quick cup of coffee and a pep talk from Jesse, Randall walked the streets of Cobble Hill with the intention of performing a long-overdue task: telling Abigail how he felt about her. On the way, he passed by a bodega, where a bunch of huge yellow flowers in a tall white bucket below a sign that said "Poms" caught his eye. He bought two dozen and had them wrapped up in pink paper, which he knew Abigail would love.

As his feet pounded the sidewalk, Randall grew more and more confident, thinking how he'd kiss Abigail when she opened the door and that would change their destiny. When he was less than a few blocks away, he was nearly running, his resolve so strong that nothing could stop him. When he saw her front door, the memories began to flood back to him: the way she'd recited that poem, the way she'd looked at her mother's funeral, that first day when he'd fallen for her over math homework, the way she'd looked when she first cut her hair off, her tiny ears sticking out like an elf's would. His body was nearly burning with the excitement of what was to come.

There were just steps between him and the staircase now. One, two, three, four. And finally, with one foot on her brick stair and one hand around the iron rail, there he was. Randall paused at the bottommost step. The full weight of what he was about to do was upon him. He savored this surge in his heart. He wanted to remember just how everything looked, that spot of light to the right, the thin, hazy cloud that partly covered the moon—directly above, it seemed, lighting the way just for the two of them. He turned his gaze to the door with a gigantic breath, hid the flowers behind his back and climbed the steps two at a time.

He rang the bell and waited. He heard the clicking sound of locks being undone. He took a deep breath and straightened his shoulders, steeling himself to accomplish this thing that had seemed so impossible not long ago. But when the door swung open, Randall nearly choked.

Nick.

"Hey, Randall," Nick said with a skeevy smirk.

"Nick." Randall couldn't mask his hostility. In fact, it took every ounce of restraint just to keep himself from punching Nick right in the face, though he didn't stop himself from imagining it: Nick falling to the ground like a hollow tree trunk, Abigail stepping right over him and into Randall's arms.

"What's up?" Nick asked, crossing his arms in front of his chest.

"Is Abigail around?" Randall somehow managed to say, the blood pumping in his ear so loudly that he could barely hear his own voice.

"She's just freshening up. We were busy setting up our apartment all day."

Randall jerked back as if he'd been kicked in the gut. Somehow he'd convinced himself that Abigail wasn't going to move in with Nick, that she had realized the ridiculousness of it and had found another solution to her problem. How could all those moments Randall had shared with her recently have left her unaffected?

Finally, he heard Abigail say, "Who's there?" He could hear her footsteps thumping down the staircase. When she popped her head out the door, her smile deflated fast.

"Hi, Randall." Abigail's gaze traveled to his arm, as if she was trying to figure out what he was hiding.

"Hey," Randall spat out. His voice had an edge of anger, but there wasn't anything he could do about it. He *was* angry—angry that Nick was here to ruin the moment he had dreamed so long about.

This anger burned even more fiercely when Randall saw Nick close his arm around Abigail's waist. But then she pushed away from Nick slightly and looked into Randall's eyes for just a second. He wanted to believe that her look had meant *I wish you were him right now*. However, Abigail turned back to Nick and the look was gone.

"I just stopped by to see if you wanted to see this band down at the Knitting Factory," Randall said. "But you're busy, so . . ." He paused for a moment and gulped. "Anyway, have a great night, guys."

He backed down the steps so neither of them would see the flowers. When he heard the door close, he let his hand fall. He slunk over to the street corner and threw them into the trash, kicking the can so that its steel mesh was bent in. Then he rode the train to the Knitting Factory by himself. He sat at a table for two, trying to ignore the couple to his right, who couldn't seem to keep their hands off each other. But it was no use.

No use at all.

24

On Sunday evening, Kate was sitting on her bed, wrapped in her favorite silk kimono and covered in paperwork. The open-mike night at the One Trick was tomorrow evening, and she was running through all the preparations, making sure she had everything under control. After dinner with her parents, she'd spent an hour on the phone calling the florist, jeweler, props store, and furniture rental company and confirming all her orders. She'd also checked the One Trick Web site to see how advance ticket sales were coming along. Kate had e-mailed Caroline and encouraged her to offer a discount to those who purchased reserved seats to eliminate last-minute ditch decisions, and so far over a hundred tickets had been sold, which was slightly more than the capacity of the coffeehouse.

The event seemed to be running smoothly, but for some reason Kate was feeling a little uneasy. She knew that none of this was what Abigail had wanted, but considering how strange her friends were acting, Kate needed to cling to any sort of normalcy. If that meant taking charge and disregarding all the humble plans Abigail had written down in her binder, then so be it. Anyway, Kate just wanted to make sure her best friend's event was a raging success. What was so dreadfully wrong about that?

Kate heard the distinctive ring tone on her phone, which was a song by the Flash. It could only be one person.

"Jesse?" Kate's heart leaped into her throat. Even though she hadn't spoken to Jesse over the weekend, she hadn't been able to get him out of her thoughts since Randall had told her about Jesse's feelings for Caroline.

"Hey," he murmured.

"Are you okay?" she asked. His voice was so strained, it was obvious that something was wrong.

"Caroline rejected me," he said simply.

Kate clamped her hand over her mouth. She *really* wanted to say what was front and center in her mind: *I told you this would happen!* But she wasn't all that happy to be right just then. She hated that Jesse was in pain.

"I feel like total shit," he added gruffly.

"Do you want me to come over?"

"Yeah. My parents left to go back to Texas already. I could use the company."

A few minutes later, Kate shrugged off her robe, threw on a T-shirt and jeans, pulled a pair of shoes out of her closet, slipped them on, and ran downstairs. "I'll be home late," she said to her parents as she grabbed her coat and bounded out the door. She nearly ran the two blocks between their homes, pulling her coat on as she dodged past a middle-aged man walking a huge golden retriever on a red leash and a teenage girl wearing a big puffy pink coat and chunky black shoes.

When she arrived at Jesse's, windblown and gasping for breath, Kate took the elevator to his floor. During her slow ascent, her mind whizzed back to last year when she and Jesse had messed around in his room. As she tightened her hand into a fist and knocked at the door, it was almost as if she could feel him pressing up against her on his bed. By the time Kate heard the lock being undone, she was trembling. She tried to think of how badly it had hurt when he'd forgotten about her on the night of the concert, and when Randall had said Jesse had finally fallen in love—with someone else, someone so fundamentally different from her.

When Jesse pulled the door open, Kate's eyes grew wide. He looked as if he hadn't slept in days. There were dark circles under his dim, lifeless eyes, and the skin on his face was red and dry in places. Kate knew he'd put on the faded Yankees baseball cap to hide his hair, which he always did when he hadn't showered. Even so, Jesse was undeniably gorgeous. She had to force herself not to notice this every time she saw him, but now that was very hard to do.

"Hey," he muttered, and slunk away from the door.

As Kate followed him into the house, she couldn't help noticing how his jeans were slipping off his hips, revealing the blue waistband of his boxers. She took off her coat and threw it on the chair next to the sofa where he'd sat down, his elbows on his knees and his face in his hands. Kate knelt in front of him and took his hands in hers. It was a while before he looked into her eyes, but when he did, Kate saw that he was crying.

"It's going to be all right, Jesse," she whispered, and leaned in to kiss him lightly on the forehead. It was a tender expression of affection that Kate rarely exhibited, but it seemed absolutely necessary at the moment. She'd never seen Jesse deeply distressed like this, and it was extremely troubling. Kate just wished she could do something to put him back together again.

But before she could figure out a way to take control of the situation, Jesse pulled her in so close that the tip of his wet nose brushed against her warm, flushed cheek. She didn't want to move an inch, because if she did, she knew she'd end up pressing her lips against his, no matter how much she would try to resist the temptation. She would never be able to forget how amazing Jesse had been the time they'd hooked up—how his kisses were deep yet soft; how his hands had run up and down the insides of her thighs; how he had unfastened the buttons of her shirt with his teeth and glided his tongue along her collarbone.

Then in a split second, Kate didn't have to remember Jesse's prowess at all. He moved that critical inch and pressed his lips against hers. Everything that had happened before happened again.

Only this time, Kate didn't tell Jesse to stop.

The next morning, Kate woke to find the sun shining into her eyes through the huge industrial wall of windows. It took a minute to realize it wasn't her own bed she'd been sleeping in, but when she turned and saw Jesse lying next to her, she rolled back over to her side of the bed with a giant smile on her face. She closed her eyes again and reflected on their passionate night frame by frame, as if it were a movie she'd watched or a dream she'd had. She wrapped the sheet tighter around her naked body when she thought of how Jesse had taken her to his room and removed her clothes as he kissed her neck and clutched at her waist. She pulled a pillow over her head when she thought of how loudly she'd moaned when they were grinding against each other.

Kate had had plenty of sex before this, but nothing could compare to last night. She had been completely out of control and had never felt better. But now, when she took the pillow away from her face and peeked at Jesse, who was still fast asleep, she noticed how he was curled up on his side of the bed with his back to her. Then she realized that he hadn't tried to cuddle with her after he'd said good night, and her stomach began to ache.

Luckily for Kate, these thoughts were put out of her mind when she heard the doorbell ring. She figured this would wake Jesse up, but he didn't stir. When it rang again, Kate grabbed Jesse's oversized T-shirt off the floor, put it on, and ran downstairs. In bare feet, she tiptoed along the slate floor and down the long hallway, turned left at the living room and made her way to the entry. She closed one eye to look through the peephole, wondering who could possibly be coming to Jesse's house at six-thirty in the morning on a Monday.

Kate was surprised by the sight of Caroline standing on the other side of the door. She was dressed in jeans and pretty navy flats, with a crisp white blouse under a giant black cabled sweater coat that hung to her ankles. Kate unlocked the door and opened it, a wide smirk forming on her face. Caroline was holding two coffees in her hands and appeared stricken with disbelief, which made Kate feel all the more powerful.

"Good morning," Kate said slyly as she put her hands on her hips and angled her bare legs in such a way that Caroline would be certain to notice them.

"Hello." The tone of Caroline's voice was weak. "Is Jesse here?"

"He's sleeping. We had a *very* late night, you see." Kate crossed her arms over her chest and narrowed her eyes at Caroline, making her point crystal clear.

"Oh." This seemed to jar Caroline so much that she was at a loss for words. "Well, can you tell him that I came by to . . . apologize? And that I wanted him to have this?" She held out the cardboard tray with the coffees, smiling weakly.

Instead of stiffening her posture any more, Kate reached out slowly and took the tray from Caroline. "Sure," she said.

"Thanks," Caroline said, turning on her heel slightly, but then stopped, dug into her pants pocket, and pulled out a silver key chain. "Forgive me, I almost forgot. Here are the keys to the One Trick Pony. I've closed it down today so that you can set up for tonight. I really appreciate your hard work."

Kate swallowed hard as a sharp tingle of remorse nipped at her skin. "You're welcome."

"Au revoir," Caroline said before darting down the hall and disappearing into the elevator.

A chill ran up Kate's spine, as she closed the door, fastened the locks, and took a seat on the cold leather sofa, gathering her legs beneath her. She looked at the coffees a few seconds, then pulled the plastic lid off the one marked "C" and gazed inside. There was a peak of foam on the top that reminded her of the homemade hot cocoa she used to love as a kid. Even though she'd always resisted drinking coffee, especially when it was made by Caroline, she was very thirsty, and the smell of this unusual concoction was so inviting.

"Here goes nothing." Kate sat back against the arm of the sofa and stretched her legs out along the length of the couch. She sipped the coffee slowly and felt the warm liquid slip down the back of her throat. The taste was decadent, like milk chocolate combined with a rich robust coffee bean. It was almost impossible not to gulp it back all at once, but somehow she managed to savor every drop.

By the time she'd finished the cup, Kate had thought twice over about everything that had happened. She couldn't stop seeing that sad look in Caroline's eyes, which reminded her of just how sad Jesse had looked when Kate had showed up at his house last night. As difficult as it was for Kate to admit it, it was quite easy to see that Jesse and Caroline had some sort of connection. Denying it wasn't going to make it go away or give her control over her world, which was drastically changing around her.

Kate took one final swallow of the coffee and wiped her mouth with the back of her hand. When she looked up, Jesse was standing right in front of her, wearing nothing but a pair of orange mesh shorts and a groggy expression. "Do you want some coffee?" she asked.

He smiled and looked off in another direction, obviously trying to avoid eye contact. "Thanks."

Kate handed the cup marked "J" to him. She noticed the way his gaze had suddenly focused in on Caroline's curly, feminine handwriting and how his lower lip started trembling.

Wow, he really is in love, Kate thought as she bowed her head and stared at the peeling nail polish on her toes. But regardless of the new awareness she had stumbled upon this morning while drinking from Caroline's paper cup, which was still in her hand, Kate made sure Jesse didn't see the "C"—she covered it up with her palm.

25

Jesse had stood before his bedroom door a good five minutes before coming out to face Kate. Even though they'd had a wild night in his room, he knew he'd made a gigantic mistake sleeping with her, especially because she had been growing jealous of his relationship with Caroline. But the night before, when Jesse had gone to call Randall and ask him to come over, he'd found himself dialing Kate's number instead. Maybe he needed more than someone to confide in. Maybe he'd even wanted to light some spark between him and a girl he was sure had some kind of romantic feelings for him, though they were hidden below the surface. Besides, if things had taken off with Kate, wouldn't that have made getting over Caroline easier?

But the truth, which Jesse saw now, in the light of day, was that it hadn't made anything easier. It had just made it painfully clear how much he loved Caroline. In fact, he was amazed that seeing something simple, like the single letter she'd written on his cup, sent him back to that one fantastical kiss, when it seemed possible that she might love him back.

He sat down carefully on the couch, making sure he didn't get too close to Kate and give her the wrong idea. But after an awkward silence and a quick sip of coffee, Jesse got up the courage to be straight with his friend. Too bad he still couldn't look her in the eye. "Kate, about last night . . ."

"You don't need to say anything," she said quickly. "I understand."

Jesse was so surprised to hear her say this that his head snapped up. How could Kate possibly understand?

"I know you love her, Jesse," Kate went on, laying her hand on Jesse's knee. "Last night was just . . . well, we can forget it ever happened."

Jesse nearly dumped his coffee into his lap. Why wasn't Kate telling him what to think and do, all of a sudden? "Are you . . . *okay?*"

"Yeah. I am," Kate replied as she glanced down at herself in Jesse's T-shirt. "I know I always get into your business, and everyone else's. But you know what? The only thing anyone should listen to is their own heart."

Jesse knew that these words weren't easy for her to say. To tell him to follow his heart after the night they'd shared, knowing that would lead him away from her, was the kind of brave act he didn't know if he himself was capable of. But in the end, beyond all the antagonistic bullshit and snide remarks, this was the reason he and Kate were friends. When it really counted, they took care of each other, no matter what the cost.

"You have no idea how incredible you are, Kate," he said, taking her hand and squeezing it gently.

Kate smiled wickedly. "Yeah, I do."

Jesse broke into an infectious fit of laughter that made Kate giggle like a little girl. Somehow she found a way to compose herself long enough to say, "Drink your coffee."

Later that morning, Jesse turned the collar up on his favorite distressed denim jacket, tossed on his pricy mirrored sunglasses, and walked his bike down the sidewalk. Just thirty-six hours ago, he had felt his heart shattered to unrecognizable fragments that even a great forensic guy could never identify. After everything he'd shared with Caroline, she had turned her back on him, and then he'd gone home to a painfully empty house. The note his father had left for him read: *Jesse, I am incredibly sorry. I am going to find a way to make this all up to you.* Apparently Jesse was supposed to find some shred of comfort in that, but instead there was just a big void that Jesse could think of only one way to fill.

Which was why he had to go to the One Trick Pony before school and convince Caroline that he was the one for her.

Once he arrived at the alley, Jesse leaned his bike against the building in back and drew in as much air as he could. But when he tried to push the back door open, it wouldn't budge.

"What the . . . ?" Jesse couldn't understand why the door would be locked. *Please let her be here. Please, God.* He hopped back on his bike and rode it around to the front door, which was locked, too. A tiny sign on a yellow piece of notebook paper was taped to the door: WILL REOPEN FOR OPEN-MIKE NIGHT AT 8 PM.

Jesse stared at it in disbelief, along with a growing crowd of people who were peering into the café with disappointment. Everyone in the neighborhood loved to come to the One Trick, especially Jesse. How could Caroline think of closing its doors, even for a few hours?

He stood there, straddling his bike, for a few minutes. Then he shifted his view up to the second-floor windows of Caroline's apartment. He rolled over to the apartment door, which was next to the One Trick entrance, and pressed the buzzer. Although it was freezing outside, beads of sweat were forming on the back of his neck.

All his anxiety was unnecessary, however. Caroline didn't answer the buzzer, not even after Jesse pressed it for a third time.

When he backed up to get a better look at the windows, fat raindrops began pummeling everything around him. Within seconds, the street was deserted, but Jesse wasn't going anywhere. He would wait for her to come home, regardless of the torrential downpour that had store owners dragging their sidewalk chairs inside and drivers pulling their cars over to wait it out.

Jesse waited for an hour, asking himself unanswerable questions, looking for some cosmic sign in the movement of water rushing down the gutters, anything that might clue him in to where Caroline might be. He was soaked through and he would probably catch pneumonia, but he didn't care. He just willed himself to stay focused, concentrating on the lyrics of one of Randall's songs.

Kick and tuck and slide, yeah, yeah, yeah, you
*   can,*
though you don't think it, you can.
You can, my baby, you and me.
Together we can.
Sway leaf and hail cab and sweep the floor.

Jesse stayed afloat in this shallow puddle of hope for another twenty minutes, but Caroline didn't come home. When he finally pedaled away, there wasn't a song on his mind or any life in his heart.

Now he knew why Caroline had left France and never looked back.

26

After school on Monday, Abigail put her backpack down in the front hall and hung her coat on the brass hook her mother had hung for her when she was five years old. It was too low for her coat now—the hem of it skimmed the floor—but Abigail loved the ritual so much that she'd never asked her father to adjust it. She hadn't spoken a word to him since their argument, which was why she nearly gasped when she ran into him on her way to get a bottle of water from the refrigerator. The last thing she needed on the night of her big performance was to have another fight with him.

He didn't say anything at first, but when she stood at the open refrigerator door, the cold blasting in her face, he cleared his throat. "I'd like to talk with you about the other night."

"Okay," she said, turning around slowly and crossing her arms in front of her chest. She softened when she saw how disheveled her father looked even though he was dressed in a three-piece suit. His eyelids looked heavy and his expression weary.

"Abby, I'm sorry I've handled this all so poorly. Your mother—" He blinked away some tears and tried to keep his hands from shaking by shoving them into his pockets. "She was *everything* to me . . . and I know how amazing she was with you, how much you loved her. I just . . . I just didn't know it was going to be this hard."

"Dad, you don't have to do this," Abigail said, her eyes stinging at an old memory of her father in a tuxedo and her mother in an elegant black cocktail dress. They were walking hand in hand down the steps, leaving Abigail in a cloud of their cologne and perfume.

"Yes, I do. I thought I could run away from the hurt, and when I met Ginny, I don't know, it seemed better to be with someone who made me feel . . . secure and safe. I'm sure that's difficult for you to understand."

Abigail sighed deeply as she took a few steps toward her dad. "I do understand."

Her father grinned. "Well, you were always very intuitive. You get that from Penny, you know."

It was obvious by the way he rocked back on his heels that it was torture for him to say her name. All this time, Abigail had been so quick to judge her father and measure his grief, and here he was, vulnerable and pained and in despair. Just as she was.

"Anyway, after all our fights, I was able to see how this has been such a big burden on you. And I don't want to take you away from your friends and your life," he said. "So we're not going to Aspen, honey. We're staying right here, together."

Abigail was so stunned, her water bottle almost slipped right out of her hands. *We're staying. We're staying!*

"Are you happy?" her father asked as he moved closer and tucked a strand of hair behind her right ear.

She surprised both of them when she grabbed him and hugged him tightly, which she hadn't done since her mother's funeral. The distance between them didn't seem that important now. Nothing did: not her reservations about Nick, or her anxiety about open-mike night, or even her hatred of Ginny. And that was when Abigail knew.

"I don't think I've ever been happier."

But when suddenly she thought of Randall standing on her doorstep with that unique crooked smile of his, Abigail wondered whether what she'd just told her father was true.

The line that began at the front of the One Trick Pony snaked all the way to the corner. As Abigail approached the café, dressed in her favorite dark denim jeans and a heather-gray T-shirt with the words LOVE IN printed on it, her body hummed with nervous energy. She'd be up on that stage, performing for all those people. When she passed all the ticket holders and headed for the door, she saw Kate sitting on a stool, holding a clipboard and checking off the names of incoming guests. A knot immediately formed in Abigail's stomach when she thought about how she'd left things with Kate. She wasn't sure she could take the tension right now, considering how anxious she was about reading her poetry tonight.

"Okay, go ahead in. Enjoy," Kate said to a couple of young guys Abigail recognized as underclassmen, before looking up and smiling in Abigail's direction. Kate was wearing cute black jeans and heels and a casual but expensive cowboy-inspired blouse with red piping on the pockets. But what stood out the most was the large paper cup with lipstick marks on the lid that was tucked between Kate's knees.

Wait a second, there's no teabag string hanging from the cup. . . .

"So what do you think, Abby?" Kate asked.

"It's an unbelievable turnout. You did a great job," Abigail said, hoping that when she went inside she wouldn't be faced with too many of Kate's decorations.

"Well, it's all thanks to you," Kate said with a wink.

Abigail flinched. "Me?"

"Well, you and your binder full of great ideas."

"But . . . before . . . you said—"

"Never mind what I said before," Kate said as she leaned back toward the open door. Then she cupped her hands around her mouth and shouted, "Randall, get your ass over here and do the list for a minute!" Kate swung back around, reached into a small cardboard box that was sitting on the outside window ledge, and extended her hand to Abigail. "Here, take a couple of buttons," she said, placing two in Abigail's palm.

A wide grin stretched across Abigail's face as she read them both. One said, I DIDN'T PERFORM AT THE ONE TRICK,

BUT I HAD A DAMN GOOD TIME and the other said, I PER-
FORMED AT THE ONE TRICK AND LIVED TO TELL.

In all the years Abigail had known Kate, she'd never imagined that her friend would be able to swallow her pride and give in to someone else, especially when it came to party planning. While Abigail was a bit shocked by this turn of events, she was more surprised to see this shimmering glint in Kate's eyes, which Abigail hadn't seen before now. Instead of looking like the weight of the universe was pinning her down, Kate appeared truly content and at peace with herself, smiling like an optimist instead of rolling her eyes like the cynic Abigail knew her to be. It was an unbelievable yet welcome change.

"Sorry the type is so messy. I was kind of in a rush." There was Randall, leaning against the door frame, wearing a light-blue button-down shirt with the sleeves rolled up.

Abigail felt her shoulders and neck tighten the moment they locked eyes. "You made these?"

"Yeah, I did." He shifted his weight nervously from his left leg to his right and then scratched the back of his head before leaning in and kissing her on the cheek. "You look amazing," he whispered into her ear.

Abigail stepped away and turned toward Kate so that Randall wouldn't see her cheeks flush ten shades of red. These growing feelings of hers were getting more difficult to hide, and though she wanted to lean on Randall because she was worried about performing, she was even more worried about putting their friendship in a jeopardy with a silly new crush. That was what it was. A crush, right?

Thankfully, she didn't have too much time to obsess about it. Kate handed Randall the clipboard and pulled

Abigail inside the door, where an excited hum of low talking and whispers filled the café. There were so many people at the tables and standing along the walls that it took her a minute to realize that Kate hadn't followed through on any of the plans she'd railroaded Abigail with at their meetings. There was no lacquer furniture, no gift bags, no ruby red curtains, light-up marquee, or huge potted plants.

Instead, the place looked exactly like Abigail's sketch come to life. There were the mismatched strands of colored Christmas lights over the makeshift plywood stage. There were the tubs of ice dotted with retro soda bottles, a cracked mirror behind the platform stage and a tall stool for the artists to sit on. The poster Abigail had painted and made copies of at Mr. Gold's office was plastered all over the walls like concert posters on a New York street.

"So . . . you like?" Kate asked as she put her arm around a stunned Abigail.

"Oh my God, Kate. It's every single thing I wanted."

"I know," Kate said, and pulled Abigail in for a full-on hug. "Your ideas were much better suited to this crowd. I should have listened to you."

Abigail was so shocked that she nearly collapsed in Kate's arms. First, her father had surprisingly come through for her, and now her bossy, no-nonsense friend was admitting she'd been wrong? And Abigail was sure she smelled the sweet aroma of Caroline's coffee on Kate's breath. Maybe Jesse had been right. Maybe there was some ethereal magic going on right under their noses. Sure, she'd sort of believed it before, but at the moment, it seemed more fact than fairy tale.

Kate left Abigail's side a few minutes later to join Randall at the door. Abigail had sat down at one of the tables halfway back from the stage when a unkempt-looking Jesse emerged from behind the counter, where he'd been doling out coffees and sodas and a selection of delectable desserts.

"Drinks for artists are on the house," he muttered, and passed Abigail a piping-hot mug of coffee.

"Thanks." Abigail took a long sip. "Where's Caroline?"

Jesse shrugged and then let out a few coughs. "I have no clue."

Abigail raised her eyebrows with concern. "Are you okay? You look like you might be coming down with something."

"I'm fine," Jesse replied, tossing a towel over his shoulder with a deeply defeated expression that made Abigail worry even more. But before she could coax anything out of him, Jesse cocked his head toward the door. "Looks like your better half has arrived."

Abigail followed his gaze and saw that Nick and a bunch of his friends were handing Kate their tickets and throwing buttons at each other. She looked back at Randall, who rolled his eyes. By the way Nick and company were laughing and carrying on, she could tell they'd been drinking. Then again, she'd been drinking, too. Only, her intoxication was much more than just a rush of caffeine or adrenaline. Abigail was nearly halfway through her mug and all the blurriness of her life was clearing up to reveal a sky glittering with stars, a sky she knew she could touch if she just stood on her toes like a ballerina—like her mother—and reached for it.

Nick and his friends went directly to the back of the

room while Randall, Kate, and the last few guests sauntered in. Abigail slouched in her seat and covered her face with one of the programs that had already been distributed on the tables. She didn't want anyone around to encourage her, because that would only make her more anxious. Which was why she'd asked her father not to come. Abigail was on such an emotional ledge these days, and falling off the ledge in front of all these people just wasn't an option.

When Jesse dimmed the lights, Kate took to the stage and approached the microphone with her signature poise and confidence. "Ladies and gentlemen, artists and wannabes. This is your chance to show us what you're worth. Audience members, you're not off the hook, either. You have to show your support to the acts you like, so make sure we hear you. Got it?"

A nice roar of applause erupted from the crowd as Kate grinned. "That's great, guys. Now, let me hear it even louder for one of my best friends, who helped make this entire evening possible. A brilliant poet, a compassionate soul, and a true warrior, Abigail Jones!"

"Woohoo!" Nick shouted.

"We love Abigail," Randall yelled.

When Abigail approached the stage, she felt a bit wary at first, but with each Converse All-Star stride forward, her self-confidence grew. The scared little girl inside her that always sunk into the background was now cheering for the opportunity to be seen and heard. Abigail could feel that her mother was rooting for her too, encouraging her to live up to all the potential she'd been given. A surge of empowerment traveled through Abigail and wrapped around her heart when she reached the middle of the stage.

As the spotlight shone down on her, Abigail glanced at the sheet of paper and took baby steps toward the microphone. She'd planned to read a whimsical poem she'd written years ago about the fig tree her mom had planted in their backyard. That way, her mother would be part of this monumental experience. But when Abigail peered out into the crowd and saw Nick still roughhousing with his friends while Randall made his way to the front row and sat down, she knew that tonight wasn't about looking back; it was about looking forward. That meant envisioning her future, and when she closed her eyes for a second to picture who she'd be with, the person she'd envisioned by her side before wasn't there.

She opened her eyes, tucked her tree poem into her back pocket, pulled the mike from its stand, and sat down on the stool with her legs crossed. "This poem is called . . . 'No.' " She cleared her throat in the heat of the bright overhead light and just let the words come to her as she stared right at him.

> *I said I would, but I can't leave.*
> *My roots are deep beneath the soil.*
> *I won't run, but my lifeblood will,*
> *Until my voice dies out in the forest.*
> *You have fallen*
> *And maybe I'm the only one who heard.*
> *So listen hard and then let me go.*
> *There's someone else for me to hold on to.*

There was plenty of applause when she got up and took a bow, but Abigail was so consumed with guilt when she saw the surprised reaction on Nick's face that she couldn't enjoy the enthusiastic response to her spontaneous poem. The gnawing sensation in her stomach was so intense, she bolted off the stage, plowed through her adoring fans, and darted outside, where the air was cool and she could breathe.

27

Though he was supposed to perform next, Randall didn't hesitate one second to run out of the One Trick Pony, right after Abigail. It was clear from the poem she'd read that she wasn't moving in with Nick, and this was his chance to tell her that he would hold on to her forever. That was, if she wanted him to. And God, did he pray for that to be true.

When he pushed the door open and saw her pacing back and forth, Randall had to keep himself from running over to her and crushing her in an enormous hug. He could tell she was frantic about what had just happened, and he didn't want to overwhelm her. But still, there was so much he had to say to her, and his heart might burst if he didn't do anything about it.

So he just reached out and gently grabbed her by the arm. "Hey," he said, his voice light and upbeat.

Abigail shrugged him off, though, and kept pacing.

"How could I be so cruel, Ran? What's gotten into me? Nick has been nothing but—"

"Completely wrong for you?" Randall interjected. He knew he sounded angry all of a sudden, but the fact that Abigail was actually feeling remorse about Nick ripped into him like a knife through a feather pillow.

And at that exact moment, Nick marched out of the café and onto the sidewalk with his eyes blazing and his fists clenched. "Abigail? What the hell was that all about?"

Randall watched as Abigail wrung her hands and dipped her head. He was expecting her to cave in and walk off hand in hand with Nick—it had happened so many times before.

But then there was a little spark of magic.

"I'm sorry, Nick. My dad's not moving us to Colorado, and even if he was, I just . . . I can't be with you anymore," she said softly.

Nick rolled his eyes and laughed. "You don't know what you're saying, babe. You're just confused, is all."

"She's not confused. She's being brave," Randall said as he stepped in front of Abigail, hoping to take some of the heat off her.

"Oh, I get it," Nick said, slurring his words and cracking his knuckles as if he was preparing to throw a drunken punch. "After all this time of pining away for my girlfriend, you finally have the balls to do something about it."

"Back off, man, you're drunk." Randall sized Nick up quickly. He couldn't believe he was even thinking about fighting this guy, especially because he'd dreamed about kicking his ass so many times. Still, the reality of the situation was that Nick was much bigger, and his friends had just followed him outside, so Randall was also outnumbered.

Abigail sensed that the situation was getting out of control and put herself between them. "Nick, why don't we go somewhere quiet and talk?"

Nick relaxed and put his hands at his sides. Then he smiled, which seemed to calm Abigail's nerves. "How about the diner around the block?"

"Okay, let's go," Abigail said, tugging on his shirt.

"I left something inside, though, so I'll meet you over there," Nick replied, and gave Randall a sly grin.

Oh, shit, Randall thought. *This can't be good.*

"Fine, see you in a few." Abigail turned to Randall and gave him a hug, her lips lingering near his neck. "Good luck up there. Sorry I won't be there to see it. Could you ask Kate to cover for me?"

"Sure." Randall wanted to say it right then and there. *I love you, Abigail.* But not with Nick watching. Not only would the beating he knew he was about to receive be so much worse, but it would forever taint his proclamation. He'd waited this long to say it; he wasn't about to risk the specialness of the moment now.

He watched as Abigail disappeared around the corner. The first punch seemed to come out of nowhere. His eye socket exploded in a flash of heat. The rest came in a flurry of punches and kicks that he tried to fight off but couldn't. When it was over, Nick and his pals took off running while Randall stumbled to the door of the One Trick, blood pouring down his face, his head pounding. He couldn't see out of his right eye.

Without thinking, Randall hobbled through the audience and onto the stage as soon as there was a break between performers. He didn't wait for Kate to introduce him or for the audience to stop gasping at his gruesome appearance. He just grabbed his guitar, leaned into the microphone, and said, "This one is for Abigail, the love of my life."

Randall missed some notes and his fingers hurt when he pressed down on the strings. Still, Abigail's song had never sounded better, even though she wasn't there to hear it for herself.

28

Early the next morning, Kate was at the door of the One Trick Pony once again. She'd been on her way to school when she remembered that she had to drop off the keys with Caroline, who'd need them to open up for the day. As she rang the bell of Caroline's apartment above the café, Kate flashed back to all the remarkable things that happened the night before and wondered if somehow Caroline hadn't been behind a lot of it: Abigail breaking up with Nick in a poem; Randall professing his love in a song; and the most surprising turn of events yet: Kate actually seeing her own flaws for the first time, which had only begun to happen after she'd drunk some coffee from the One Trick Pony.

That could just be coincidence, couldn't it?

When Kate heard activity at the door at the top of the stairs, she felt nervous. She had told Jesse not to trust this woman, and maybe she'd been right all along. Maybe Caroline had powers that none of them could truly understand. And if that was true, maybe she should stay far away from this Frenchwoman.

"Good morning, Kate," Caroline said sweetly as she opened the door. She was wearing a black sweater dress and gray textured tights, which made her legs look more slender than usual.

"I just came by to return your keys." Kate held out her hand and opened her palm, revealing the silver key chain.

Caroline had her hand at the base of her ponytail, smoothing it back again and again, as if she was nervous. Then she took the keys out of Kate's hand. "Thank you."

"Well, it was thoughtful of you to close the place down so that I could get everything set." Kate looked into Caroline's eyes to see if she could detect anything off-kilter, but all she could see was sadness. "Anyway, the event was spectacular. Abigail and Randall stole the show. It's a shame you missed it."

"I know. You all worked very hard." Caroline swallowed hard and then chewed on her lower lip. "But I was . . . too distraught to attend."

Kate flashed back to the previous morning and how she had rubbed her presence at Jesse's house in Caroline's face. Her skin felt very hot, as though she'd been out in the sun without proper sunscreen. "Do you want to talk about it?"

What the hell am I saying?

"Perhaps. Would you like to come in?" Caroline backed up and opened the door wider.

Kate could smell the wonderful aroma of Caroline's apartment from the bottom of the steps and was unable to resist the invitation. "Sure."

When they reached the top of the staircase, Caroline and Kate stood in front of an old wooden door with a strange frosted glass cutout, like a classroom might have. Caroline fumbled with the keys in the fluorescent lighting, and after much tinkling and jiggling, she pushed her door open and Kate followed her inside.

Immediately Caroline looped around to the small kitchen, just to the left of the front door. Kate wandered into the living room and sat on the flowery sofa draped with a big red afghan. On either side of the sofa stood two unmatched tables—one in punched tin with the kind of candle on her mugs sitting on top, and the other a soft wood, curved like a barrel. Although the décor wasn't Kate's style at all, she couldn't help feeling warm and comfortable there, like she was visiting a favorite cousin.

"Do you think I could have a cup of coffee?" Kate asked meekly. She was all too aware of how she had previously turned down Caroline's brew.

"Kate, you can have anything you want in life, as long as you're not trying to control it," Caroline said knowingly while taking a fresh pot off the stove. "And when you open your heart to possibilities, there's no such thing as right or wrong."

Caroline pulled a cup from her cupboard, placed it on a matching saucer, and put a few pinches of spices and what looked like brown sugar into the cup before pouring the coffee. When she put the cup in Kate's hands, her fingertips felt nice and warm.

"Thanks," Kate replied, and took a quick sip, which led to a long, hearty gulp. Kate had wanted to savor the coffee, but it tasted so amazing—almost like a chocolate-covered cinnamon stick—that she couldn't control her urge to drink it all at once.

After she'd finished, Kate gazed at Caroline again. In front of her was a woman who had done nothing but try to help Kate and her friends. And even if Caroline could cast magic spells with her coffee, she did it to awaken people and show them how to break bad habits by turning their lives upside down. Wasn't that reason enough to trust her? Wasn't that reason enough to be honest—about everything?

"Caroline, I know you're upset about what happened with Jesse and me," Kate said with her head cocked to the side. "But he really loves you. And he's never felt that way about anyone. Please don't be mad at him."

Caroline's eyes immediately filled with tears. "I'm not mad at him."

Kate furrowed her brow in confusion. "You're not?"

Caroline shook her head.

"Well, you should be mad at *me*, then. I purposely gave you the wrong impression yesterday morning because I was . . . well, I was burning with jealousy. In fact, I told him many times not to trust you, and I only did that because I couldn't stand the way he felt about you."

"Why is that?" Caroline asked, taking Kate's hand and caressing it the way Kate's mother used to do when Kate was very young.

The words Kate wanted to say caught in her throat. Her feelings had been so mixed up in the past couple of weeks, but as the steam from her coffee floated into the air, everything seemed clear, much like it had at Jesse's place and on open-mike night. "At first I thought it was because I wanted Jesse to feel that way about me. But now . . . I think I was just scared. It was so hard to watch him spin out of control and—"

"Kate," Caroline interjected softly, "sometimes, you have to let people follow their own path, even if it brings them pain."

"And what about my path?" Kate could feel herself trembling. She had never made herself this vulnerable before. "I don't even feel like me anymore."

"It will present itself to you in time," Caroline said, letting go of Kate's hand. "You just have to be patient and allow it to come instead of trying to make it appear." She walked over to the stove, picked up the coffeepot, and returned to fill Kate's cup to the brim. "And you are more you now than you ever were before."

"I thought you were supposed to tell me your troubles," Kate said, smiling genuinely.

"My troubles will be just a memory soon." Caroline grinned back and then reached over to the end of her counter. She slid a package wrapped in brown paper, tied with bakery string, and secured with a wax seal depicting the well-known candle in front of Kate. "Take this. It's the coffee you're drinking right now. It's meant to be shared with friends."

"Thanks," Kate said, knowing that was what she and Caroline were destined to become.

29

Jesse rode over to Randall's house on his bike after school. Jesse had been shocked that he'd managed to get out of bed at all that morning, considering that he hadn't spoken to Caroline and had no idea where she'd been the night before and the night before that. Unfortunately, Jesse's parents had left town too. His father pleaded with Jesse not to be upset—he'd tried his hardest to alter their schedule, but it proved to be an impossible task. Still, when his mom and dad had been picked up in a Lincoln Town Car to be taken to JFK airport, Jesse couldn't help wondering if their understanding reaction to his little speech about them being unavailable had something to do with Caroline and her coffee—both of them had been drinking it when he'd professed his feelings. Still, staying home alone and obsessing over her hadn't appealed to

Jesse in the least, so when the sun came up, he'd crawled into a pair of dirty jeans and a long-sleeved black T-shirt, then had gone through his classes like a first-rate zombie. He hadn't even noticed Randall's absence until the very end of the day, and when he'd called his friend to check up on him, he kept getting voice mail, which wasn't a good sign.

Jesse rang the doorbell of the Gold residence, and Randall's dad answered, looking spiffy in a navy blue sweater and corduroys.

"Lookin' good, Jeff," Jesse said with a smirk. "Big date?"

"Actually, yes. I'm having dinner with a woman I met a while ago." Mr. Gold raised his eyebrows mischievously.

Jesse laughed. It was great to see Randall's dad off the couch and ready to start his life again. "Right on. I'm sure she'll be all over you."

"Yeah, right," Mr. Gold replied as he mopped his forehead with the back of his palm nervously, just the way Randall was known to do.

"How's your son holding up?" Jesse asked.

"I'm not going to lie to you. His face has looked much better," Mr. Gold joked. "I just hope he's hurting less on the inside than he is on the outside." He patted Jesse on the shoulder and pointed up the stairs. "I think Randall's in his room."

Upstairs, Randall was lying in his bed with twenty pillows over his head. The room was dark and sullen, with the black shades rotated to keep out every ray of light. "Go away," he said, his voice muffled by all the cotton and feathers.

Jesse walked closer to the bed and remembered the other day when Randall had come to help him out of his Caroline-induced depression. Boy, they were a couple of messes lately. "Come on, Ran. Hiding up here isn't going to make things better. Believe me."

He began pulling pillows off Randall and tossing them onto the floor, but when he finally caught a glimpse of Randall's face, it was not without a measure of shock. "Ouch, your eye is really messed up."

"Thanks for that news flash, man. Now get lost, okay?" Randall barked.

Jesse passed him the half-melted Ziploc bag of ice that had been on the wooden bedside table and then took a seat on the corner of the bed.

"Are you deaf, Jesse? I want you to leave," Randall said, raising the ice to his face.

"Jesus, Randall. Ease up. Can't you take a few punches?" Jesse could see that Randall was still in the clothes he'd worn the night before, one tail of his shirt out and the other tucked in loosely.

"It's not that, jerkwad." Randall threw the bag of ice at Jesse and sat up. "I haven't heard from Abigail all fucking day."

"So . . . ?" Jesse said quizzically.

"So while I was singing my heart out to everyone but Abigail, Nick was probably talking her out of breaking up with him!" Randall shouted.

"You don't know that's what happened." Jesse popped his baseball cap off and folded it in his hands.

"Well, I don't know that it didn't, because *she hasn't called me*," Randall said through clenched teeth.

Jesse really understood where he was coming from, to the point where his stomach was becoming queasy. "Maybe she just needs some time to think, man."

Randall craned his neck up to the ceiling, sighed, and leaned back against the bulky pine headboard. "Maybe. But what happens if she decides to stay with him, Jesse? I can't tell her how I feel then. She'll have already made up her mind."

Jesse felt a sharp chill wash over him, even though the heat in the room was on full blast. "No, Ran. True love can change everything."

Randall managed a half smile. "Yeah, you're probably right."

Jesse knew he was, too, which was why he told Randall goodbye and pedaled to the One Trick Pony faster than the guitar solo of his favorite Flash song.

Now that he was within minutes of seeing Caroline, Jesse found terror trickling up through him and gripping his throat. What if this last inkling of hope he'd allowed himself turned out to be a dead end? At the alley, he heard the familiar gravel crunch beneath his tires. The sound reminded him of logs crackling in a fire, and it brought him back to that night when he'd been courageous and put out the flames at the One Trick. He knew it was adrenaline that had given him the power to be so fearless, and as he locked his bike around the gate at the back, he prayed he could tap into that same power right now.

He took his time adjusting his bag behind his back and straightening his shirt, as if the longer he took to prepare, the better chance he'd have of finding that fearlessness. This was the moment: he was going to tell Caroline again how he felt about her and face his destiny, for better or worse.

Jesse put his hand on the doorknob, but it didn't budge. Just when he was about to turn around, he saw something out of the corner of his eye. Peeking out from the bottom of the door was a red envelope.

He reached down to pick it up and saw his name written in Caroline's perfect cursive. He turned the envelope over and stuck his thumb under the wax seal to open it. Inside was a sheet of parchment paper.

Dear Jesse,
Please go to your house. I have left a package
there for you, with your doorman.
With my heart,
Caroline

With my heart?

Jesse had to get home. Now.

He unlocked his bike, hopped on, and jammed himself right into street traffic, ignoring blaring car horns and angry shouts from annoyed drivers. He pedaled furiously and then glided down the slight downward slope of Smith Street until he turned right onto his block. All he could think about was what might be inside the package. Maybe it was a note about where to meet her. Maybe there were two tickets to France—he could leave for a month and his parents wouldn't even know. His mind raced with all the possibilities until his bike pulled up in front of his building.

After Jesse retrieved the package from the doorman in the lobby, he clutched it under his left arm. When the elevator opened at his floor, he raced to open the door. Once inside, he jumped onto the sofa and tore the paper open. There was a red box inside, and on top of it was another of Caroline's envelopes. He slid his thumb under the wax seal, just as he had at the café, and read what she'd written.

Dear Jesse,

As I told you, I came to Brooklyn with a broken heart. I didn't think there was room in it for someone else, but there you were—with your bright blue eyes and your own heart, broken in a different way.

After those few lines, Jesse had to look away for a second and catch his breath. Perhaps his dream was about to come true.

You took me by surprise, to say the least. But I have not worked out all the things I need to. And so, I must leave for now.

He was going to be sick. Where would she go? How, if all those things were true, could she go?

I will be back, but I don't know when. However, there is only one person in this entire world I could trust with the One Trick Pony. Jesse, please take care of it, and yourself, until I return.

Jesse let his head fall into his hands and closed his eyes. Through all the pain, one thing became clear: it wasn't a rejection. Caroline hadn't said she didn't love Jesse back. Besides, he knew how important the café was to her, and for her to hand over the responsibility for it was no small thing.

He lifted the lid from the box. On the very top was a black-and-white photograph of him and Caroline. They were behind the counter together, Caroline's chin resting daintily on her hands, Jesse leaning against the giant coffee roaster. They were both in semiprofile, and there in their eyes was that unmistakable look, the one Jesse had dreamed of one day having.

He set the photo on his thigh so that he could still look at it out of the corner of his eye as he pulled the tissue paper back to reveal Caroline's keys—the ones she'd kept hanging near the pen and bakery string. He clasped his hand around them, thinking of that very first day, when she'd been fumbling with them, when she'd turned around and he'd seen her face for the very first time.

She'd also tucked in the accounting books—the ones Jesse had straightened out for her—along with the bankbook, the company credit card, and a book of business cards of all the vendors she worked with—the laundry company and the coffee distributor and the paper-goods salesman.

Somehow, Jesse steeled himself, gathered everything back into the box, and rode back to the One Trick. He locked his bike, walked around to the front, opened the gate, and went straight for the chalkboard. He wrote: "The waiting is the hardest part.—Tom Petty." Next, he opened the doors, went behind the bar, and taped the picture of him and

Caroline in a spot where only he would see it. Then he scooped a great hill of green beans and started the patient work of roasting them, listening carefully for the two rounds of cracks, hoping that if he kept Caroline's coffee brewing, more people would be as touched by its magic as he had been.

30

When Abigail was a child, she had loved to build sky-scrapers with her blocks and then knock them down. Her mother used to kneel with her on the floor in the living room, among Abigail's favorite playthings. "Go ahead, Abby, make them go boom," she'd say with unbridled en-thusiasm. But Abigail would never make a move unless her mother had started the process by flicking her palm dar-ingly at the topmost pieces. Once she'd seen her mother do that, she would smash the blocks with a mighty blow and watch them tumble all around her in pure delight. "Now you can make something brand new," her mother would say. "Anything you want."

As Abigail chewed a mouthful of eggplant parmigiana while sitting at the dining room table, she thought that per-forming at the One Trick Pony the night before had been a lot like trashing those block buildings with her mother. Not only had she managed to achieve a breakthrough with her father, but she'd also found her own voice, a voice that people listened to and respected, even if it took a little convincing—for example, with Kate. Abigail smiled uncontrollably when she thought of how the café looked with all her suggestions implemented and how she felt when she'd stepped onstage. *Luminous.*

"What are you so happy about?" her dad asked from the other end of the table. He was being extra-attentive tonight, forgoing his issue of *Variety* and sending Ginny out to the movies so that he could have some quality time with his daughter.

"Everything. Yet nothing in particular," she said wistfully. It was something Abigail would have said to her mother, but tonight, it didn't hurt as much that her father was the one she had to confide in. "Does that make any sense?"

Her father smiled as he traced his thumb along the stem of his wineglass. "I know exactly what you mean."

Abigail's eyes widened. Was her father truly beginning to understand her? She'd have to wait and see, of course.

As she pushed some tomato sauce–covered fettuccine around with her fork, Abigail heard her cell phone go off in the kitchen, where it was charging on the counter. At first, she wanted to ignore it—she'd tried to lie low that day in school because she'd been kind of embarrassed by how many students had come up to her and asked about her poem. She hadn't even talked to any of her friends. But curiosity got the better of her, and she excused herself from the table and went to see who was calling. When the caller ID flashed NICK, she let out a distressed sigh. He'd already called her three times that afternoon. She couldn't bring herself to respond or to listen to his messages. She had felt so guilty for breaking up with him in such a cold, public way. Although they'd had a brief, civil discussion over grilled-cheese sandwiches at the diner about their relationship and her father's decision not to move to Colorado, she was upset that she'd treated him even the least bit callously. The only thing Nick had done was love her in his own simple way.

"Hey." Abigail answered the phone softly.

"Hi, cutie," Nick said, his voice light and breezy, as if nothing had happened the previous night.

She shook her head in confusion. "So . . . what's up?"

"I was just wondering when you were coming over. I'm lonesome without you."

Abigail couldn't believe this. He was asking her to come over after she'd told him she didn't want to see him anymore? "Um, I don't think that's a good idea, Nick."

"Why not?"

"Well, fooling around with your ex is never a smart thing to do," Abigail explained as her palms became sweaty.

There was an awkward silence until Nick cleared his throat and spoke up again. "Your *ex*? What are you talking about?"

Abigail was so stunned she could barely talk. "We broke up last night. Don't you remember?"

There was a crashing sound that indicated that Nick had dropped the phone. But he came back on the line, laughing hysterically. "Babe, I took some killer shrooms yesterday. I still can't think straight."

If this isn't a red flag, I don't know what is.

"Okay, but I can," she said flatly. "And I don't want to be your girlfriend anymore, Nick. I'm sorry."

He mumbled a few curse words and then growled. "Is this about that retard friend of yours, Randall?"

Abigail bristled but managed to keep calm. "Maybe it is."

"I always thought you had a thing for him," Nick barked. "Luckily, the one part of last night I do remember was kicking his scrawny ass."

"*What?*" Abigail yelped, her heart speeding up at his revelation. "Is he okay?"

Nick was quiet for a second, as if he were regretting both what he'd just said to Abigail and what he'd done to Randall. But then he said icily, "Don't worry about me, Abby. I'll be just fine," and hung up the phone.

Abigail stood there motionless for a minute, imagining Randall being roughed up by Nick and his friends. Her stomach lurched at the thought of Randall getting hurt at her expense, but then she doubled over in pain when she contemplated what would happen to her if Randall ever left her behind, the way her mom had.

She was in tears when her phone vibrated in her hand. She looked at the display and saw Kate's name. Abigail couldn't even say hello, she was sobbing so hard. The one syllable she could get out was "Ran."

"Randall's fine, Abby." Kate comforted her immediately. "Jesse says he's a little bruised, but nothing major."

"Oh, thank God."

"There's something I need to show you," Kate said urgently. "Can I meet you at your house in fifteen minutes?"

Abigail swallowed hard and wiped at her eyes. "Get here as soon as you can."

* * *

Ten minutes later, Kate showed up on Abigail's doorstep with her camera in one hand and a cardboard tray with two coffees from the One Trick in her other. "This is for you. Lead me to your television," she said, pushing past Abigail and heading straight to the living room.

"I didn't think you drank coffee," Abigail said, blowing her nose into a Kleenex and following close behind Kate.

"I do now. Caroline gave me this recipe. She said it was something to share with friends. So here I am." Kate hooked up her camera to the TV and spun around with one eyebrow raised. "You ready for this?"

"I guess," Abigail muttered as she plopped down on the sofa. Kate kept her perch alongside the television, watching the video footage from there.

Soon Randall appeared on the screen. He was on the stage at the One Trick Pony, standing in front of the microphone, his chest heaving, blood dripping from a nasty-looking cut on his cheek and his eye swollen and red. Abigail's heart swelled with a mixture of anxiety and desire.

"Just wait," Kate said with an enormous smile.

Randall gazed out into the crowd, as if he was waiting to see someone he recognized. But when he didn't, he bowed his head a little and said very clearly, "This one is for Abigail, the love of my life." Abigail shuddered in shock and then gaped at Kate, who couldn't stop grinning.

"I know this is none of my business," Kate said. "But he's been waiting for the right moment to tell you."

Abigail turned her attention back to the video footage, which had closed in on Randall's hand, strumming the strings on his Fender. He was amazing. Each chord progression transformed into a rich blend of sounds, and then the camera zoomed out, and there was Randall, singing with his eyes closed, as if the lyrics came from his heart. But soon she realized that the words were from inside her own.

> *But life and the words.*
> *Kick and tuck and slide, yeah, yeah, yeah,*
>   *you can,*
> *though you don't think it, you can.*
> *You can, my baby, you and me.*
> *Together we can.*
> *Sway leaf and hail cab and sweep the floor.*

When the song was over and the crowd applauded like crazy, Abigail was overtaken by a thrill so intense and genuine that she couldn't even bear to think about taking a sip of Caroline's coffee, out of fear that it might affect her feelings. Abigail realized that she had been wanting someone to understand her this way for so long, and here Randall was, standing by her side, keeping her grounded no matter what happened. Kate paused the video and Abigail looked directly into Randall's bright eyes. Her heart began to cave in like a tower of building blocks, and before she knew it, she was hugging Kate so tightly that she nearly squeezed all the life out of her friend.

"I love him, too," Abigail said, trembling.

Kate pulled away from their suffocating embrace and giggled. Then she tucked a strand of hair behind Abigail's ear and said, "So go get him."

31

That night, Jesse had some coffee delivered to Randall's place via bike messenger with a note: "Give up and I'll kick your ass worse than Nick did." Randall chuckled when he read it, but once he'd drunk two cups of Caroline's delectable French vanilla brew, the sentiment resonated with him in a way that only one other event had: playing his song for Abigail at the One Trick Pony. Even though Randall hadn't gotten a chance to tell her he loved her, he'd told a whole roomful of people, and if by some twist of fate she and Nick had mended fences, then he'd have to be satisfied with that, right?

Randall's heart led him to answer no—that kind of satisfaction was merely settling, and he couldn't allow himself to get back into that cycle. So without reservation or thinking too much about it, he threw on a pair of cords and a sweatshirt, then went to see Jonathan Sizemore.

It was after eight p.m. when he arrived at the tall gleaming building, but Randall knew that most people in music were night owls and there was a good chance Mr. Sizemore was still holed up in his office, listening to demos and the opinion of his A&R reps. Randall stepped into the lobby, feeling as if he could take on the world with his disgusting eye, his guitar, and his charming personality. It was as if the person he had been that morning had been banished from his kingdom for all eternity. "Hi, I'm Randall Gold. I'm here to see Jonathan Sizemore, please," he said to the skinny bespectacled receptionist.

"Do you have an appointment?" she asked.

Randall swallowed hard. "No, I'm just stopping by."

The receptionist gave him a displeased look and then called Mr. Sizemore. To his great relief, after she'd hung up, she gave Randall a temporary ID card and pointed him toward the elevators.

When he arrived at the twenty-first floor, Randall took a seat in the waiting room and stared at the platinum records hanging on the walls. There wasn't one musician's name on there he didn't recognize. In fact, it seemed almost as if Randall could channel their energy just by clutching the arms of the chair.

He snapped to attention when he heard a young woman say, "Mr. Sizemore will see you now."

When he rose, a pinch of doubt and worry grabbed hold of him and wouldn't let go. *Oh my God, what the hell am I doing?*

"Hey there, Randall," Mr. Sizemore said as he shook his hand.

"Thanks for seeing me, Mr. Sizemore. I know my appointment isn't until a week or two."

"Not a problem, I was just ordering some Chinese food. And please, call me Jonathan," he insisted.

Randall smiled and tried to let go of his worry. "I was just hoping that you could listen to the demo I put together. I know I could have mailed it in, but it's very . . . personal to me."

Mr. Sizemore put his hands in his pockets and grinned. "Sure, let's have a listen in the studio."

Randall practically floated behind the legendary Jonathan Sizemore into the studio where real, meaningful music that had touched his own soul, never mind the souls of millions of others, had been made. It was surreal, to say the least.

Once they had settled into the studio, Mr. Sizemore popped the CD into the gigantic sound system. The first song was Abigail's, and the next was titled "Magic." Randall considered it a good sign that Jonathan Sizemore was listening so intently well into the third track—he was tapping a pencil on the desk and letting his head bounce from side to side with the music.

After about ten minutes, Mr. Sizemore turned the volume down and said, "You've got something here, Randall. But I think I need to hear you play live before I can really judge your material one way or the other."

Randall had a feeling that, when he strapped his guitar to his chest and began to play, Abigail's song would come pouring out of him. He couldn't stop thinking about the sound of her voice on the "Kiss Me Now" track and how it radiated through the room now, even though he could only hear her in his mind. His eyes closed tightly, and when he inhaled, he could almost smell her: a sweet mix of vanilla and baby powder. It was strange—a few minutes later he opened his eyes, and from the way Mr. Sizemore was clapping enthusiastically, apparently he'd strummed his way through Abigail's song. The only thing that stayed in Randall's mind, though, was an image of Abigail, smiling at him under the moonlight.

"That was phenomenal," Mr. Sizemore said, placing his hand on Randall's shoulder. "I need to give your demo to a couple of people here, and then I'll get back to you with a response. Just give me a couple of days before you drop by again, okay?"

Randall chuckled and shook his hand once again. "Deal."

Outside, the night sky was incredibly clear. Randall could see the flicker of airplane lights above, and although a brisk breeze was funneling through Brooklyn, he felt warm all over. Everything that had just happened seemed as if it had come out of a dream. In fact, Randall was starting to think he might have been sleepwalking. His head was a little fuzzy, as if he were waking up, groggy after being given anesthesia at the dentist's office.

But when Abigail suddenly came into view, wrapped in a crocheted sweater that was a size too big and smiling as if she'd just uncovered a secret, nothing in Randall's life had ever felt more real. She walked toward him slowly, each step small and steady yet full of purpose. Randall couldn't

274

remember if she'd ever seemed this confident and self-assured before. It was as though she had finally become the very person he knew she was, deep down in places she'd been afraid to look.

When Abigail stood no more than a few inches from him, Randall realized that he'd had a premonition in Mr. Sizemore's office. Here she was, standing in the moonlight, so close he could lean down and kiss her.

"How'd it go?" Abigail asked as she took his hand.

Randall could feel in every nerve ending of his skin the electricity that was all around them. "How'd you know I was here?"

"I just knew," she replied, a hint of cinnamon-flavored coffee still clinging to her clothes.

Randall squeezed her hand tightly and gazed at her face, which was glowing like a firefly. He knew something, too, and he had to tell her, regardless of whether Nick might be in the picture, regardless of the possibility that she would reject him. The time was now, and he wasn't going to let it slip through his fingers.

"I love you, Abigail," he said, closing his eyes as soon as the words were spoken, shaking so much that his guitar case rattled.

And then Randall felt the sweetness of Abigail's lips against his own. He mindlessly set his guitar down with a loud thump and pulled her in as tight as he could. He put his arms around her and they began kissing so deeply that he could taste the delicious coffee on her tongue. Randall felt so light, as if his feet were rising off the ground. But now he also felt that Abigail would hold on to him forever and keep him from drifting away. She didn't have to say she loved him back. She didn't have to tell him it was over with Nick. Actually, Abigail didn't have to do anything but keep kissing him, and Randall would know everything he needed to.

And that was exactly what she did.

32

Two weeks later . . .

"Jimmy, dude, for the last time, the green coffee beans aren't rotten," Jesse said, shaking his head in mock annoyance.

"That's Jimmy *the* Dude," his old friend said with his old Brooklyn attitude. Miami hadn't changed him a bit.

It was great to have Jimmy back, managing the One Trick Pony while Jesse was at school all day. Of course, Jimmy had given Jesse some lip about the place being all fruity now, but Jesse could tell he liked it.

It hadn't been difficult to lure him back, either. "It's too freaking hot here," Jimmy had said when Jesse phoned him in Florida. "And I'm too fat to be in a bathing suit all day. I don't know why I didn't think about that before moving here."

But after being back in his element for a while, Jimmy

looked a little slimmer. Jesse had been working the guy pretty hard, but that was only because he took his responsibility to Caroline very seriously. She'd trusted him with her coffee, which was her passion, and although he hadn't heard from her yet, Jesse believed that Caroline would make good on her promise and come back, perhaps healed enough that she could be with him in the way he still thought about every single day. Customers hadn't forgotten about her, either. They were still crowding the café at all hours and traveling in from the other boroughs, asking about her whereabouts. Nevertheless, they kept returning to this intriguing spot in Cobble Hill, and this gave Jesse a lot of pride, as well as hope that he'd see her once again.

In the meantime, Jesse knew there were some things you held in your heart no matter where you might go. His parents had made that clear to him when they'd come back from their most recent trip and told him they were on sabbatical until the new year—great news that was better than any souvenir they'd ever bought him. Also, one glance at the photo of him and Caroline always reminded Jesse that feeling alive had everything to do with reaching out and making a connection with someone, regardless of the consequences.

Randall and Abigail knew this to be true, too. Lately, they would come into the One Trick Pony all glassy-eyed and dreamy, with their arms around each other's waist. Even now, sitting at a table right across from Kate, they'd kiss each other whenever they thought their friend wasn't looking. It didn't freak Jesse out one bit to see them like this, but he had a feeling that it might get under Kate's skin. She was the jealous, control freak type, and all their relationships were continuing to change. In fact, next year they would all be on their own paths, going to college or finding jobs. But whatever they decided to do and wherever they decided to go, Jesse knew that if Caroline hadn't come into their lives, they'd just be stuck where they had been, going absolutely nowhere.

The tiny spray of gypsy bells at the door jingled, and Jesse caught a glimpse of the customer who'd just walked in. He had blond hair that was darker in some spots, as if he'd spent too much time in the sun. Jesse's first thought was that this guy was some airhead surfer who might be looking for someone else to pick up his tab. Jesse watched as he approached the bar, and he noticed how Kate's eyes followed the stranger the entire distance. She tried to avoid eye contact as she took a long sip of coffee, but it was no use. She'd caught Jesse's glance and the second she put the cup down, she stuck her tongue out at him. Jesse just threw his head back and laughed. And at the end of the night, as he was closing up, he wrote this on the café's outdoor chalkboard:

"The love that's shared between good friends is worth its weight in coffee."